Stern & Lilland

P. 28 Borish w/Tudor
   29 Clem Stone

CYCLES

CYCLES

BY

SAMUEL A. SCHREINER, JR.

DONALD I. FINE, INC.
New York

Library of Congress Cataloging-in-Publication Data

Schreiner, Samuel Agnew.
Cycles / Samuel Schreiner, Jr.
p. cm.
ISBN 1-55611-162-2
1. Cycles—Popular works. I. Title.
Q176.S3 1989
116—dc20   89-45438
                                                         CIP

Manufactured in the United States of America

10 9 8 7 6 5 4 3 2 1

Designed by Irving Perkins Associates

For Dorrie, who went cycling with me.

CONTENTS

Contents

INTRODUCTION

MORE THAN FIFTY YEARS AGO, E. R. Dewey began his journey into the world of cycles. This journey led to an all consuming passion that became his life's work and resulted in the founding of a worldwide educational and research organization. Dewey came to realize that cycles were both vast and mysterious and that they touched nearly every major field of study, from biology to physics to the economy. He believed that their mysteries, when unlocked, would bring us to a deeper understanding of the world we live in.

Although Dewey brought the study of cycles to the level of a science, he was neither the first nor the last person to become fascinated with cycles. Since the dawn of history, mankind has used cycles and speculated about their origin. In Egypt, Babylon, India and Greece, cycles were followed, often in relation to agriculture.

Cycles have a wonderful quality to them; they give us a sense of what to expect in the future. The advantage of this knowledge is obvious for both the individual and humanity. In the 1940s, Dewey projected the cyclic outlook for stocks until the year 2000—a forecast that has been uncannily accurate, including the 1987 crash. In the 1960s, he forecast higher interest rates for the next twenty years.

The story goes on and on. And cycles are a story, an amazing story. Cycles are like a play that is still unfolding, in which characters continually step on and off the stage. In this new book, Samuel A. Schreiner, Jr., brings the reader right onto this stage and into this fascinating tale. The key to understanding cycles is in its characters, and they are brought to life in this book.

But the book is more than simply an account of people interested in cycles. It is a book of ideas that will both challenge and illuminate the minds of its readers. As you read these pages, you will experience, through the eyes of those conducting the research, the new potentials that the world of cycles portend.

Cycles is a great journey, and Sam Schreiner brings his readers right to the borders of a fascinating frontier.

—Richard Mogey
Executive Director
Foundation for the Study of Cycles, Inc.
Irvine, California

CHAPTER

1

DISCOVERING CYCLELAND

IT'S EARLY MORNING of the day that I've picked to start writing this book. I'm finding it difficult to plunge into a subject as intriguing but difficult to bring into sharp focus as cycles. So I do what writers do best in such circumstances. Instead of sitting down to the typewriter, I brew a second cup of tea and sit in front of the TV to catch the news. I also rationalize. This is the time of troubles in China, and the latest bulletin about the rapidly changing news in that great nation is something a writer can't afford to miss.

My set springs to life in the middle of the business news. While pictures of foreign nationals crowding the Chinese airports in an effort to flee the country roll across the screen, an announcer with a clipped British accent delivers a report from London to the effect that British business interests are likely to keep their operations going in China despite the exodus, despite that government's violation of all international standards of human rights. The reason for

1

this bit of business as usual is summed up by the reporter in a single sentence: "The world economy is now determined by what goes on in the Orient."

I am enthralled. Just the night before in the course of my research I had come across a prediction made nearly forty years ago by a leading figure in the strange and wonderful world of cycles, the late Raymond H. Wheeler: "The next five hundred years of history will belong to Asia." The night before that I had interviewed Dr. Theodor Land-scheidt, director of the Schroeter Institute for Research in Cycles of Solar Activity in Nova Scotia, who told me that the turbulent events in China were understandable and pre-dictable because they were related to solar cycles.

Now, as I watch cycles so dramatically shaping history, I feel that writing about them is an imperative. I switch off the TV and go to the typewriter . . .

Cylces are at work everywhere and in everything. It's more than a possibility that the study of cycles will one day reveal the long-sought-after unifying principle that will en-able man to understand how the universe really works. It's already a certainty that cycles have proved to be a reliable predictive device in financial investment, weather forecast-ing, political prognostication, religious recruiting, psycho-logical development, natural disaster, and many other matters. Becoming involved with the study of cycles is not an exercise to be taken lightly. It can change your entire outlook, shatter long-held beliefs because it does away with comforting preconceptions about how the world works.

I have to confess to having been totally unaware of the significance of cycles for most of what's getting to be a fairly long life. The word was familiar, of course. I'd heard it used in connection with the ups and downs of the economy, the changes in weather, the movement of the heavenly bodies. Like any other human being, I was conscious of cyclical action, whatever it might be called. I counted on seeing the sun or its diffuse light for roughly half of every date on the calendar. In stillness, I could hear the regular beat of my heart. As a sometime sailor, I was attuned to the rise and fall of tides, which I knew to be somehow related to the phases of the moon. But my involvement with cycles was almost subliminal. I never gave their workings a conscious thought.

When an editor suggested that cycles might be a subject worthy of investigation, my instant reaction was: What? Why *me?* Curiosity about everything is a reporter's stock in trade, however, and I took myself over to the local library. Even the few so-called popular articles I could find seemed to confirm the wisdom of that initial reaction. Following cycles would lead me into unfamiliar realms of finance, mathematics and science where I might be totally lost. With nothing at risk in the markets, my personal attention to money matters had been limited to taxes, interest rates on charge accounts and home mortgages. My academic background in economics consisted of one freshman course in college. It was even thinner in math and science—only algebra and a general science course in high school. But I found that references to cycles did pop up in relation to politics, psychology, sociology, medicine and even the arts. So with some trepidation, I decided to follow the cycle trail, one step at a time.

Paradoxically, my ignorance was my main source of confidence. During forty years of experience, I had learned that, next to curiosity, ignorance can be the most effective tool in a reporter's kit. The reporter's job is to bear the news of an interesting event or development to a broad public that presumably knows little or nothing about it—and thus couldn't care less. The reporter who is in the same fix as the people he is trying to serve has a better chance of making the message clear. In an increasingly technical and specialized culture, a great deal of simple truth gets lost in vocabulary. Whether it is essential to understanding or whether it is a form of elitism, each scholarly discipline

3

develops a language of its own, and even the erudite in one field have difficulty understanding what's being said in another without the aid of a translator. Like a traveller visiting a dozen foreign lands, all of whose languages he cannot hope to master, the ignorant reporter has to find a way of getting around language to learn the facts that are needed to make the journey. It's the only way to create a guide book for other similarly handicapped venturers.

Fortunately, the important sign posts—the seminal ideas in any field—that point toward a happier, wiser way of life stand above all such artificial barriers as language. Even if they don't articulate this thought, people feel it. Consider the fact that, as I'm writing these words, the most enduring best-seller in America bears the insightful title, *All I Really Need to Know I Learned in Kindergarten.* Unfortunately, the call for technicians to keep the machinery running in a complex world has turned most education above kindergarten into an exercise in learning the laws and language of some special land on the map of academia. But an indelible memory from my own school days gave me confidence that I would see the sign posts in cycleland.

In that high school algebra class, my last effort at comprehending mathematics, what kept me awake was the sight of the teacher, a young and attractive woman just out of college, and my only motivation for doing the work was to please her. After all, memorizing equations and writing them down in proper order wasn't any more difficult, or very different from, memorizing Latin and its English equivalents. Then one day this dazzling teacher chalked a problem out of the book on the blackboard and asked a quiet, retiring classmate named Roger to come up and solve it. Without a word, Roger quickly wrote down a couple of equations that none of us had ever seen before and arrived at the right answer. Before Roger could get back to his seat, the teacher was rubbing out his work, shaking her head and saying, "That won't do." Not shy in matters of the mind,

Roger literally stood his ground: "Why not? The answer's right, isn't it?" The teacher was unfazed: "Yes, but you got it the wrong way. It isn't what is in your book." Roger sat down, shaking *his* head. This was a flash of enlightenment for me—not Roger's equations, which I didn't comprehend any better than the teacher, but the realization that understanding has nothing to do with rote learning or, for that matter, good looks.

Although I wasn't fully aware of it at the time, that incident armed me against being intimidated by the legions of the learned. Truth is something other than the mastery of the terminology and techniques of any intellectual discipline or trade. Such mastery has value, of course. For instance, I have no doubt that that teacher made it possible over the years for legions of people to function in areas where some grasp of algebra is required, a task at which Roger with his leaps of the imagination would have failed. The world we've made wouldn't work at all without skilled specialists, but, unfortunately, acquiring even one skill takes most of the time and energy most people have to give. Simple survival calls for accepting the *how* of most things on faith, but the whole human being in search of understanding shouldn't shy away from asking the *what* and *why* simply because he or she doesn't know how. I would make no effort to make mathematicians or physicists or biologists or astronomers or psychologists or stock market analysts out of myself or my readers in my exploration of cycleland, but I wouldn't let the jargon of the specialists scare me. I could hope to create a few Rogers.

The first encouraging development in my early probing into cycles was the discovery of an institution called The Foundation for the Study of Cycles. The Foundation had, in fact, been in business for nearly fifty years, a strong indication that the subject of cycles possessed both depth and staying power. When I got in touch with the Foundation and learned that its executive director, Jeffrey H. Horovitz, was a psychiatrist who had become involved in cycles as a result of dealing with human emotions, I knew that the subject also had breadth. The Foundation had recently moved from Pittsburgh where it had been associated with the University of Pittsburgh, to Irvine, California, where it was in the process of establishing a relationship with the local branch of the University of California. It was obviously an institution with considerable credibility. Possessed of a file of more than four thousand cycles, it was also a unique resource center—the only place of its kind in the world. If nothing else were to come of my efforts, a report on this center of cycles would be bringing news to most readers. I made arrangements to go to Irvine.

En route I tried to prepare myself with background reading. The Foundation was started in 1940 by Edward R. Dewey, a Harvard-educated economist, who remained its director and guiding spirit until his death in 1978. Dewey's interest in cycles was born of necessity. After a stint in the Commerce Department during the Hoover Administration in the course of which he was asked to look into the causes of the Depression, he went to work for Chapin Hoskins, a former managing editor of Forbes, who was selling to industry his analyses of business cycles. Dewey had to learn about cycles to persuade clients of the need for Hoskins's services. In the course of that effort, he came across an account of an international conference on biological cycles held in 1931 at the summer camp of Boston financier Copley Amory in Matamek, Quebec. Some of the cycles in living things such as Canadian lynx, snowshoe rabbits, and Atlantic salmon, looked enough like cycles in the markets to raise an intriguing question in Dewey's mind: might not all cycles come from the same source? The more he thought about it, the more Dewey felt that this was a question in need of an answer, and the only way to find that answer would be to study the whole range of cycles.

Dewey wrote to Amory proposing a foundation for this

study and received an enthusiastic response. Not only did Amory put up five hundred dollars in seed money but he agreed to serve as chairman of the Foundation, in which capacity he helped recruit a distinguished executive committee. Among its members were Dr. Julian S. Huxley, secretary of the Zoological Society of London; Dr. Harlow Shapley, director of the Harvard Observatory; and Alanson B. Houghton, chairman of the Corning Glass Works and a former Ambassador to Germany. As director of the new foundation, Dewey parted company with Hoskins but not with economic cycles as his primary concern. In order to fund his operations, Dewey continued to sell research to corporations and, on the side, publish what general information he encountered about cycles. From the point of view of scientific investigation, this method of operation left much to be desired. The saleable economic research took most of Dewey's working time and that of the small staff he had assembled. Dewey's clients, the businesses that paid for his research, didn't want it published so their competitors could glean it for free. By 1950, with his own curiosity about cycles as a universal phenomenon increasing, Dewey decided to gamble on getting out of commerce and turning the Foundation into a non-profit membership organization that would be free to pursue and publish whatever seemed relevant to its mission. Although he kept the headquarters in New York for a while, he eventually moved the whole operation to a site near the University of Pittsburgh where his chief researcher, Gertrude Shirk, was already established and where he would be near an ancestral estate he had inherited at Brady's Bend, Pennsylvania. There the Foundation remained, quietly accumulating cycles, publishing two magazines—Cycles and the Journal of Interdisciplinary Cycle Research—and a number of books, until Dr. Horovitz came on the scene in 1986.

Although he is a native Pittsburgher, Dr. Horovitz decided early on that the venerable foundation needed a new outlook in a physical as well as a philosophical sense. There were, according to Dr. Horovitz, a number of practical reasons for moving clear across the continent to California. Although the Foundation's 2,500 members are sprinkled throughout fifty-seven countries, more of them are clustered in California than anywhere else. The facilities in Pittsburgh were inadequate, and with Ms. Shirk about to retire a new research staff would have to be recruited. Whether subconsciously or not, Dr. Horovitz may have been motivated to make the move by cycle theory itself. At least Gary Bosley, the new managing director of the organization, thinks so. A disciple of Wheeler and Landscheidt, whose predictions I found echoed on my TV, Bosley says, "This is the border of the Pacific rim. With the center of human activity shifting from the West to the East, we are on the exciting boundary where changing cycles mesh."

From my point of view, no more perfect place could have been found for an operation that is dedicated to delving into the secrets of the universe in order to predict the future. The whole Irvine area is in the process of being developed; it has a futuristic feel, a sense of becoming. Lying athwart the freeway between Los Angeles and San Diego, it is a checkerboard of close-clustered, high-priced housing enclaves pinned down by the steel and glass spikes of a few high-rise office buildings and hotels. With the mountains only a blue shadow to the east and the sea just below the horizon to the west, the land is a featureless plain. Irvine is still without the character that comes from experience, but it is not without a personality. There are no crumbling ruins, no honky tonks, no mom-and-pop stores, no slums, no smoking factories, no billboards, no graffiti, no polyglot swarms of people or animals afoot to take the shine off the pristine scene. The needs of living are served by modern, multi-faceted malls; all that moves is encased in steel—the automobiles that jam the freeway and its cloverleaves, the airplanes and helicopters hovering over

Orange County's John Wayne Airport and an Air Force field nearby. Irvine's human component seems to consist of interchangeable young men and women dressed in business suits—all on the move, all working with the mind, all full of high expectations.

This is more than a fuzzy impression. Even before I visited the Foundation offices, our hotel gave tangible evidence of the Irvine personality. An austere and functional mass of concrete with steel piping as ornamentation, it was so new that the plaster was hardly dry. There were two similar hotels and two more a-building within sight. To come upon so many reasonably large hotels in a place that was not a city in any familiar sense of that word was puzzling, but not for long. As we were led to our room, we passed door after door opening onto scenes of earnest, suited young men and women gathered round conference tables, wrestling with graphs and figures on charts or slide screens. They came from all over, as their accents and the license plates in the parking lot would indicate, and they never left the premises, seldom got out of uniform and into the pool. The cocktail lounge was usually abuzz by six, and the evenings were given over to large, speechifying gatherings. What missions these people were on we never knew, but a few months earlier we would have found ourselves in the midst of a conference of cycle enthusiasts from all over America and abroad. Having such a hotel within walking distance of the Foundation and within a short drive of an airport was a factor in selecting the Irving site; conferences are, after all, the way business is done in the information age. Significantly, the hotel emptied so rapidly and completely on weekends that management offered lower rates in an apparently vain effort to stem the exodus.

The building in which the Foundation offices were housed turned out to be a lofty metallic silo that looked like a hangar for a spaceship. It rose starkly alone from a manicured carpet of industrial parkland across the freeway from the hotel. Since the report that nobody walks in California was verifiable by a glance out of the window of our room, there was a hint of charming eccentricity in cycleland when Director Horovitz instructed me on the phone, "Oh, you can just walk over. There's a footpath on the freeway crossover and then a hole in the fence on the other side you can get through and come right across the park. A lot of our visitors at the convention walked . . ." I opted to stick with the old saw that goes "when in Rome . . ." and pilot my rental car. In a four-block, five-minute journey I managed to get into the wrong channel of a flow of traffic on a road called Jamboree that had already built to three full lanes before eight o'clock in the morning. As a consequence, I missed my exit and was lost in the featureless landscape for half an hour. I wondered whether it was an omen of my future in cycleland.

Inside its sun-sheened skin the silo was relentlessly modern in design and appointments. Hidden behind a door leading off a glass-walled, carpeted mezzanine, the Foundation's modest quarters were clean and efficient. A large room accommodated secretaries' desks, a research library and study table; three individual offices along the window wall accommodated Dr. Horovitz and his professional staff—Bosley; Richard Mogey, research director; and Diane Epperson, managing editor of Cycles. On each and every desk sat the tool that is revolutionizing the study of cycles as well as most other activities that are related in any way to the mind—a personal computer. There was a reassuring ambience of solid, serious business in progress, the kind of business that was immediately relevant to the world outside the windows.

Bearded, bouncy, ebullient, Dr. Horovitz had a salesman's contagious enthusiasm for his product—the knowledge of cycles. I could well appreciate how he had managed to get cycles back into the pages of the popular press and onto TV screens after a long lapse. His effort in that regard

10

was enhanced by a bit of serendipity in the form of the worst stock market crash in sixty years. After it was discovered that Cycles had accurately predicted the movements of the market in 1987 as early as March of that year, Dr. Horovitz became something of an instant media star. Although happy that his field could be of such interest and practical use, Dr. Horovitz was quick to focus on aspects of cycles that have broader implications for humanity in general and are more in keeping with his own scientific background.

One of the Foundation's ongoing projects, for instance, is grandly called GLOBAL 2000. It is a twelve-year worldwide study of mental health cycles; the concept grew directly out of Dr. Horovitz's specialty. He holds a B.S. degree in biology from the University of Pittsburgh, an M.S. in radiation biology from the University of Miami and an M.D. from the University of Miami School of Medicine. Before becoming involved with cycles he was chief resident in psychiatry and clinical assistant professor of psychiatry at the University of South Florida School of Medicine and a commissioned officer in the division of Radiological Health Physics of the United States Health Service. But Dr. Horovitz's vision of the potential in cycles went far beyond that study. Jumping up to pace and gesture out of sheer nervous energy, he told me:

"Even after fifty years, I feel we are just kicking the top of icebergs. It seems that all systems have their characteristic recurring patterns. All systems we have studied here—and we've identified over four thousand recurring characteristic patterns. Just start with this office—this office, this floor, this building, this city, this county, this state, this country, all the countries of the world, the world, the moon, the sun, the stars, the planets, the solar system, the galaxy, the universe—all are made up of recurring patterns, repeating cycles . . ."

Dr. Horovitz suggested that I could get a feel for the

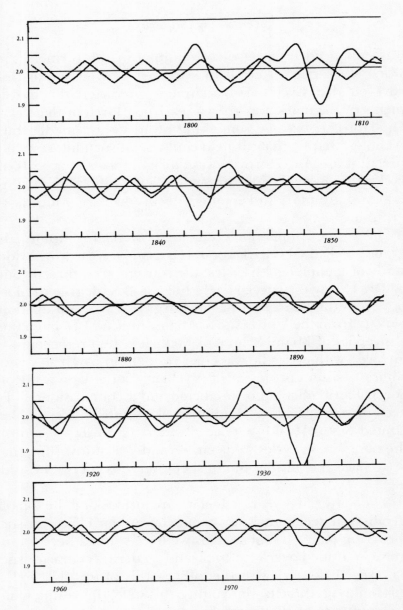

One of the most celebrated cycles in the 4,000-cycle bank of the Foundation for the Study of Cycles at Irvine, California, is the 40.68-month cycle in stock prices, shown here in graph form. It was this cycle that enabled alert cycle enthusiasts to get out of the rising stock market before the 1987 crash. *(Cycles Magazine)*

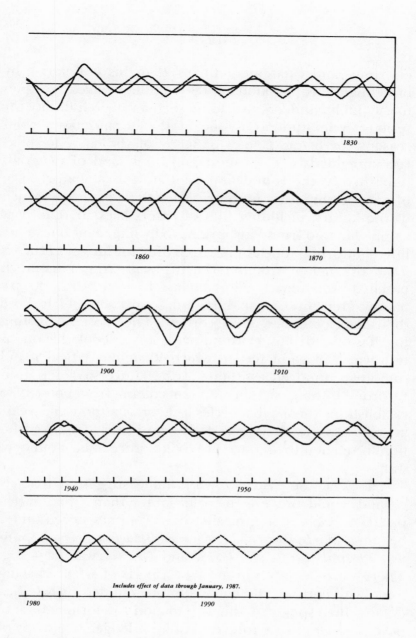

1830

1860   1870

1900   1910

1940   1950

Includes effect of data through January, 1987.

1980   1990

13

enormity and excitement involved in his enterprise by browsing the Foundation's library and files, which are open to the public. Indeed, providing such a research facility for serious cycle students is one of the organization's chief reasons for being. Copies of many of the current books recommended by the Foundation's staff and of materials published by the Foundation itself are for sale; a privilege of membership is reduced prices for these materials. Much of the library, including files of letters back to 1940, was shipped in toto from Pittsburgh. An incongruous but somehow comforting touch in research director Mogey's office is a set of ancient wooden file drawers from Pittsburgh perched atop new metal cabinets. In these drawers are handwritten three-by-six-inch index cards on which those thousands of cycles are recorded. The most fascinating touch is provided by a custom-made ledger book that opens to a width of eight feet in which Raymond Wheeler and some two hundred assistants at the University of Kansas recorded by hand significant events dating from 600 B.C. to establish his theory that cycles as long as a thousand years are operative in all aspects of human history from revolution to religion to architecture to literature to economics to war.

A look at the Wheeler book alone suggested that cycleland would prove to be a lot larger than I had anticipated. A glance along the shelves of volumes stored under headings like *Business and Economics, Biological Science, Statistics, Physical Science, Medicine,* and *General* was daunting. There were books on brand new aspects of science having to do with entropy and chaos and one entitled *Global Mind Change* that spoke to the Foundation's determination to position cycles in the forefront of knowledge. The scope of the subject was inspiring and a little intimidating. A quick examination of the contents of those wooden drawers revealed that they contained many fascinating details.

The cycle cards are filed according to disciplines and time

spans, beginning with seconds. In that first category, there is a card recording the basic sound frequency of bees (Biology) at 250 cycles per second; another noting the "coalescing of H_2O molecules into structures" (Chemistry) at ten to thirteen seconds; yet another phasing waves in Los Angeles harbor (Hydrology) at five to six seconds. The file runs on through increasing time spans to 200 to 250 million year Ice Age cycles (Climatology). It is very much a living file in that many of the cards identify work yet to be done. Cards of cycles for which statistical analysis had found significant probability are marked "verified," and those noting cycles where probability had not been established are marked "hint." The scientific caution that has characterized the Foundation's approach to cycles through all its history is spelled out on an identification card inserted into a plate on the face of each drawer: *Cycle Allegations.*

By the time I sat down on one of the comfortable swivel chairs around the library table in the Foundation for the Study of Cycles, I knew that I would be entering a kind of wonderland. Encompassing as it did all of the separate principalities of knowledge, cycleland ought to include within its boundaries territories of interest and vital concern to everybody, including me. In offering this book, I submit that it does.

CHAPTER

2

A CYCLE IS A CYCLE IS A CYCLE—OR IS IT?

ONE OF THE more interesting ways of defining something came from the pen of Gertrude Stein when she wrote that "a rose is a rose is a rose." If I read her right, she meant that a rose, or anything else, is unique, singular. William Shakespeare was conveying much the same thought when he wrote that "a rose by any other name would smell as sweet." These perceptive poets may have been right about roses, but they would have found it difficult to capture cycles in one such memorable stanza. Although a major objective of the study of cycles is to show that they are as definite and recognizable as a rose, a complete definition of this phenomenon has been somewhat elusive. This is not to say that there aren't valid guidelines for recognizing a cycle when you see one or experience its effects.

The founder of what he called "the science of cycles," Edward R. Dewey, offered this fairly straightforward definition in one of his central books on the subject: "'Cycle'

17

comes from a Greek word for 'circle.' Actually, the word 'cycle' means 'coming around again to the place of the beginning.' It does not, by itself, imply that there is a regular period of time before it returns to the place where it started. When there is such a fairly regular period of time, the correct word to use is 'rhythm,' from another Greek word meaning 'measured time.' Tides are rhythmic; your heartbeat is rhythmic; so is your breathing. A cycle, when we refer to one, will usually mean a cycle with rhythm." Accordingly, he stated that the business of the science of cycles was to deal with "events that occur with reasonable regularity" whether they could be found in nature or commercial activity or anywhere else.

In a sense, Dr. Jeffrey H. Horovitz, until 1989 the most visible spokesman for the science of cycles as director of the Foundation for the Study of Cycles, echoed Dewey when he told me: "Cycle by definition means circle—one complete turn of the circle until you get back to the same spot on the circle." Then Dr. Horovitz quickly added: "The circles we look at are not particularly round, and when you show them like frequencies they are not necessarily sine waves. When the Foundation was started the definition was periodic rhythmic fluctuations. Now we have come to realize that there are recurring *patterns* that you can identify and that there are systems based on them, including human behavior."

It quickly becomes evident that it would be a mistake to visualize cycles exclusively as either perfect circles or smoothly undulating waves. The most distinguishing feature of a true cycle is statistically significant regularity. Except for the self-evident natural ones like the twenty-four-hour cycle of the day, it often takes rigorous and extensive examination to detect this all-important feature of a cycle. Because even true cycles manifest themselves in an infinite variety of shapes, sizes and rhythms, it's easy to be deceived by occurrences that appear to have a cyclical character but may only be accidents or coincidences. As a probable example of this, Gary Bosley, managing director of the Foundation, cited intriguing circumstances surrounding the 1989 Kentucky Derby. At forty-four degrees, it was the coldest since 1957; it was the slowest since 1958, and there was a winning California horse as in 1958. In those previous years there was a sunspot high as there was in 1989; the thirty-one/thirty-two-year time stretch represents approximately three eleven-year sunspot cycles. Bosley shrugged off the Derby events as coincidence—so far. These circumstances coincided only twice, which isn't enough to suspect there is a cycle or cycles at work, but it also doesn't rule out the possibility . . .

Even an established regularity isn't enough to furnish a precise definition of a cycle. The most regular of cycles are subject to confusing changes. One example—a cycle, as Dewey said, "to keep scientists humble"—was a 40.68-month cycle in industrial common stock prices that kept the same shape from 1871 to 1946 through all sorts of economic crises and two world wars only to do a complete flip-flop. After faltering briefly, the cycle returned to a forty-one-month rhythm in the 1950s, but it traced a mirror image of its behavior on the graph. At least one convincing reason for this is postulated by cycle students: there is no such thing as a single cycle.

"When we study any system, whether it is the stock market or animal populations or rainfall or temperatures or earthquakes with our mathematical tests, we find that most characteristic systems have a number of characteristic cycles within them," Dr. Horovitz explains. "Sometimes all the cycles peak at the same time and create a tremendous high; sometimes they bottom at the same time to make a tremendous low. At other times they cause all sorts of frequency interferences like static in a radio signal. When they interfere with each other, cycles give you the total mathematical addition or subtraction of their different influences.

19

"Take tides, which may be the greatest example of the kind of thing we study. They are the respiration of the ocean, a breathing in and out. It's rhythmic. Still people are always screwing up on predicting the tides. Sure, they get high tides plus or minus ten minutes and plus or minus a foot or so—but not exactly. The world authority on tides—Fergus Wood—lists 136 representative cycles in the sun-moon system that have a bearing on tides. And then you have to bring in other factors like the shoreline. Where I'm living at Laguna Beach the tide is different than at Newport Beach six miles away."

In an effort to describe what she was doing, Gertrude Shirk, the first research director of the Foundation once wrote: "We can say that the Foundation for the Study of Cycles studies figures for evidence of regularity in the ups and downs in those figures (where we have regularity we have predictability); it tries to find out in which cases the regular ups and downs have meaning, and in which cases they are just the result of chance; it tries to find the causes that could create such behavior if it is not the result of chance. The particular kind of figures which we study are called *time series*. Time series are just figures that are written down for successive periods of time. Continuous daily temperature readings make a time series. Yearly figures on pig iron production make a time series. The average monthly sunspot record makes a time series. A cycle is the characteristic of a time series to get back to where it was before. In our definition, we used the term, 'regularity in the ups and downs.' That is, we look for rhythmic cycles, figures that tend to get back to where they were before with some degree of rhythm, with a sort of beat."

Ms. Shirk's successor, Richard Mogey, who now heads the Foundation, elaborates on her definition: "A cycle has to repeat the data a certain number of times before being considered a true cycle. A bare minimum is five times, but I think that's too low. I prefer at least ten times. I like to go back into the 1600s and 1700s when I can. I know it will get out of sync, and I want to see what it does when that happens. I want it to get back into the same beat, to pick up that beat that it left behind. Even when a cycle gets off, it should return to its original phasing. For instance, the forty-month cycle that Dewey and Shirk worked on so long has been out of phase occasionally but when it comes back it is right back where it should be."

Cycles are easier to identify—or, at least, to substantiate—when hard data, such as records of the stock market or of the types of time series cited by Ms. Shirk, are available. But believers in cycles are convinced that they can be seen in processes that are more difficult to reduce to numbers. One of America's leading geographers of this century, the late Ellsworth Huntington of Yale University, defined cycles in the broadest of terms when he got around to writing his masterwork, *Mainsprings of Civilization:*

"The whole history of life is a record of cycles. In the vast geological periods plants and animals of one great order after another rose to importance, flourished, and declined. In prehistoric times successive species of manlike creatures passed across the stage. In the historic period nations have risen and fallen; types of civilization have grown great and decayed; science, art, and literature have been full of vigor and originality only to fall into deadly weakness and conventionalism. In modern business few things are more disturbing than the cycles which seem to become more extreme as time goes on. In each of these examples some form of existence or type of activity starts in a certain condition, goes through a series of changes, and comes back to essentially the same condition as at the beginning. An explosion, for example, sets still air in violent motion. There is a loud sound and buildings fall. Then the whole thing dies down. The air may be full of smoke and dust, but so far as motion is concerned, it has returned to its old condition of stillness. The life cycle of plants and animals

21

also illustrates the matter. It starts with non-existence, passes through many stages, and ends once more with non-existence."

Despite the wide angle of his lens, Huntington claimed that he could see the same characteristics that Dewey, Shirk, Mogey & Co. describe. Some aspect of "coming around to the place of beginning" is basic to a definition of a cycle, but thereafter there are other factors that must be taken into consideration, according to Huntington. One of these is repetition, which he illustrated with reproduction. A plant or a person or a nation can go through a life cycle and disappear without leaving a successor. But if a plant, say, produces seeds that take root, a new life cycle arises from the old, and this can go on indefinitely. Thus there are both individual cycles and reproductive cycles. Another factor is regularity, or rhythm. An explosion might create a cycle in the air, but there would be no rhythm involved unless a similar explosion occurred at regular intervals. Akin to rhythm but more precise is "periodicity," about which Huntington wrote:

"By this we mean a regular recurrence at specified and hence predictable intervals. The day with its phases of light and darkness is of this kind. So are the seasons and tides. Many people are beginning to suspect that definite periodicity goes much farther than this. They think that it is found in cycles of business and even in the rise and fall of types of civilization and the long eras of geology. This definite periodicity is supposed to have its origin in purely physical conditions which repeat themselves as regularly as the motions of the planets or the waves of different lengths which constitute heat, light and electricity. Such physical cycles are superimposed upon one another in bewildering profusion. The length of some is only a fraction of a second and that of others millions of years. When the effects of all these periodic cycles are added to those of rhythmic but not periodic cycles, the result is bound to be highly complex.

For that reason many events which are really due to the combined effect of many periodic causes are commonly supposed to be hopelessly irregular and unpredictable."

Among those who share Huntington's belief that there are some cycles that don't arise from mathematical analysis alone is historian and sometime presidential adviser Arthur M. Schlesinger, Jr. His most recent book is, significantly, entitled *The Cycles of American History* and is an elaboration of a thesis put forward by his father, also an historian, fifty years ago. A surprising proponent of cycles is Lee Iacocca, the wizard of Chrysler, who offers a rather jaunty definition of cycles in *Talking Straight*: "Life is full of all sorts of cycles. Some of them are predictable—night follows day; fall follows summer; tides follow the moon. Those are the ones God takes care of. Then there are the ones people take care of: business cycles, energy cycles, automotive cycles. Those we manage to screw up good."

The French have a saying—"*Plus ça change, plus c'est la même chose*" or "The more things change, the more they stay the same"—that would seem to be one possible definition of the cycle. But it doesn't fit any better than a perfect circle or a sine wave. Cycles or no, things do change. This has been a cause for skepticism with regard to cycles. A clear case in point can be made about the stock market for which the hardest of hard data for statistical analysis is available. If cycle proponents could crow about foreshadowing the 1987 crash and connect it with historic downs, such as 1929, their critics could counter with: "How can you talk about cycles when nothing's really the same this time? Just for instance, the low was around 384 in 1929 and only 1616 in 1987 . . ." Harvey Wasserman, who sees cyclic rhythms in the softer data of history, came up with a visual image that neatly solves the paradox of change within sameness. For his book *American Born and Reborn* he drew a spiral rising in ever tightening circles to accommodate the so-called progress and the perceived acceleration in human events that make today's America so very different from that of Pilgrim times and yet still cyclical in character. The spiral analogy—I personally see it as a spiral staircase—can also accommodate natural history with its evidences of evolution. The spiral made so much sense to me as a layman with regard to all aspects of cycles that I tried it out on each member of the professional staff of the Foundation for the Study of Cycles and found them largely in agreement.

There is yet another aspect of the cycle that makes it harder to define than the rose—its individuality. As Mogey explains it: "Cycles are idealized. They're a little like Platonic ideas. Plato used to say that there is an idea of man but no man is like that idea. Uniqueness is more significant than similarity in the way a man develops. In a cycle you have an ideal rhythm, but the unique way in which a cycle works out its uniqueness is much more critical." Mogey was discussing cycles in the financial markets, but in *Cycles of Becoming* Alexander Ruperti was dealing with cycles in human affairs when he wrote:

"If a cycle is reduced to a closed circle of repetitive events, it cannot have the creative, evolutionary meaning it possesses when understood to be the expression of a creative process. And yet, as a matter of fact, both interpretations of a cycle are correct. The *structure* of a cycle in time, i.e., its duration, repeats itself. A day cycle repeats itself every twenty-four hours; the lunation cycle, on which the month is based, repeats itself at each New Moon; the year cycle repeats itself every twelve months. But those who limit their understanding of the significance of a cycle to such a repetitive sequence of time values—days, months, or years—forget that what *happens* during a given day, month or year, does *not* repeat itself exactly. The way we act and the meaning we find in a particular experience during a given cycle represent the creative, individual element."

The fact that the cycle doesn't lend itself to simplistic definition is one reason why it might prove to be the clue to solving many mysteries of the universe. However cycles may be seen or described, their presence and influence has been felt by mankind throughout all of recorded history. Using the standard image, Ralph Waldo Emerson, the sage of Concord, expressed this thought in words that rival those of Shakespeare or Stein: "The eye is the first circle; the horizon which it forms is the second, and throughout nature this primary figure is repeated without end. It is the highest emblem in the cipher of the world."

CHAPTER
3
THE ROTHSCHILD SECRET

FOR REASONS THAT become easily understandable in any investigation of the subject of cycles, the board of directors of the Foundation for the Study of Cycles has been dominated by businessmen throughout its fifty-year history. Although the non-profit foundation's mission is scientific inquiry into the phenomenon of cycles wherever and whenever they can be found, cycle knowledge as a practical tool for living has so far been put to more use in business than in the other affairs of man. The great House of Rothschild is, in fact, credited by cycle scholars with discovering the value of this predictive device more than a century ago. The Rothschilds did not look upon cycles as a science but as a business secret that improved performance in their investment enterprises, and they guarded it as closely as manufacturers do their inventions and special processes.

From the literature, it is evident that the cycle tool didn't become a property of the general business community until the stock market crash of 1929 and the subsequent Great Depression prompted businessmen and economists alike to look for new answers to their problems. These events led directly to the establishment of the Foundation by Edward R. Dewey whose efforts had a lot to do with revealing the significance of cycles. In the beginning, however, even the Foundation followed the Rothschild rule of secrecy in order to raise money by selling cycle analysis to corporations. Fortunately for the existence of the Foundation, there has continued to be enough business interest even in shared secrets to account for the institution's ability to recruit the support and participation of men like its present chairman, Peter Borish, vice-president, research, Tudor Investment Corporation of New York.

Borish's immediate predecessor was Clarence Coleman, vice-chairman and director of the Coleman Company, Inc., Wichita, Kansas, who remains on the board. Other current board members include Walter Bressert, vice-chairman of the Foundation and president of HAL Management Company, Frisco, Colorado; Edward S. Dewey, son of the founder who acts as treasurer of the Foundation and is president of Management Advisors, Inc., Boston, Massachusetts; Gene Engleman, senior chairman and advisory director of the Texas Commerce Bank, Fort Worth, Texas; L. A. Hyland, chairman emeritus of Hughes Aircraft, Los Angeles, California. This is only a sampling of the business types serving on Foundation boards, past and present, but it is sufficient to show that cycles are taken quite seriously by presumably hard-headed money men.

This was not always so. Dewey, a man who was able to view what became his obsession with a healthy sense of humor, liked to recount two tales of his early efforts to interest businessmen in what an awareness of cycles could do for them. A man he called Charlie, vice-president of one of the nation's ten top corporations, listened to Dewey with

28

interest and then said, "I think you really have something, but I don't want to get in bad around here."

Charlie called the company's comptroller into his office and asked, "Bill, how much can I spend for a crazy idea and be able to laugh it off if anything ever comes up about it?"

"Five hundred dollars," Bill replied.

"That's what I thought, too," Charlie said and turned to Dewey. "All right, Mr. Dewey, make a study for us of the cycles in our industry. Hold the cost to five hundred dollars and send the study and bill to me."

Dewey carried through, got the five hundred dollars but no follow-up. In another case the vice-president of a New York bank also seemed interested but finally said, "I believe in astrology. I never take any action without consulting my astrologer. When were you born?"

When Dewey gave him the date, the man said, "I'll send this date on to my astrologer. If he approves, I'll contact you further."

Dewey never heard from the man, which may account for the fact that the Foundation to this day does not consider astrology, as popularly publicized and practiced, a proper part of the science of cycles. But Dewey had no cause to be discouraged in view of the caliber of the men he was able to recruit.

One of the most enthusiastic and longest serving chairman of the Foundation was W. Clement Stone, the millionaire Chicago entrepreneur, who resigned only recently by reason of age. Stone's support for the Foundation was in gratitude for the kind of experience anybody can appreciate—the making of his millions. He told the story of his personal involvement in his own publication, Success: The Magazine for Achievers:

"Many years ago, I had a large loan at the American National Bank and Trust Company in Chicago. One day, Paul Raymond, vice-president in charge of loans, telephoned me and said, 'Clem, I am sending a book to everyone who has a large loan with us.' I laughed and responded, 'I can read. What's the name of the book?' He said, '*Cycles* by Edward R. Dewey and Edwin F. Dakin.'

"Because I had developed the habit at an early age to recognize, relate, assimilate and apply principles from what I read, saw, heard, thought and experienced, I discovered a missing ingredient on how to predict my future and make a fortune—and not lose it. When I see my business leveling off, I use a principle learned from *Cycles:* Start a new trend with new life, new blood, new ideas, new activities. That's why I now predict that I shall increase my wealth by a few hundred million dollars in the next five years.

"You, too, can predict your future and make a fortune if you are willing to study, learn, and apply the principles of cycles and trends and daily engage in creative, positive thinking time."

Borish's entry into cycleland came about in a manner very much like that of Stone's. In 1985, after a stint at the New York Federal Reserve Bank, he joined Tudor where, as he puts it, "My first marching orders were to learn as much as I could about cycles and seasonality, because we felt that if the market, whichever market you are looking at, behaves in a cyclic manner, it should be relatively fixed in terms of periodicity." A study of the data over a 220-year period has, for example, established a 17¾-year cycle in cotton prices; a study begun in 1860 has fixed a 3½-year cycle in corn prices. In each case, the peaks are that far apart on average. Borish's research into cycles was not only convincing enough to lead him into active participation in the Foundation but to widen his view of its function. "My idea is to make the Foundation an interdisciplinary medium for exchange of information on all cycles, not just in the market," he told me.

Like the board and membership, most of the staff of the Foundation came out of the business world, starting with

Dewey and running right down to the newly appointed executive director, Richard Mogey, and his managing director, Gary Bosley, both of whom learned to use cycles in the markets. The first research director, Gertrude Shirk, something of a pioneer in both cycle analysis and careers for women, graduated with a degree in business administration from the University of Pittsburgh and went to work in the department of economic and statistical analysis at Westinghouse Electric Corporation. In a foreshadowing of the Borish experience she was told by her boss, Frank Newberry, vice-president in charge of new products and a cycle enthusiast, to look into using cycles to add time-period analysis to econometric analysis.

By the time Ms. Shirk left Westinghouse to go to work for Ford Motor Company in Dearborn, Michigan, as an analyst in marketing, she had learned enough to feel that she was bringing the effective tool of cycle analysis to her new tasks, but she was in for the same kind of treatment that Dewey had experienced. "In the automobile industry, cycles was a naughty word," she says. This, of course, was in the days before Lee Iacocca, an avowed proponent of cycles, surfaced as a power in Detroit. Moreover, Ms. Shirk sensed the same kind of conservatism, which would now be called discrimination, with respect to the employment and promotion of women. It wasn't long before she packed her bags, went back to Pittsburgh and signed on with Dewey for the duration of her career.

It says something for the fascination of cycles that Ms. Shirk could tell me, "One of the considerations I had in looking for a new job when I left Ford was that I never wanted to be bored. Any job has a lot of dog work, of course, but overall the work at the Foundation was never, ever boring." In addition to seeking out and testing cycles through statistical analysis, Ms. Shirk became the voice of cycles as editor of the Foundation's magazine. Hers can be a delightfully blunt voice. When, for instance, I asked why there was so much concentration on economics in the Foundation's work, she said, "People are always concerned about money, aren't they? As a matter of fact, writing was invented to take care of numerical transactions, wasn't it?"

However close to the heart, concern about money is itself cyclical, according to Ms. Shirk. "Public and professional interest in cycles seems to come and go with the times. When things are prosperous, people are not concerned about a downturn; they think things will go up forever. But when there is a downturn, people are interested in the possibility that it might be rhythmic in nature," she says. This shortsighted fickleness could create a problem—a kind of reverse cycle—for a Foundation dependent upon membership fees and contributions from interested parties.

Quite apart from the interest that money-related topics generate, a concentration on economic information in cycle literature is the natural result of an available wealth of data. Ms. Shirk's contention that writing was first used to record economic data suitable for statistical analysis extends further back into the history of almost every country than data in any other discipline. In fact, historically, America has paid more attention to business than to that proverbial conversation starter, the weather. Although useful price figures date from 1720, regular meteorological records didn't start for another century.

Some cycles in business are so natural and obvious that people make use of them instinctively. In this category would be the recurring seasonal demand for things like fuel, clothing, toys, recreational equipment. Although there are some complicating marketing factors, commodities tend to have a structure imparted by the cycles of nature. Ms. Shirk cites soy beans, which have an annual cycle that is 70 percent accurate. In view of the fact that the odds in pure chance are 50-50, an investor who uses a 70-30 predictor as a guide over a long period seems bound to win. There are even more reliable cycles, some of which lurk in the tangle of data produced by the frantic daily trading on Wall Street. These are neither natural nor obvious, and are usually arrived at by mathematically minded observers armed with computers. But Dr. Anthony F. Herbst, a professor of finance at the University of Texas, who designed a software program that the Foundation sells, rates the accuracy of computer assisted cycle analysis thus: "On a scale of one to ten with ten being perfect accuracy and one being worthless, I'd say probably seven to nine, in that range. That's very good."

With odds like that available, why aren't there more winners on Wall Street? Why are there so many business and banking bankruptcies? Why aren't people breaking down the doors of the Foundation and the offices of commercial cycle analysts? In terms of the numbers of people actively employing cycle theory as compared to the millions upon millions of people involved in business, the cycle might as well still be the Rothschild secret. (Investors close to the Foundation who heeded its forecast of stock market action in 1987 did very well with their personal funds in that year's crash.) There are a number of factors involved in the neglect of cycles, many of which will surface as important themes in the unfolding story of this phenomenon.

The first of these factors is that cycles study has not yet found a firm place in the curriculum of economics—or any other discipline. "In higher education, in economic and statistical analysis, the emphasis is on systems analysis, on econometric analysis rather than on time series themselves," says Ms. Shirk. "In courses in economics you study cause and effect. For instance, take copper prices. The thinking goes: deliveries of copper are going down so we expect the price to be cut." Ms. Shirk acknowledges an increasing interest in the methodology of time series analysis in academic circles, but people like Professor Herbst who introduce cycles into college courses are still pioneers.

One professor, now retired, who taught a course in time

series analysis at the University of West Florida for fifteen years is Dr. A. Bruce Johnson. Dr. Johnson turned to cycles as a way of dealing with a puzzling paradox in the stock markets. "When I first got interested in the stock market, I found the news misleading," he recalls. "If a piece of good economic news comes out, instead of the market responding positively it responds in a negative way. This set me to thinking. There must be something more to this than just economic news and economic forecasts—the fundamentals, that is. That something else is mass psychology which may be expressed as periods of mass optimism and other periods of mass pessimism regardless of the economic outlook, and they appear to go in cycles. Now I say forget the news and try cycles."

Dr. Johnson's feeling that cycles might reflect the human element in the economic data was shared by Paul A. Volcker, a former chairman of the Federal Reserve, when he delivered the 1978 Moskowitz Lecture with the interesting title, "The Rediscovery of the Business Cycle." His remarks were prompted by the shock of a 1970s recession that seemed to come out of nowhere to stem an economic tide that had been rising steadily since World War II. "The evidence seems to me pretty clear that there is some tendency toward swings in the tempo and mood of business activity over relatively long periods of time—say periods of ten to twenty years," he told his audience. "Those swings may be influenced by a variety of more or less objective events, such as changes in population, wars and their aftermath, waves of technological innovation, and so on. But those swings also appear to be influenced by less tangible, even psychological phenomena. Specifically, a long period of prosperity breeds confidence, and confidence breeds new standards of what is prudent.

"For a while, the process is self-reinforcing, sustaining investment and risk taking. But it may also contain some of the seeds of its own demise: eventually natural limits to

34

some of the trends supporting the advance are reached, and the advance cannot be sustained so easily. We find ourselves with more houses and shopping centers and oil tankers and steel capacity than we can readily absorb. Financial positions are extended, and the economy has become more vulnerable to adverse and unexpected developments.

"As a result we find that a business setback is not coped with so easily by policy changes that served so well in a more buoyant underlying environment. So the mood turns conservative and uncertain: we rediscover the business cycle. Viewed in this light, we need look no further than human nature to find some explanation for recurrent swings in business activity in a market economy."

Volcker managed to put a wry twist on Gertrude Shirk's blunt statement about turning to cycles in times of trouble. He also recognized another facet of human nature that begs to rule out cycles: people, especially those with political motivation, want to believe good news will go on forever. The Republican Administration's chant after 1929 that "prosperity is just around the corner" still rings a sour note in many living memories, but Volcker stuck to quoting more current pronouncements in the same key. Listen to Arthur Oken, who was named Chairman of the Council of Economic Advisers in 1968, as quoted by Volcker: "When recessions were a regular feature of the economic environment, they were often viewed as inevitable. . . . Recessions are now generally considered fundamentally preventable, like airplane crashes and unlike hurricanes." Or listen to an earlier Council Chairman, Walter Heller, who, according to Volcker, said in 1969 that there was "a constantly deepening conviction in the business and financial community that alert and active fiscal-monetary policy will keep the economy operating at a higher proportion of its potential in the future than in the past; that beyond short and temporary slowdowns, or perhaps even a recession—that's not ruled

35

out in this vast and dynamic economy of ours—lies the prospect of sustained growth in that narrow band around full employment." Volcker notes, too, that in the surging sixties the Department of Commerce changed the title of its monthly statistical publication from Business Cycle Developments to Business Conditions Digest. In those optimistic times, cycles, like God, were considered dead. Who needed them?

In quoting those statements, Volcker was caught up in form of cycle himself; and he was more prescient than he may have known. Another rising economic tide after the low ebb of the early 1980s (which was caused by Volcker's own policy at the Federal Reserve of wringing out inflation) provoked another round of official optimism. In March 1989 columnist George F. Will wrote of some interesting exchanges during public discussion of shaky bank loans such as the $21 billion that some eleven banks had put out to finance leveraged buyouts. Kenneth J. H. Pinkers of Moody's, a Dun & Bradstreet subsidiary, told Congress that "there *is* a business cycle," and expressed concern about such loans "*when* the business cycle returns." On the other hand, Michael Boskin, another chairman of the Council of Economic Advisers, was quoted as saying that no recession is necessary, that it is a misreading of economic history to suggest that either the frequency or amplitude of recessions is predictable, that he knew of "no economic law mandating that economic expansion died of old age." Columnist Will waffled on the issue. Even as he admitted that Boskin's statements could be true, he pointed out that there had been eight recessions in the past forty years, an average of one every five years.

The debate on the value of cycles would seem to be as eternal and predictable as adherents claim the cycles themselves are. At least one reason for this is clear. Just about anyone engaged in economic activity is reluctant to give up on the econometric models based on cause and effect that dominate the discipline, which is sometimes called a science. For the scholar, they provide a way of organizing and manipulating data to arrive at a rational thesis. For business people, they offer theoretical support to a desire to feel in control of both personal and corporate destiny. For the economic advisers to politicians, they document the pleasing assurance that leaders can have the power to improve the economy by following certain policies. The thought that an uncontrollable cycle can wipe out an intellectual construction cemented with research and logic like a tide can crumble a stone sea wall is threatening. Yet it happens all the time. Consider this example that Volcker reported laconically with respect to the 1970s recession: "Econometric models of consumer behavior no longer seem to fit the facts of the emerging situation. For example, the consumption function developed by Albert Ando and Franco Modigliani for the FRB-MIT-Penn model overpredicted consumption by \$6 billion in mid-1973, and by about \$13 billion by the end of that year—a sizable error." Still, it runs contrary to human nature to expect that people who have invested a great deal of money or a painstakingly acquired reputation as experts in the system will surrender easily their conviction that they should be able to manage it to their taste and advantage.

More often than not cycle enthusiasts are looked upon by people in charge of things as the bearers of bad news, and the fate of such messengers is well known. The most dramatic instance of this in cycle history took place not in capitalistic America but in communistic Russia. During the 1920s an economist named Nikolai Kondratieff, laboring quietly in a Moscow institute, set out presumably to prove the instability of capitalism by a detailed study of prices, wages, interest rates, foreign trade, bank deposits, and other economic data as well as factors related to social and cultural life in capitalistic countries throughout the nineteenth century. Kondratieff concluded that capitalism was subject to periodic recessions, but he claimed that it also enjoyed periodic highs. What he saw in the data was a wave of between fifty and fifty-six years duration undulating up and down—a visualization now known in cycle circles as the Kondratieff Wave, the K-wave, the long wave. Stalin, who wanted a prediction that capitalism was doomed, found the Kondratieff message so distasteful that he banished the messenger to Siberia. It is one of the more delicious ironies of history that Stalin's economics is being submerged by perestroika while Kondratieff's wave goes on cresting.

In an odd way, Dewey's discovery of cycles two decades later mirrored Kondratieff's. He, too, was working for the government and was assigned in the midst of the Depression to find out why capitalism had suffered such a crippling blow. Before he could reach any conclusions, he was swept out of his office in the Commerce Department by the broom of the New Deal. The assignment did, however, give Dewey an opportunity to talk to economists all over the country. As he later told Gertrude Shirk, he was disappointed to learn that nobody in the field agreed with anybody else and that none of them could elucidate the causes of the Depression clearly enough to be dealt with in the future. It was like seeing the proverbial light at the end of the tunnel when he finally encountered Chapin Hoskins, who had studied the economy from his desk as managing editor of Forbes, and was then in the business of cycle analysis. Hoskins told Dewey, "I can't tell you *why* depressions happen, but I can tell you *when* they will." Dewey gave up on his search for an answer as to why and went to work with Hoskins in what was the beginning of a lifelong search into the mysteries of when.

If optimists and economic activists resist yielding to the use of cycles in their monetary affairs, so do the intellectually lazy. Stone's prescription for making millions with the use of cycles rather significantly includes the order to "daily engage in creative, positive thinking time." As with any effort to create a model or abstraction of a living organism, the cycle analyst has to find a way through a tangle of ambiguities, contradictions, surprises, disappointments. Bafflement begins with the acknowledged circumstance that there is no such thing as a single cycle at work in any given situation.

Even before the computer was available to ferret out the multiplicity of cycles in a mound of data, Harvard's Joseph Schumpeter noted in his seminal and monumental work, *Business Cycles*: "There is no reason why the cyclical process of evolution should give rise to just one movement. On the contrary, there are many reasons to expect that it will set into motion an indefinite number of wavelike fluctuations which will roll on simultaneously and interfere with one another in the process. Nor does the impression we derive from any graph of economic time series lend support to a single-cycle hypothesis. It is much more natural to assume the presence of many fluctuations of different span and intensity, which seem to be superimposed on each other." Schumpeter's assumptions have become gospel today in the light of what the better tools for statistical analysis are revealing as well as in the reflection from broader theoretical concepts of the nature of cycles.

Among the cycles that have to be taken under consideration in a business context are the K-wave and a newer long wave theory postulated by R. N. Elliott which is based on the same observation that there is a natural ebb and flow of human economic activity. Then there are a variety of shorter cycles that might be relevant to the product or market in question. These days, too, a cycle analyst tends to ponder the increasing evidence that economic cycles may be linked to natural cycles such as those of solar activity. Because the graphs of solar-planetary activity show periodicities similar to those in the markets, a theory has developed that cycles in energy coming from the sun are a factor in the "psychological phenomena" that Volcker sees in the markets. Dr. Johnson, for instance, has recently begun using planetary cycles in conjunction with other cycles to make long-range forecasts of turning points in the stock market. The key to correct analysis, according to Richard Mogey, is to "know where you are within a basket of cycles."

The basket is a full one. Using hourly data, daily data, weekly data and on up the line of time, Mogey has so far proved that at least 230 cycles in the stock market are statistically valid. But statistical validity only tells the analyst that the cycle is probably not random. "Statistical validity isn't as significant as importance," Mogey explains. "I'm interested in the fewer number of cycles that account for the greatest movement in the market. It's a little like the situation where 20 percent of your business brings 80 percent of the profits. There are what I call economic cycles and cycles unique to the market you are dealing with. In seasonal markets, for instance, take soy beans. In the soy bean market you will not find a lot of short little cycles. Six months after the beans are in the ground, they know what the crop will be and therefore the market becomes immune to short term variation."

Mogey claims that deciding which cycles are in control of a given market at a given time is a fairly straightforward process that involves a number of established steps and techniques. One of the most important of these is to determine a cycle's history. "It's just like a doctor taking a patient's history," he said. "If you have blood pressure of 90 over 130 the doctor might think it's high. But if, in fact, your blood pressure had been 100 over 150 he might take a different view of it. So in the same way you have to know about the cycle. Every cycle produces a change above and below the trend of an approximate percentage. Looking at the whole data, you must know what the mean change was for that cycle, and you also have to know what the deviations have been and whether or not that cycle is ever a part of another cycle."

Mogey cited the hypothetical case of a thirty-week cycle and a ten-week cycle. If you're looking at a thirty-week cycle and find another cycle with similar phasing three times, or every ten weeks, within it, the ten-week cycle has to be part of the thirty-week one. Ten is a harmonic of thirty, i.e. $3 \times 10 = 30$, so these cycles can be seen to be part of the same system whereas nine- or eleven- or twelve-week cycles could not. When examined, the history of the ten-week cycle might show a mean percentage change in amplitude (or height) of seven with deviations as high as nine above and ten below. If this cycle goes over 9 percent or down to 11 percent, chances are that another cycle is at work. If the cycle fails to turn as it has in the past, chances are that another cycle is dominant. In this case, according to Mogey, it is a 90-percent certainty that another cycle has taken over.

Aside from the numbers of cycles involved, the analyst has to determine from history what might be called the cycle's probable shape. Although the sine wave is often used as a model for a cycle, it is inadequate. The sine wave is supposed to move 50 percent above and 50 percent below a given line over a period of time. A two-year cycle that behaved like a sine wave would be expected to go up a year and down a year whereas in the market, as Mogey explains, "a real two-year pattern probably moves up a year and a half and probably goes sideways and down for less time." Out of his long and close study of cyclical history, Mogey recommends paying close attention to the down side of cycles. His reading of the market movement in 1987 is illustrative:

"It was a three-and-a-half-year cycle that topped in July 1987, and that assumes a year and a half or year and three quarters up and the same time down. But when the cycle high came so close to the exact high it told me that the

41

chances were that the low would come very early in the cycle. It's a tendency I've observed. I knew that the market wasn't going to go down for a year and three quarters. This just doesn't happen, even in the worst times. The market barely did it back in the 1930s. So the chances were that there would be rallies in between. By the same token, when the market continues to go higher after the ideal topping time, the chances are that the low will be on time. But that you learn from taking a careful history."

In the actual event, it was a very cautious reading of the puzzling 40.68-month cycle in stock prices by Gertrude Shirk that made it possible for alert Foundation members to take advantage of the 1987 crash. This is the cycle that, in Dewey's words, could "keep scientists humble." Acknowledging that the cycle had flip-flopped after World War II, Ms. Shirk nevertheless said in her landmark Cycles article in March 1987: "In spite of this latter day anomaly, subsequent analysis using weighted moving average to filter the

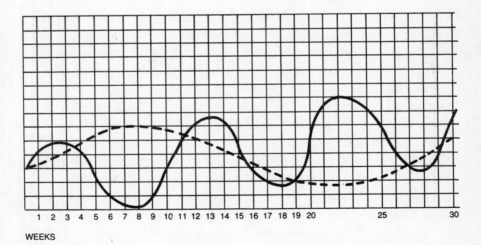

WEEKS

In a hypothetical "basket of cycles," there is a rising trend line criss-crossed by 30-week and 10-week cycles that rise and fall by three points. Sharper rises and drops show that a new dominant cycle is in control.

data more precisely, confirmed the 40.68-month period as a statistically significant cycle. The next benchmark on the cycle is at July 1987. This point in time is the critical month around which actual prices will reveal whether or not the cycle is again effective. July 1987 is not a forecast—it is the checkpoint against which we can measure the behavior of the 40.68-month cycle." Experienced cycle watchers weren't fooled by her caution and knew better than to stay in the market much beyond that "critical" month.

Complicated as it may sound, cycle analysis for business purposes can be learned, as in the case of many other pursuits, by doing. Obviously, it would help to have a good grasp of—or at least a keen interest in—mathematics as well as some computer literacy. The new software available from the Foundation should facilitate do-it-yourself analysis, but nobody claims that it will be easy. It certainly isn't a matter yet of rote learning or employing mechanical methods. A great deal of judgment and/or intuition is involved. When

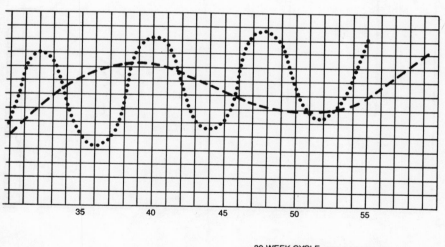

| 35 | 40 | 45 | 50 | 55 |

30-WEEK CYCLE — — — — —
10-WEEK CYCLE ——————
NEW DOMINANT 8-WEEK CYCLE ••••••••••••

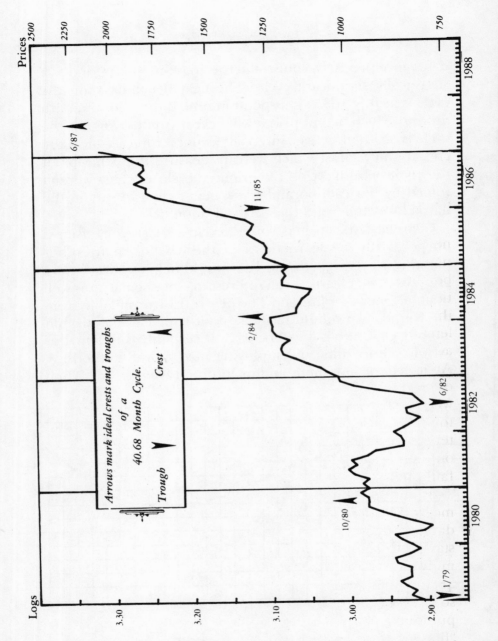

One of the graphs used to forecast the 1987 market crash showed the monthly average of the daily close of the Dow-Jones Industrial Average as compared with the ideal 40.68-month cycle. *(Cycles Magazine)*

Dr. Johnson first introduced planetary cycles into his mix of statistical cycles and other economic factors, he got a nearly perfect forecast of the movement on the New York Stock Exchange for 1988, but it went awry in 1989. He takes the setback philosophically. There are thirty-six planetary cycles, according to Dr. Johnson, who is still experimenting with selecting the five or six most influential ones to use in a composite for forecasting. "Cylces is still an art and still needs lots of work, but it is the only way to go," he insists.

Fortunately, a technical mastery of cycle analysis isn't necessary for anyone who wants to make use of it in business or investment. The results of a variety of analyses can be obtained from the Foundation or from private practitioners. What's needed is an attitude about cycles. Knowing that cycles are out there when you are dealing with problems in economics is analogous to knowing that doctors are available for consultation when you have health problems. An interesting aspect of this analogy is that medicine is often referred to as an art rather than a science, even by its wiser practitioners. Nevertheless, most people go to doctors, and cycle believers are incredulous when they encounter the unfortunately widespread ignorance or indifference on the part of people who could benefit directly from the faith the cycle believers espouse.

Examples abound, but a fairly typical one was recited to me by Foundation managing director Bosley. Because of the damage droughts have done lately, the Foundation has started to collect data on drought cycles in the American midwest. When I talked to Bosley, the Foundation had some 48,000 weather observations dating from 1865. One of the sources for this data was a utility company that had already put it on a computer disc. Bosley was so delighted with the "find" that he approached another utility in the hope of obtaining similar data. He was told by the company's marketing department: "By law we have to keep six years of data but we don't fuss with that stuff." The story was totally believable to me since I had tried to get records from my own water company dating back only five years and discovered that they had all vanished into thin air. I also found Bosley's reasoning flawless. "On which of those two companies would you bet?" he asked. "The first company has to be given an *A* for coming up with that data and working with it to anticipate the demands that could be put upon them."

When it comes to appropriating the Rothschild secret for personal use, a conversation I had with Richard Mogey is worth repeating almost verbatim:

Q "Can an ordinary citizen use cycle analysis?"

A "The average person couldn't analyze the cycles. It takes a good deal of training in statistics and computers to do it. But people with computers can get a program from the Foundation and try to produce an analysis themselves. It's like anything else—some people are better at it than others. I've never done anything that there wasn't somebody better at it than I."

Q "What's *your* batting average on analysis?"

A "Somewhere between 80 and 90 percent. I think that's about what you can expect out of cycles. But back to your original question, the average citizen can use what comes out of cycle analysis. For instance, if he or she had known that sometime in July or August of 1987 there would be a major top in the market, that would have been very useful information. That's why we have a membership magazine.

"Cycles are concerned with timing, and most brokerage houses are not. The last thing they want to see is everybody out of the stock market. It's not in their self-interest to tell people we are going to have bad times for the next two years, and you shouldn't be investing in stocks. So they've taken another tack—and it's a reasonable tack. They say they're going to find the best quality stock for you in terms of company performance, and some of them do a very good job at this. Even in bad times, a good stock can perform well. Stock picking and timing are two entirely different things. Most of the major brokerage houses are focused on stock picking.

"An investor has to be very clear about his objectives. The average investor is much better off buying and holding except in major moves of the market. So there's a certain degree of timing. To have been in good stocks in 1982 and gotten out in early 1987 would have been perfect. And the investor who did that should probably be on the sidelines now [spring of 1989], in Treasury bills waiting for a new cycle to begin which should be in 1991 or so. Get in before a new rise. Cycle lows are the beginning of new strength in the market, and cycle highs are the end of the strength and the beginning of weakness.

"Despite the fact that we are approaching all time highs for Dow Jones and S. & P. [Standard and Poor's], the majority of investors should take a look at the value, at the average. It isn't all that high. If you were in some of the thirty Dow stocks or some of the S. & P. 500—not all, because I could show you some very fine stocks from very good companies that have done nothing—you might have done well. In a bull market, it is hard not to pick the right stock, but in a market like we have now picking is critical. If you can get 9 percent with no risk at all, you shouldn't be greedy; you should take the 9 percent."

As Mogey's comments would indicate, cycle theory is not a guide to quick killings in business or the markets, nor is it advice on how to outsmart everybody else. That it was once a secret of the long-lasting Rothschilds seems symbolic. The real secret of cycles as a business tool was spelled out in language reminiscent of Ecclesiastes by Dan Ascani, editor of the Elliott Wave Commodity Forecast, when he wrote in an article for Cycles:

"The natural laws of the universe remind us once again that, for every action, there is a reaction. For every upwave, there is a downwave. For every expansion, there is a contraction. For every bull market, there is a bear market. Survival comes to those who understand, accept, and prepare for these natural swings."

CHAPTER

4

GETTING IN—AND OUT OF— THE MOOD

IN DECEMBER 1988 there appeared in the New York *Times* a remarkable document by William Styron, author of several best-selling novels, including *Sophie's Choice* and *Confessions of Nat Turner*. Styron was explaining and defending the action of an Italian writer, Primo Levi, who had committed suicide by jumping down a stairwell the year before. Other commentators had expressed disillusionment and disappointment that a man who had survived Auschwitz and written inspiringly about it could kill himself, as if the act represented a form of moral failure. Styron argued that Levi was a victim of clinical depression, an illness as real and painful and often fatal as a heart attack. Styron's argument was unusually convincing because it was based on personal confession.

Just a year before Levi's death Styron had committed himself to a mental hospital in order to keep from killing himself. His graphic description of the torture that drove him to this decision bears repeating:

"The pain of the depression from which I had suffered for more than five months had become intolerable. I never attempted suicide, but the possibility had become more real and the desire more greedy as each wintry day passed and the illness became more smotheringly intense. What had begun that summer as an off-and-on malaise and a vague, spooky restlessness had gained gradual momentum until my nights were without sleep and my days were pervaded by a gray drizzle of unrelenting horror.

"In depression, a kind of biochemical meltdown, it is the brain as well as the mind that becomes ill—as ill as any other besieged organ. The sick brain plays evil tricks on its inhabiting spirit. Slowly overwhelmed by the struggle, the intellect blurs into stupidity. All capacity for pleasure disappears, and despair maintains a merciless daily drumming. The smallest commonplace of domestic life, so amiable to the healthy mind, lacerates like a blade. Thus, mysteriously, in ways difficult to accept by those who have never suffered it, depression comes to resemble physical anguish.

"Most physical distress yields to some analgesia—not so depression. Psychotherapy is of little use to the profoundly depressed, and anti-depressents are, to put it generously, unreliable. Even the soothing balm of sleep usually disappears. And so, because there is no respite at all, it is entirely natural that the victim begins to think ceaselessly of oblivion."

Styron's words make chillingly vivid the individual agony involved in mental disorder, one of the most pervasive afflictions of human beings worldwide. Consider this doleful drumbeat of statistics issued by the National Institute of Mental Health in the same year that Styron was stricken:

— In any six-month period, approximately 29.4 million adult Americans (18.7 percent of the population) suffer from some form of mental disorder.

— Between 1958 and 1982, a total of 587,821 persons in the United States ended their own lives by self-inflicted injuries.

— For males, the most frequent disorders are alcohol abuse/dependence, phobia, drug abuse/dependence, and dysthymia (abnormal condition of the mind).

— For females, the most frequent disorders are phobia, *major depressive episode without grief,* dysthymia, and obsessive-compulsive disorders.

— In the year of 1980, total expenditures for mental health care in the United States were estimated to be between $19.4 billion and $24.1 billion, approximately 7.7 percent of the total expenditure for general health care.

In view of the massive individual and collective suffering caused by mental disorders, it would seem necessary to take seriously any theory that can throw light on the functioning of the complicated human psychological system. In the case of clinical depression, for instance, Styron reports that the cause remains a puzzle despite modern medical advances. There is a confusing mix of probable factors—chemical, genetic, environmental, psychological. With no sure cause, there is no sure cure. But Styron sounds a note of hope with respect to clinical depression that could have come straight out of cycle literature: "Depression's saving grace (perhaps its only one) is that the illness seems to be self-limiting: Time is the real healer and with or without treatment the sufferer usually gets well."

It was the promise that cycle theory offers for dealing more effectively with both normal and pathological mental states that led Dr. Jeffrey Horovitz, a practicing psychiatrist, into the surprising career change that made him the executor director of the Foundation for the Study of Cycles. While he was an in-hospital resident in Florida, Dr. Horovitz became intrigued by a rhythm he detected in psychiatric admissions. At first it was a casual observation. When he couldn't find a bed for a patient he would call another hospital and ask, "Do you have any room left over there?" More often than not, they would say, "No, we're packed here, too." A few days later, the other hospital would call back and report, "We have plenty of beds open now. Do you need any?" By then Dr. Horovitz's hospital would also have beds to spare. Keeping tabs on such incidents, he discovered that there would be a day or two of massive admissions to all the psychiatric facilities in the city every three to nine weeks. In addition, he observed that more than 50 percent of admissions were recurring—patients who had been hospitalized before.

Like many a thinker who wanders off on a new trail, Dr. Horovitz had a lonely time of it for a while. Whenever he broached the subject of these admissions patterns to medical colleagues, the response was, "Sure there are big days, but so what?" A man who enjoys spreading his enthusiasms, Dr. Horovitz talked to patients about it, too. One of them, an economics professor, brought in a pamphlet from the Foundation for the Study of Cycles having to do with cycles in the stock market and said, "I thought you might find this interesting since you've talked so much about recurring patterns in human behavior." Even then, Dr. Horovitz let the pamphlet gather dust since there seemed to be no connection between the money markets and medicine. But he picked it up when he became interested in investing and began discussing cycles with brokers. When one of them suggested that there was a correlation between cycles in solar activity and those in the market, Dr. Horovitz had a wild thought: would the patterns in psychiatric admissions that he was toying with look anything like stock market or solar cycles?

Dr. Horovitz first tried comparing a graph of solar activity with his own of hospital admissions. There was enough of a fit to be interesting, but the real eureka moment came when he picked up a *Wall Street Journal* and saw that the chart of the ups and downs on the market looked very much like the other two. He rushed to the office of a medical professor who had been skeptical about his interest in admission patterns but who was a keen follower of the market. Handing the professor a graph, Dr. Horovitz asked, "What does that look like?"

"It looks like the Dow Jones average over the past three or four months," the professor replied.

"It is solar activity adjusted to try to forecast psychiatric admissions," Dr. Horovitz said.

"What?!"

Although he didn't become an instant convert, the professor was astounded and enthralled. Actually, Dr. Horovitz's initial results didn't prove anything in the long run, because he didn't have the necessary data. He now admits that they could have been a case of coincidence, but the spark they struck turned into flame. "I actually had tears in my eyes when I thought it was working," he recalls. "There was a hint in those look-alike cycles that there was something more to the universe than I was told in school. Somebody left something out. There had to be some connecting link."

So instead of being discouraged, Dr. Horovitz gave up his practice, went to Pittsburgh where the Foundation was then located, signed on to work there and eventually replaced Dr. John T. Burns as executive director. Dr. Burns, a chronobiologist, wanted to return to teaching at Bethany College, but he continues as secretary of the Foundation's board of directors. Like Dr. Horovitz, Dr. Burns is primarily interested in cycles in living creatures and a firm believer in the important role they play. Dr. Horovitz also resigned as executive director in 1989 mainly to pursue, in conjunction with the Foundation, a study he launched to collect worldwide data on the cycles in mental health.

Surprisingly, this has proved difficult. Hospital chains in

the United States have declined to provide records of psychiatric admissions for the Foundation's study, stating that they didn't want to reveal their numbers to their competitors. Even promises not to disclose the sources of information have so far been ineffective. Perhaps the hospitals have more reason to worry about business than they actually know. Dr. Horovitz's conviction is that, once there is enough data to establish the cyclical nature of mental illnesses, much hospitalization can be avoided. "For instance, if we know one of those waves of admissions is coming up at a certain time, doctors can tell patients to increase their medication to a therapeutic dose—perhaps double—to stabilize them through the stress period," he says.

Since discovering cycleland, Dr. Horovitz's confidence that he can eventually prove his thesis has understandably increased. Although work has only begun on what might be called the mass aspects of mental health, the Foundation's files are stuffed with fascinating material on studies over the last fifty years that show cycles at work in the individual psyche. The existence, if not the cause, of cycles in normal mood swings as well as in pathological states has been well established.

Much of the work in this area is being done these days by chronobiologists, specialists in the effect of time on living systems. In a recent overview of this field Susan Perry and Jim Dawson, in their book *The Secrets Our Body Clocks Reveal,* report discoveries about clinical depression that illuminate Styron's experience:

"Clinical depression—a severe mood disorder that is typified by intense feelings of sadness and often accompanied by serious disturbances in normal body functions—is also a recurrent illness.

"Sometimes the cycles of clinical depression are short and, thus, easy to spot. This is especially true of manic-depressive psychosis, a type of mental illness in which depressive episodes alternate with periods of mania or excessive excitement, hyperactivity, and rapidly changing thoughts. For example, several cases of people with forty-eight-hour manic-depressive cycles (episodes of depression and mania falling on alternate days) have been reported in the medical literature. In one famous case, a salesman in Washington, D.C., became so morose and apathetic on his depressed days that he was unable to leave his car once he arrived at the offices of his clients. On his 'up' days, on the other hand, he was the ideal salesman—loquacious and aggressive. He worked around his illness by making appointments with clients on alternate days.

"Such short cycles are relatively rare, however. Clinical depression is more often characterized by annual cycles. It is most common in spring. Not surprisingly, spring is also the peak season for suicides.

"Researchers have found that the circadian [daily] rhythms of depressed people are different from those of nondepressed people. For example:

- Body temperature tends to peak earlier in the day in depressed people than in nondepressed people.

- The daily rise of cortisol [adrenal excretion] begins earlier than usual in depressed people—specifically, early in the evening rather than late at night.

- Levels of thyroid stimulating hormone (TSH), which indirectly affects mood, fall to their lowest point at night rather than in the morning, as is the case in nondepressed people.

- The daily peak of the hormone melatonin occurs earlier in the night in depressed people than in nondepressed people.

"All this seems to point to the depressed person's body clocks being out of kilter."

The reference to the effect of spring is an acknowledgement of one of the external—or exogenous, as they like to

55

call them in cycleland—influences on mood that is clearly cyclical and so generally accepted as to need no proof of its existence. In fact, Dr. Henry Schneiderman, an internist and pathologist at the University of Connecticut Health Center, told the New York *Times* last spring that the phenomenon known as "spring fever" is a "human diagnosis" rather than a medical diagnosis. Its symptoms, he said, are loss of concentration, wistfulness, failure to focus, restlessness—"an unwillingness to work on assigned tasks with the outbreak of good weather after the passage of a confining winter"—and everybody gets it. On the whole, Dr. Schneiderman considers spring fever a natural feeling that people should accommodate as much as possible by changing their schedules, but he adds, "If there is a stress present, I think spring fever can exacerbate it. So can cabin fever in the winter and a heat wave in the summer. Anything that takes us from our ordinary patterns of life can exacerbate a psychological problem."

The enormous effect of the great natural cycle of the changing seasons is a factor in every facet of cycle theory and observation. In the matter of moods, it is like a shifting backdrop against which the drama of inner—endogenous—cycles is played out in the individual. These emotional cycles in normal people were first studied scientifically more than half a century ago by Rex B. Hersey, an assistant professor of industry at the University of Pennsylvania. Hersey was engaged to investigate the effect, if any, that mood swings in workers had on safety in a number of industries. Over a period of twenty-three years, he studied more than a thousand individuals, two hundred of them intensively, in America and Europe. His work is still cited because, oddly, it has not been duplicated. One reason for this neglect may be the logistics involved. In one study, Hersey and his assistants virtually lived with twenty-five men in the plant of a utility company for thirty-six weeks,

interviewing each man four times each day to get the necessary quantity of data.

From the point of view of his specific assignment,
Hersey's results were decisive. In a sampling of eight hundred accidents, he discovered that 60 percent of them occurred when the worker was "in a worried, apprehensive,
or other low emotional state." For the long term, Hersey's
insights into emotional cycles in general are even more
valuable. In a summary of his study, he wrote:

"All the male workers studied over long periods showed
an 'emotional cycle.' This means that emotional tone varies
not only from time to time during the day but also exhibits
longer recurrent fluctuations based on internal phys-
iological functioning rather than external causes. This does
not mean that every person or even any person will suffer a
severe case of the 'blues' at regular intervals. It means
rather that there will be a lowering of a person's emotional
resistance and his capacity for integration and response
which may for any definite 'low' merely mean that he is less
happy than during the 'highs' both preceding and following. How acute the depression experienced in the 'low' may
be dependent not only upon the internal condition of the
person but also on his relation to his outer environment.
These recurrent emotional fluctuations in the workers
studied in America averaged about five weeks in length,
though it varies with the individual. The cyclical emotional
'low' can be expected to cover only about 10 percent of the
cycle, i.e., between two and four days in a thirty-five-day
cycle."

Aside from evidence of the existence and periodicity of
cycles, some other surprising and significant insights came
out of Hersey's work. Consider these few:

— In working out with his subjects a rating scale to describe
their emotional states, Hersey concluded that "the most de-

structive emotion, that which more than all others tends to bring men to an abnormal state, is without doubt worry."

— Although cycles vary as between individuals, an individual's cycle is never more than a week off his average. For instance, a person with a five-week cycle might occasionally have a six- or four-week cycle, but "never, in spite of all the buffets of misfortune, in spite of difficulties at home, in spite of great pleasure and unusual success, does this periodicity depart more than one week either way from its norm."

— Emotional "highs" are characterized by a sense of physical well-being, a drive toward activity, making pleasant plans for the future such as earning more money or buying a new car. "Lows" are characterized by lethargy and a reluctance to tackle any task requiring creative energy. The way to stimulate a person on high is to give him a problem to solve; the same person at a low would have difficulty solving the same problem.

— During an emotional high, a man "feels he is more powerful than his environment; he is master of his destiny." Yet, ironically, many men got less actual work accomplished during high periods because their energy and enthusiasm bubbled over into socialization, into sharing their well-being and creative thoughts with fellow workers.

— In their high periods, the men slept less, ate less—and had less sex, despite feeling a stronger sex drive. "This anomaly," Hersey opines, "seems caused by a restlessness at night, which the sex activity tends to quiet, rather than by an energic force driving the worker on."

Cycles related to sex are as commonly and instinctively accepted as those related to the seasons. Every woman lives with a menstrual cycle that has an average length of 29.5 days and recurs approximately four hundred times during a woman's life. As with any other cycle, the menstrual cycle is subject to irregularities. For most women it tends to be about thirty-five days during their teen years and shortens to twenty-eight days in their thirties. Certain external factors such as crash dieting, prolonged use of oral contraceptives, prolonged strenuous exercise such as long-distance running, emotional stress, tranquilizers and a number of ailments can change the timing or even cancel out the cycle. Premenstrual syndrome is an acknowledged mood regulator that has found its way, rightly or wrongly, into public controversy over women's roles in business and politics. In this connection, it is interesting to note that the menstrual cycle also shares with other cycles the fact that it is not functioning alone. In one of his bits of research, Professor Hersey determined that mood cycles often run along independently of the menstrual cycle. If a woman's mood cycle is, say, five weeks and her menstrual cycle four weeks, there will be times when happiness will be at its peak to dampen the sometimes negative premenstrual effects.

Men have sex-related cycles, too. There is a short cycle of rise and fall in sperm count, peaking for most men every three or four days. Then there's the fact that beards tend to grow most on Sunday and least on Wednesday about which Perry and Dawson theorize: "Because beard growth seems to be triggered by testosterone levels (which rise during sexual activity), this weekly increase and decrease in beard growth may be the result of increased sexual activity on the weekend."

So far it has proved difficult to subject mood cycles to the same sort of statistical verification and widespread practical adaptations that are possible with, say, economic cycles. They elude what is generally accepted as "scientific" measurement for a variety of reasons. Moods are by nature subjective and hard to describe in exact and broadly applicable terms. The only laboratory in which moods can be examined is the human psyche, and few people are willing to undergo the rigors necessary to arrive at reliable data. The exercise requires testing and recording emotional states on a daily basis over a long period of time in a manner analogous to keeping watch on bodily temperature. A few interested and determined individuals have tried to make laboratories of themselves with results that are more teasing than satisfying.

On January 1, 1959, Jack Dorland, a businessman who served on the board of the Foundation for the Study of Cycles and was founder of his own Society for the Investigation of Recurring Events, embarked on a fifteen hundred-day experiment throughout which he recorded his emotional state each day before the evening meal. When the graph of his emotional cycle was analyzed, it revealed a seven-day cycle in mood with the high on Wednesday and the low on Sunday. When Nancy B. Brinker reported on the Dorland experiment in the magazine Cycles in the early 1970s, she opined: "It seems probable that the seven-day week causes or induces the cycle. However, it is possible that the seven-day emotional cycle is universal and that it may have caused the adoption of the seven-day week."

Subsequent research in the field of chronobiology is tending to support the latter conclusion. The socially decreed seven-day week, dating from the Biblical account of creation, is acknowledged as an exogenous influence on moods. But there is evidence that a seven-day rhythm is stubbornly rooted in biology, in the natural cycles that all living organisms seem to share with the sun and moon. A seven-day cycle is roughly a fourth—a cycle within a cycle—of the monthly lunar cycle. Two experiments in human engineering without regard for nature's structure are worth pondering. After the French Revolution, the nation's new rulers tried to substitute a rational ten-day week for the seven-day week which they thought to have been ordained only by religious superstition. But the French people simply ignored the government decree and continued to take a rest every seven days until the decree was rescinded. More than a century later, not willing to learn from either nature or history, the leaders of the communist revolution in Russia tried to change the week to five days and then to six before yielding to the people's refusal to abandon their seven-day cycle.

Among others who attempted to reduce mood cycles to usable data is Albert Edward Wiggam, a best-selling popularizer of psychological findings. Wiggam arrived at a personal mood cycle of thirty-six days. He found the knowledge useful: "After you chart your cycle, you will find that you can tell within three or four hours when you are plunging down into a low and when you are about to come up again for air." But John Steinbeck, more aware of ambiguities as a Nobel prize-winning novelist, reported on his own experiment in an exchange of letters with Jack Dorland:

"I read of your mood cycles with interest. Some years ago, I kept a complicated record somewhat similar. Every morning, on going to work I noted such things on a scale from one to ten in several categories: 1) purely physical; 2) mental (alert, dull, inventive, sluggish, etc.); 3) what you might call spiritual (optimistic, pessimistic, pleased, angry, generous, spiteful); 4) relational (by this I meant did I feel close to other people and to my habitat—rejected or rejecting). This was a kind of ecological index.

"I kept this record for over a year. Cycles were certainly indicated, but not necessarily parallel. It would be easy to jump to conclusions after such a record, but rather dangerous, because there were not enough hundreds of thousands; and, since I showed the record to no one, the computing machine and the programming agency were the same, namely me. Fortunately I had no thesis to warp my findings to. An outside diagnosis might have been interesting, but only that."

Although he was not a mathematician or scientist, Steinbeck recognized the need for "enough hundreds of thousands" to arrive at reliable generalizations from individual mood charts. So does Dr. Horovitz. Along with efforts to

61

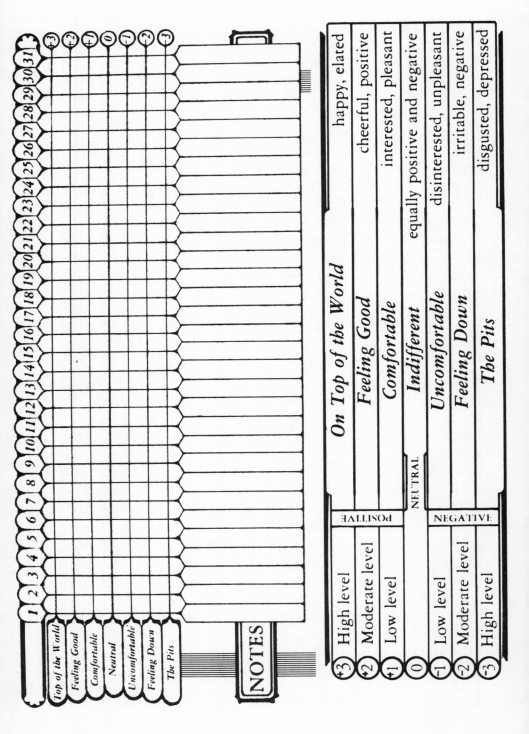

	1	2	3	4	5	6	7	8	9	10	11	12	13	14	15	16	17	18	19	20	21	22	23	24	25	26	27	28	29	30	31
Top of the World (+3)																															
Feeling Good (+2)																															
Comfortable (+1)																															
Neutral (0)																															
Uncomfortable (-1)																															
Feeling Down (-2)																															
The Pits (-3)																															

NOTES

POSITIVE	+3	High level	On Top of the World	happy, elated
	+2	Moderate level	Feeling Good	cheerful, positive
	+1	Low level	Comfortable	interested, pleasant
NEUTRAL	0		Indifferent	equally positive and negative
NEGATIVE	-1	Low level	Uncomfortable	disinterested, unpleasant
	-2	Moderate level	Feeling Down	irritable, negative
	-3	High level	The Pits	disgusted, depressed

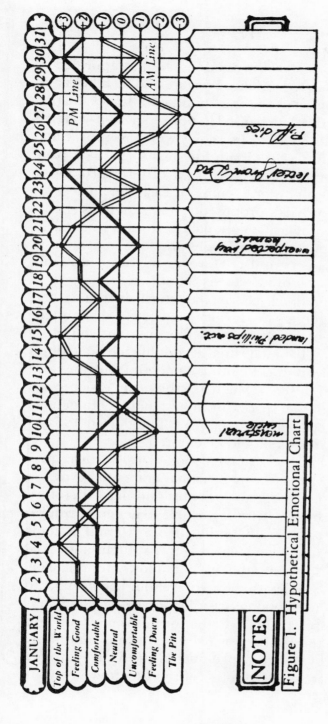

Figure 1. Hypothetical Emotional Chart

Dr. Horovitz's do-it-yourself mood charts: The hypothetical emotional chart he created for a young working woman shows the kind of notes you should make to indicate outside influences on your moods as, for instance, her high when she gets a bonus on the 20th or her low when Puff dies on the 27th.

63

obtain data from medical institutions, he has appealed to individuals to emulate Dorland, Wiggam and Steinbeck and send the resulting charts to the Foundation for evaluation and inclusion in the data bank. He devised a do-it-yourself rating system and chart to go along with his appeal and published them in Cycles. Using the blank chart on page 62, for each month, place a dot in a different color for morning and afternoon or evening of each day in accordance with Dr. Horovitz's proposed rating system as shown below in the hypothetical emotional chart for a woman. In order to get enough repeating highs and lows to produce a statistically reliable curve, Dr. Horovitz advises twice daily entries over a period of at least six months.

Keeping an emotional chart takes stern discipline, and Dr. Horovitz suggests "toothbrush charting"—making entries when you brush your teeth morning and night or perform any other habitual ritual at roughly the same times of day. Using different colors to connect the morning and evening points of the chart will make the cycles easier to see and evaluate. In the space for notes, both endogenous (menstrual period) and exogenous ("I got fired today") forces affecting moods should be entered.

In a bow to Steinbeck's perception, Dr. Horovitz says that, in the act of measuring personal emotional cycles, a person is both guinea pig and scientist and must therefore maintain as much objectivity as possible to get good results. After charting for several months, the way to find cycles is to look for repeating trends, peak to peak, highs and lows. A cycle exists if the peaks, the highs and lows, are relatively equal. With these cycles established, it should be possible to predict your own emotional weather in advance and thus make the effort rewarding, whether or not you extend it to participating in the Foundation's study, which is continuing under Dr. Horovitz's guidance and in need of volunteer data. Dr. Horovitz suggests a few of the uses to which your charts can be put:

"From these results you derive the enormous benefits of being able to forecast your feeling trends and cycles, and to prepare for these changes comfortably and intelligently. Not surprisingly, this has a number of ramifications for you and all of the people who interact with you. Couples who are aware of each other's cycles certainly are able to avoid or eliminate those uncomfortable periods that occur all too often. The same goes for employer-employee relations. Business people can use their cycles to improve their judgment and decision making. The potential benefits are broad, indeed."

Although the Foundation study is too new to be able to report significant results, it is probable that they will echo Professor Hersey's discoveries when they are available. Not surprisingly, Hersey used on himself the same system that he developed to measure the emotions of thousands of workers. In concluding his report, "Emotional Cycles in Men," he wrote: "I am able to forecast the general appearance of my own low periods, with advantage to myself. My cycle runs between 5½ and 6½ weeks. During my low period I am in a very critical mood and do not like to be bothered. At such times I enjoy solitude, and employ the time as much as possible in research work or in the laboratory. I refuse to accept engagements where I shall have to talk in such a way that it is a question of giving myself away. During my high period, I enjoy consultation work and activities that require a lot of energy and vitality. Unfortunately I sometimes become too restless to confine myself to a long-continued task requiring careful minute work. In many ways I have to be more careful of my high period than my low period, or else may be led into trouble."

Whether and to what extent a chart of personal emotional cycles might help in instances of pathology such as clinical depression is not yet known. But it does seem probable that becoming aware of the cyclical nature of all life would generate faith in that "saving grace" that William

Styron noted. For so-called normal people who ride a gentler emotional roller-coaster day by day, the chart would be a potent reminder that "the pits" aren't endlessly deep as well as an antidote to the self-accusatory guilts over feelings of personal inadequacy that so often accompany the down swing of the cycle. The dark holds far fewer terrors when there is light at the end of the tunnel.

CHAPTER

5

THE MUSIC OF
THE SPHERES

A GREEK PHILOSOPHER named Pythagoras who lived and thought in the century before Christ is credited with first claiming that the heavenly bodies make music. He, or at least his followers who were known as the Pythagorean school, meant this quite literally, and their reasoning was based on the fact that they had discovered what is now called harmonics (more about this connection below). In those days thinkers about the workings of the universe did not have the tunnel vision that too often results these days from the separation of modern science into different and sometimes competitive disciplines. Thus, Pythagoras was a farsighted pioneer in both mathematics and astronomy, and the areas of thought he opened up still have an important place in cycle theory.

Astronomy may well be the oldest of the sciences, and it certainly reveals some of the most basic and all-prevailing cycles in science. Cycles and overlapping or interacting systems of cycles are to be found everywhere in astronomy, from the movement of the solar system through the galaxy to the orbits of the planets to the recurrence of sunspots. There is ample evidence that human beings in prehistoric societies made practical use of their observation of the heavens for telling time, navigating and planting crops. Many of them made valiant efforts to understand and measure their observations. One theory about the curious construction of massive sandstone blocks in England known as Stonehenge is that it was an astronomical calculating device since its inner ovoid points to the place on the horizon where the sun rose on Midsummer Day in 1680 B.C. In his classic *Conquest of Peru,* historian William H. Prescott noted of the Incas:

"In astronomy they appear to have made but moderate proficiency. As their lunar year would necessarily fall short of the true time, they rectified their calendar by solar observations made by means of a number of cylindrical columns raised on the high lands round Cuzco, which served them for taking azimuths, and by measuring their shadows they ascertained the exact times of the solstices. The period of the equinoxes they determined by the help of a solitary pillar, or gnomon, placed in the center of a circle, which was described in the area of the great temple and traversed by a diameter that was drawn from east to west. When the shadows were scarcely visible under the noontide rays of the sun, they said 'the god sat with all his light upon the column.' Quinto [*sic*], which lay immediately under the equator, where the vertical rays of the sun threw no shadow at noon, was held in especial veneration as the favored abode of the great deity."

As in this instance, religion and astronomy have always been closely associated. For the sake of survival, human beings have had to be aware of the forces exerted upon them and their environment by the sun and the moon and the stars. Not only were these forces for the most part an

unfathomable and uncontrollable mystery of vital importance to every individual but the heavens in which they
moved were also a source of awesome beauty. Historically,
religion has served mankind as a device for coping with
mystery and awe, and the Inca meld of worship and calculation was typical. Unfortunately, religion has also historically acted as a brake on new discovery and fresh thought.
Learning new truth about natural laws generally results in
dethroning either the gods or mankind, or both. The revelations of Pythagoras were a case in point.

By the time of Pythagoras, scholars in China, Egypt,
Babylonia, Greece and quite probably the Americas, had
identified recurrent cycles in the movement of heavenly
bodies and had crudely charted many of them. It must be
assumed that Pythagoras was reasonably well acquainted
with the body of knowledge in the so-called civilized world
since he moved around physically as well as mentally. Born
and educated in Greece, he visited Egypt, which was another center of learning, and later settled in southern Italy
where he founded the Pythagorean brotherhood. His contribution to astronomy was to postulate that the earth was a
globe hung freely in space and travelling in a circular motion with all the other heavenly bodies. Previously, earth was
widely held to be a flat disk, stationary with respect to the
inferior bodies moving above and across it.

Pythagoras's astronomical insights were brushed aside by
his fellow Greeks. Aristotle in the fourth century B.C. and
Ptolemaeus in the second century went along with the concept of a stationary earth at the center of the universe. It
was what's been called a "homocentric" system, and it dominated western thought for nearly two thousand years,
partly because it fit so well with Christian theology's view of
a universe especially created by a personal God for man's
enjoyment and dominance. Only when Nicolaus Copernicus, a Polish astronomer of the fifteenth century A.D.,
came along to describe a system in which a spherical earth

rotated around a spherical sun did Pythagoras come into his own. But not immediately. Copernicus's "heliocentric" theory was condemned by the Inquisition and his book placed upon the index of prohibited books; both God and Man were in danger of losing power. Now, of course, the Copernican system is, in essence, what we still accept to be the astronomical truth.

But Pythagorean thinking has been even more influential in creating a mathematical and physical basis for cyclical theory than it was in astronomy. Pythagoras was fascinated by numbers and the way in which they could serve as an abstract expression of concrete occurrences. Indeed, Aristotle said that the Pythagoreans held numbers to be the first things in the whole of nature and the elements of numbers to be the elements of all things. One result of their working with the properties of numbers is a theorem known to every school child today (including the author in *his* day, even though he, like many, shunned the study of mathematics and science): i.e., the square of the hypotenuse of a right-angle triangle is equal to the sum of the squares of the other two sides.

The discovery that set Pythagoras afire and still sheds light down through the millennia was the relationship between the vibrations that can be heard in a plucked, stretched string and their numerical equivalents. Whether in a violin string set to vibrating or in a tuned electrical circuit, there are other vibrations with a frequency—or rate of vibration—that are multiples of the fundamental vibration. They are harmonics, or overtones. For example, the first harmonic vibration on a fundamental frequency of one hundred cycles per second would be one of two hundred cycles per second—what's called an octave in the eight-tone musical scale. As a test of his faith in the wonders of numbers, Pythagoras divided a monotone string according to the arithmetical ratios 1:2, 2:3, 3:4, 4:5, 5:6. When he plucked it—lo and behold—out came consonant overtones.

This is analogous to the placement of frets on the neck of stringed instruments like violins and guitars; by pressing a finger against a fret, the player changes the length of the vibrating string to produce a different tone. In Pythagoras's case, the ratio of 1:2 produced the octave (C-C in the key of C), 2:3—the ratio of the entire length of the string to two-thirds of its length—produced the fifth (C-G) and so on. Pythagoras postulated that only ratios of integers up to six produce consonant—i.e., agreeable—harmonics. Although the whole range of harmonics was unknown to him, he was very close to being right. Theorists since have included 5:8 which creates a minor sixth, and 8 represents the equal sounding octave. The present consensus is that the third, fourth, fifth and sixth are the consonant intervals.

Because they thought that the heavenly bodies were separated from each other by intervals with the same mathematical ratios as the harmonics in sound, it was logical for the Pythagoreans to think of the spheres as singing. But the Pythagorean brotherhood was involved with what were viewed as less-than-logical beliefs such as the kinship of men and beasts that made them into vegetarians, and their heavenly harmony was put down as a form of mysticism that became the property of poets rather than scientists. Shakespeare referred to "music from the spheres" in *Twelfth Night,* and Sir Thomas Browne wrote that "there is music wherever there is harmony, order, or proportion; and thus far we may maintain the music of the spheres."

Now, however, a very serious scientist who is a prominent figure in cycle research is suggesting that the Pythagoreans were hearing something very real—at least insofar as the mathematical and musical harmonies are equated and related. He is Theodor Landscheidt, director of the Schroeter Institute for Research in Cycles of Solar Activity and a member of the Academic Advisory Board of the Foundation for the Study of Cycles. Like Pythagoras before him, Landscheidt takes an interdisciplinary, holistic approach to the puzzles presented by the workings of the universe. By dictionary definition, holistic thinkers adhere to "a theory that the determining factors especially in living nature are irreducible wholes," and they abound in cycleland. But Landscheidt's broad background makes him unique, even there. Born in Bremen, Germany, he studied philosophy, law and natural sciences at the University of Goettingen where he earned a doctorate. He entered the legal profession and became a West German High Court Judge until his retirement. For him, the law was a rational way of making a living, of earning money to establish the Schroeter Institute; his real profession was studying the universe.

"I got into cycles to understand what is going on," he told me. "Physicists tell you that everything is vibrating. Electrons vibrating around nuclei and so on and so on. If you find this already in physics at a very basic level, it should emerge at higher levels, too. So I began to look for cycles. When I found some, I got intrigued because it is a possibility to make predictions. I began that research twenty-five years ago. While I was a judge, I was always working in all these fields—astronomy, statistics, psychology, economic cycles and all that. I needed special mathematics, too, and I got it; I studied it."

Recently, Dr. Landscheidt retired to devote all of his time to the study of cyles. He moved to Nova Scotia because "Europe is too crowded" and there he wrote an intriguing book *Sun-Earth-Man* in which, among many other exciting propositions, he makes a new case for heavenly harmony. Computing intervals in the energy wave from the sun over a period stretching from 5259 B.C. to A.D. 2347, Dr. Landscheidt found mathematically consonant intervals equivalent to the major sixth (3:5) and minor sixth (5:8) in music emerging. Moreover, he reports that a study of growth rings of Bristlecone pine trees in the White Mountains of California dating back to 3431 B.C. shows intervals coinciding with his solar energy chart's consonant intervals with a ratio of 5:8, the minor sixth. In discussing an analysis of the periodic alignment of Jupiter, the sun's center and the solar system's center of mass, Dr. Landscheidt writes:

"It is intriguing that the ratio of the superimposed harmonics 4:5:6 is that of the major perfect chord in musical harmony. Kepler [16th-century German astronomer, Johann Kepler] had found just this chord C-E-G when he analyzed ratios of the velocities of different planets at aphelion [most distant from the sun] and perihelion [nearest the sun]. Kepler's finding is also valid for the outer plants Uranus to Pluto. Thus, the major perfect chord turns out to be a fundamental structural element of the planetary system. The results presented here are a new substantiation of the Pythagorean harmony of the spheres."

The Pythagorean harmony is apparently there, but so far it has yet to be heard except in the informed mind. Meanwhile, the Copernican concept of a heliocentric solar system comprised of bodies in cyclical motion, has been confirmed and enlarged upon by observation and experience. Almost daily, new discoveries are made through finer instruments and space exploration, and they are often treated as front page news.

Cycle enthusiasts with a mathematical bent or training can feel themselves part of this astronomical symphony as they work with their equations and computers. But anyone equipped only with a reasonably good eye, a clear night, a spot to stand on with a view near the horizon in all directions and a dollop of patience can experience a physical sensation of cyclical movement. Looking east, an observer in the middle latitudes of the northern hemisphere, would see stars rising and moving to the right at about fifteen degrees an hour; in the west, stars would appear to move right and downward; at the horizon north or south, the stars would move right but neither rise nor fall. Since what the ancients thought was a movement of heavens is really the spinning of the earth—at speeds up to a thousand miles an hour—the observer will find the movement slowing as the eye travels upward from the northern horizon and stopping entirely in the area of Polaris, the bright North Star, which is only a degree away from the pole. In the southern hemisphere, movements would be in reverse.

With the cycles of heaven so obvious, regular and influential, it's not surprising that their action is the substance of much of the study and speculation of cycles scholars and analysts. Edward R. Dewey, the founder of the Foundation for the Study of Cycles, liked to dazzle readers with computations of the great cycles. "You are," he once wrote, "at this moment spinning around at speeds up to 1,000 miles per hour on a ball that is flying at 66,000 miles per hour around a sun that is traveling 481,000 miles per hour around a Milky Way that is rocketing at 1,350,000 miles per hour around a supercluster of galaxies. And all of this in a pattern of cycles so exact that it is possible to predict our position in the universe a thousand years from today." That pattern results in a cycle of 23 hours, 56 minutes and 4.09 seconds for earth's rotation relative to the stars; a cycle of 365.242 days for the earth's orbit of the sun; and a cycle of 230 million years for the whole solar system to circle the Milky Way.

Just as there are frequencies within frequencies to create harmonics, there are innumerable cycles within cycles in the starry skies. Many of these have been translated into reliable numerical values that are finding increasing use in such matters as stock market and weather prediction. Francis J. Socey, a Weems, Virginia, professional meteorologist for more than fifty years who still earns a living forecasting for almanacs and the commodity markets, puts great store in the relationships among the planets, the moon, the sun, the earth. The time it takes them to complete their orbits has become fixed in his mental computer. Talking to me, he reeled these cycles off from memory—Mercury 88 days, Venus 224.7 days, Mars 687 days, Jupiter 11.86 years, Saturn 29.46 years, Uranus 84 years, Neptune 165 years. Tidal authority Fergus Wood uses a composite of 136 representative lunisolar cycles to create a table of the maximized gravitational forces on earth. Economist A. Bruce Johnson is stirring half a dozen planetary cycles into a mix of economic cycles and other data to come up with a foreshadowing of the Dow Jones averages on the stock market.

Typical of a well-established and hard-worked celestial cycle is that of the spots on the sun. The importance of this phenomenon is, of course, related to the sun's controlling power in the solar system. Consider a few of the impressive facts about this star:

— It is 93 million miles distant from earth.

— It has a diameter of 865,000 miles.

— It's mass is approximately two billion billion billion tons, and it comprises 99 percent of the solar system's matter.

— It burns this matter at the rate of four million tons per second, generating temperatures of 6,000 degrees centigrade on the surface and many millions of degrees at the core.

— It rotates in a cycle like the moon, but not as a solid ball since the period of rotation is only twenty-five days at the sun's equator and thirty-one days at seventy-five degrees of latitude.

Small wonder that this fiery ball that energizes all life on earth has been an object of awe and worship for human beings. Man has kept an interested eye on the source of his being despite its brilliance and no doubt detected the blemishes that appear from time to time on its surface long before there was any science of astronomy. Although their presence can be detected with the naked eye, sunspots couldn't really be seen until the telescope was invented in the seventeenth century. One of the first people to open up the heavens with that instrument was Galileo Galilei who included sunspots among the fresh phenomena he observed. But it wasn't until the early nineteenth century that a German amateur astronomer, Heinrich Schwabe, looking through a two-inch telescope detected a rhythmic pattern—a cycle—in the appearance of sunspots with a frequency of approximately ten years. In a thirty-year analysis of sunspot activity since the year 1527, the Foundation for the Study of Cycles refined Schwabe's calculations to fix the average sunspot cycle at 11.11 years.

The nature of sunspots isn't fully understood, but Dewey, who directed the Foundation's study, described them thus: "Sunspots are whirling vortices of cooler, seemingly dark gas that blemish the surface of the sun. They can appear singly or in groups, but they usually show up in pairs. Their size is immense. One group, which appeared in 1946, covered an area sufficient to swallow over one hundred earths. Sunspots are sometimes accompanied by bright flares spitting thousands of miles into the corona and emitting strong doses of ultraviolet, charged particles, and X rays. Sunspots usually appear and vanish within a few days but frequently they endure for many months, disappearing from our view with each rotation of the sun and reappearing again approximately two weeks later. Sunspots are also magnetic, and one of their most mysterious characteristics is that when they are in pairs or small groups they act as if they were the positive and negative poles of huge horseshoe magnets embedded in the sun. In one cycle the leading spots of each pair or group in the northern hemisphere will have a positive polarity while the leading spots in the southern hemisphere will have a negative polarity. In the next cycle the situation reverses itself and the leading spots in the northern hemisphere will be negative while the leading spots in the southern hemisphere will be positive."

Clearly the sunspots have an effect on the sun's emission of energy and thus an effect on life on earth. Because the cycle has been so well established at eleven years, it provides a bench mark against which to measure all sorts of cycles and events. Throughout the development of cycle theory,

Sunspot Cycles

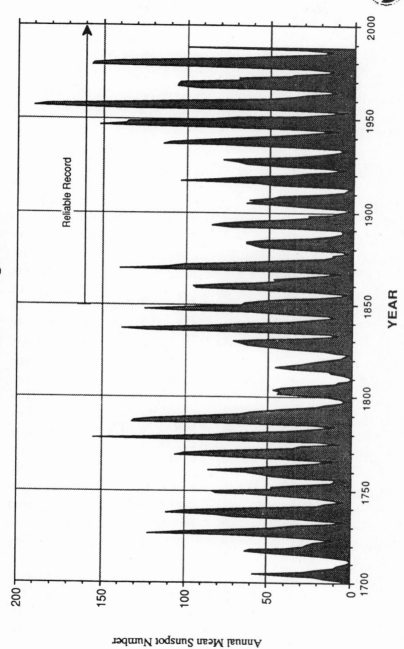

The cyclical nature of sunspots, which have a dramatic and demonstrable effect on life on earth, is clearly evident in this chart of the annual mean number of sunspots from 1700 until the present.

77

the sunspot cycle has been attributed as a factor in every-thing from the ups and downs of the money markets to changes in weather and emotional states to wars and revolutions. As Dewey noted dryly, "In the past century attempts have been made to link nearly every behavior on this planet to these mysterious eruptions." Some of these attempts will be explored further in this book; if they are not entirely persuasive, many are provocative of deep thought.

If there is nothing new under the sun, there are some new discoveries about the sun and its behavior that are changing the course of cyclical theory. Rhodes W. Fair-bridge, a leading thinker in the field of cycles, is professor of geological sciences at Columbia University and consultant to NASA's Goddard Institute for Space Studies. He and a number of colleagues such as John E. Sanders and James H. Shirley, an independent researcher in solar physics, have recently come up with what a Fairbridge and Sanders paper called "some aspects of celestial mechanics that we think are significant and that seem to have been either ignored by astronomers or cast in the completely wrong terms of a sun-centered system."

The mechanics begin with the action of gravity—the force which holds the celestial bodies in orbit and which is determined by the body's mass. Because of the sun's great mass compared to its satellites, it is commonly thought of as a body at rest in the center of the circling solar system. But the fact is that the sun is as much a body in motion as any other, and the nature of its motion, according to the new thinking, exerts an important influence on solar activity. To describe the motion Shirley uses the analogy of a dumbbell with weighted ends being thrown into the air with a spin. The ends of the dumbbell will spin around each other, one in an irregular path. But traced over the whole flight, the dumbbell's point of balance, or center of mass, will make a regular arc, a parabola. In the solar system, there is a similar center of mass—the barycenter—that orbits the center of the Milky Way around which the sun loops like one of the weighted ends of the dumbbell. Each orbit takes from ten to twenty years in varying diameters; at times, the sun can be as far as a million miles from the barycenter.

After a study of the sun's orbit from A.D. 750 to 2050, Fairbridge and Sanders postulate: "The sun is forced into an orbit around the center of mass (barycenter) of the solar system because of the changing mass distributions of the planets. Irregularities in the solar orbit generate cycles that have periods ranging from a few years to several hundred years. Much of the solar orbit is a response to the movements of Jupiter and Saturn, which change angular relationships by ninety degrees in just under five years. A fundamental rhythm is the Saturn-Jupiter-Lap cycle of 19.859 earth years. Solar-planetary-lunar dynamic relationships form a new basis for understanding cyclic solar forcing functions on the earth's climate."

Landscheidt is also convinced that the planets have a lot to do with the sun's orbit and rate of rotation and, in turn, its output of energy. Significantly, it was the analysis of one alignment of Jupiter, the center of mass and the sun's center over a period of time in which he found the harmonics of the major perfect chord. This sort of detection and analysis of heavenly cycles is a new direction in the understanding of the universe that offers great promise for predicting, if not controlling, celestial forces. It might be either a comfort or a disappointment to people with apocalyptic vision to learn that the more cycles are comprehended the more they seem to confirm the insights and intuitions of the Pythagoreans and poets.

In the seventeenth century, John Dryden included uncannily prophetic lines in "A Song for Saint Cecilia's Day":

> From harmony, from heavenly harmony,
> This universal frame began;
> From harmony to harmony
> Through all the compass of the notes it ran,
> The diapason closing full in Man.

CHAPTER

6

TAMING THE TIDES

I DIDN'T QUITE understand why this particular overnight sailing race on Long Island Sound was scheduled to start well after dark. Maybe the organizers' top priority was to enrich their club's treasury with the festive dinner for a hundred or so guests preceding the event. More likely it would be more "sporting" than a daylight start. They were right about that!

I was crewing on a thirty-foot sloop from another club. The starting line was established between a buoy and a committee boat—both nothing but dim presences in the pitch black before moon rise—and the area was unfamiliar to us. The skipper assigned tasks as we jockeyed for position behind the line with some twenty other boats ranging from twenty-five to fifty feet in length. We were all trying not to become one of those things that "goes bump in the night." Knowing that I had qualified in the U.S. Power Squadron courses for the rating of junior navigator, the skipper asked me to plot our course for after the start and then to time the start.

It seemed then like a gift from the gods. During the pre-start turmoil and tension, I would be down below studying the charts and, as the expression goes, out of harm's way. It was breezing up, and at the very last second before the start, the deck crew would have to raise the spinnaker. (For those unfamiliar with sailboats, an enormous sail that balloons around the boat's bow, which looks beautiful in pictures but is the devil's own job to manage on a boat of any size because of the power it generates.)

We were starting in the mouth of a harbor opening out to the Sound. There was a long spit of sand on our right which we were supposed to round and keep bearing right to head east. These were well-charted waters, and the charts told me the depth of water we could expect under the boat at low tide. My job was to plot a course that would shave as close to the spit as possible without getting into shallow water. A piece of cake. We drew about six feet, and I laid a line that would take us over no less than eight feet at mean low water.

I called the course up to the skipper, set a stop watch in accordance with the series of guns booming from the committee boat and stood on the companionway steps to call the time to the skipper a few feet above me in the cockpit. With a lot of effort and a little luck, our timing crossing the starting line was excellent. The crew even cheered. We were on the right side in relation to most of the fleet, but the riding lights and ghostly pillow-shaped spinnakers of several competitors could still be seen between us and the sand spit.

Having stopped the watch, I don't know to this day how long the burst of euphoria over our chances of doing well in the race lasted. It could have been a few seconds or a few minutes—no longer. Suddenly the boat shuddered to a dead stop. A few surprised crewmen lost their footing. The jolt and the still wind-stretched sails put such strain on the rigging that a stay popped out of the spreader. We were unmistakably hard aground! Fortunately, there was no grinding of rock beneath the hull; we were in the soft grip of sand. Just before I hit the deck to join in the flurry of activity to get the spinnaker down and rock the boat free, I glanced to starboard and saw that the other boats closer to the sand spit were no longer moving either.

Although we were able to continue, we had lost the advantage of a good start, and we were crippled. It was not a happy voyage as we trailed the rest of the fleet around the course. As navigator and presumably cause of it all, I was especially miserable, even though our skipper never reproached me. Considering what he stood to lose in face with the racing fraternity, not to mention in money for repairs, I still think that he should be President Bush's coordinator of a kinder, gentler America.

There was some very small consolation in discovering at the end of the race that one of the other boats that had grounded at the start was captained by no less than the commodore of the host club who presumably knew the harbor waters like the back of his hand. But I knew that being a club commodore wasn't necessarily synonymous with being a good sailor. Thus, I carried with me feelings of failure about that ill-fated voyage for fifteen years until I got involved in writing about cycles.

As Dr. Jeffrey Horovitz told me early in my investigation, "Tides are the greatest example of the kind of thing we study." That being the case, I couldn't avoid looking into the cyclical nature of tides. During that process, I learned that the tides of earth were so low on August 17, 1974, that it represented an event recurring only twenty times in three hundred years. It's hard ever to forget a failure, and my navigational error was still such a burr in my mind that I rushed to the informal journal that I, like most writers, keep. The date coincided with a brief journal notation about the race. So there it was at last! Both the commodore and I had been using smart navigational tactics in blissful ignorance of an abnormal tidal situation that could have been predicted if enough attention were being paid to knowledge that was even then available to people who understand cycles. It was not the first, nor the last, instance of realizing the very immediate application of cycle theory to my own personal life.

My brief grounding in a sailing race is only a small symptom of what remains a serious state of ignorance about tides. It seems strange that it has taken so long to understand the mechanism of tides since they have written much of the history of all the sea coasts in the world. A tide similar to the one that caught me unawares played a part in the naval war during the American Revolution. The event took place just at the eastern end of the same body of water, Long Island Sound, but on the Connecticut shore. Even as the reverse of a very low tide is a very high one, so, in a sense, that eighteenth century tide had a reverse result to mine.

In September, 1776, one of the first warships funded by the Continental Congress—the twenty-eight-gun frigate *Trumbull*—was launched from the shipyard of John Cotton in East Middletown, Connecticut. Unwittingly (it's to be hoped), the builders made that classical error of amateurs who construct a boat in the basement and then have to tear the wall down to get it out. The draft of the completed frigate was about eighteen feet; the shallowest water level in the ship channel of the Connecticut River is shown on charts of that time as six to eight feet at mean low tide which means that it would only rise to about twelve feet even on a spring tide. Inevitably, the *Trumbull* grounded on a bar on her way to the Sound. To the chagrin of Congress and no doubt to the delight of the British Navy, the *Trumbull* remained stuck on the bar until August 11, 1779, when the same sort of rare tide that grounded me lifted her. Some

84

indication of how the fortunes of war might have been altered is the *Trumbull's* record when she finally did get to sea. She was continually in action—her engagement with the British privateer *Watt* was rated the second worst naval battle of the war—and she was called "the celebrated rebel frigate named *Trumbull*" in a notice of her arrival in New York at the end of her service in the summer of 1781.

The *Trumbull's* story is only one of the many fascinating instances of the influence of tides on the affairs of men related in *Tidal Dynamics: Coastal Flooding and Cycles of Gravitational Force* by Fergus J. Wood. This book, which was first published by Kluwer Academic Publishers in 1978 and updated in 1986, represents a remarkable breakthrough in understanding a threatening natural phenomenon, a breakthrough that should result in saving countless lives and untold losses in property damage. Wood himself is recognized as the leading authority on tides in the United States, and perhaps the world, and, despite being officially retired, he is still hard at work on studies that might have equally far-reaching effects.

Wood is an astronomer by discipline. After graduating from the University of California at Berkeley with a degree in astronomy in 1938, he did post-graduate work at California, Chicago and Michigan universities until his studies were interrupted by the outbreak of World War II. Commissioned in the AAF Technical Training Command, he received special training at the Institute of Meteorology, University of Chicago, and served as a flight weather officer throughout the war. His postwar career included stints of teaching at the universities of Maryland and Johns Hopkins; service as Aeronautical and Space Research Scientist and Scientific Assistant to the Director, Office of Space Flight Programs, NASA; and Research Associate, Office of the Director, National Ocean Survey, National Oceanic and Atmospheric Administration.

In 1962, while Wood was working for the U.S. Coast and

Geodetic Service before moving on to NOAA, there was a tidal disaster along the east coast of United States of historic proportions and of obvious concern to his agency. In two and a half days between March 6 and 8, flooding at high tide claimed forty lives and destroyed some $500 million worth of property. "I thought there was more than met the eye in that flooding event," Wood told me. "We knew that there was a strong wind present which made possible the actual flooding. But what made possible the actual high tides which in turn made possible the cupping action which in turn made possible the sweeping of the waves toward shore?"

Being an astronomer, Wood started looking for answers up in the skies. It would be a natural place for anyone contemplating this question to look. The relationship between the moon and tides is the kind of natural knowledge we all absorb at mother's knee. Nobody living near tidal waters has to read a book to understand it. Tides vary visibly with the phases of the moon in a rhythm that is nearly as regular as that of day following night. The mechanism involved is the force of gravity. This force holds the heavenly bodies in orbit around each other, and the closer they are the stronger it is. The moon, our nearest neighbor, exerts more of this force than any other heavenly body. This force is neither even nor regular. Although the tides do rise and fall in a twice daily rhythm, their range varies according to gravitational forces. Twice a month—at new moon and full moon—the earth, moon and sun are in alignment. Astronomers call this alignment syzygy (pronounced siz-a-gee). In syzygy, the sun's lesser gravitational pull is added to the moon's stronger one to create what are known as spring tides. The word "spring" has nothing to do with the season but is descriptive of the tide's action in rising higher and faster. Like the earth's orbit of the sun, the moon's orbit of earth is not circular but elliptical. Once each revolution, at a point on its orbit known as perigee (closest to earth), the moon's gravitational pull will be stronger than normal. Either syzygy or perigee will raise tides by about 20 percent above normal. But when, infrequently, they come within a day and a half of each other, their combined increase in force creates a perigean spring tide that is 40 percent higher.

Beyond these rather well-known variations, there are many different degrees of perigee that cause further fluctuations. If it is separated by only a matter of hours from syzygy—quite a rare event—the resulting gravitational force draws the moon into an exceptionally close orbit and raises tides even higher. This would not be a negligible increase. Contemplating the 1962 disaster, Wood had a hunch that something like this must have happened. If so, the greater amount of water lifted into the path of the strong offshore wind that was blowing at that time would account for the flooding. Unfortunately for people caught in subsequent floodings, it wasn't until 1973 when he moved to NOAA that Wood was given the time and facilities to follow up on his hunch.

Wood began his study by asking the Naval Observatory in Washington to use its mainframe computers to provide a listing of all instances of perigee-syzygy coincidences back to the year 1600. With these dates in hand, Wood buried himself in the Library of Congress to see what might have been recorded in the way of tides, weather and flooding. It proved to be a thrilling exercise. "It was like popping pieces into a jigsaw puzzle," he recalls. Eventually, Wood came up with one hundred cases of major tidal flooding over a 293-year period that contained all the elements of the 1962 incident and presented a cyclical picture into which 1962 fitted neatly.

In the process of his study, Wood accumulated enough data on what he calls lunisolar cycles to be able to project his tide tables into the year 2164. He was also able to isolate those instances within the cycle of perigee-syzygy alignment when the small time differential resulted in an exceptionally close approach of the moon to earth. With due apology to linguists, he borrowed *proximate* from Latin to stand for close, and combined it with the Greek *gee* for earth to coin new words to define this situation—i.e., *proxigee-syzygy* and *proxigean spring tide*. What he was learning seemed like new territory to Wood, but he suspected from the history of science that somebody might have been there before him. He didn't want to undergo the rigorous labors of turning his findings into a book until he made a computer search of worldwide literature in the field. To his surprise the number of books was "nil," and a singificant number of the relatively few papers on the subject of tidal flooding dealt with hurricanes, which have their own special characteristics. Wood had come upon a seemingly obvious and logical process of nature that, in his words, "had never been brought to the attention of the public for no known reason."

As a public servant, Wood felt that he couldn't wait to share his knowledge through the long process of writing and publishing a book. According to all calculations, there would be conditions for a repeat of the 1962 flooding in early 1974. Wood so informed the press. Because destructive flooding is produced by a combination of tide and weather, Wood would not issue a "prediction." He is still leery of using that word; he prefers "advisory." The problem is that, while lunisolar cycles controlling the tides have long and predictable time intervals, the weather moves in tighter, swifter cycles. The lead on a science story in Time for January 7, 1974, reflects both the novelty of Wood's revelation and the caution of his approach:

"If there are severe storms in either the Atlantic or Pacific oceans around January 8, Americans living in coastal areas may well be hit by bad floods. This unusual warning was sounded last week by federal scientists [identified later in story as Fergus J. Wood]. Why January 8? Because of a relatively rare combination of circumstances, tides will be abnormally high around that time. Although the tides alone will not cause flooding, strong, persistent onshore winds accompanying a coastal storm would pile the water even higher, spilling it into lowlying areas."

In that particular instance, the east coast was spared because of relatively mild weather. What happened on the west coast is described in the headline and excerpts from an article in the Los Angeles *Times* on January 9, 1974 by Dick Main and Tom Paegel:

GIANT WAVES POUND SOUTHLAND COAST, UNDERMINE BEACH HOMES

". . . A local emergency was declared for all of Los Angeles County earlier Tuesday by the Board of Supervisors. 'Conditions of extreme peril to the safety of persons and property have arisen,' the board said in its resolution.

". . . At least eight homes in the Beach Road community of Capistrano Beach were damaged, as waves washed sand away, exposing or damaging seawalls, foundations and pilings. Breakers wiped out wide sections of many beaches, exposing pilings of lifeguard headquarters at both San Clemente and Newport Beach. Part of Pacific Coast Highway was flooded in Huntington Harbor and in Newport Beach.

". . . The morning tides are abnormally high because the present alignment of the earth, sun and moon exerts a stronger than usual gravitational pull upon the ocean. Tuesday morning's peak tide came at 9:22 a.m. and measured 7.1 feet. A 7-foot tide is expected this morning and Thursday's tide is expected to measure 6.5 feet.

Even with this striking fulfillment of Wood's prophecy, little was made of his warning that the same tidal conditions would return in August. The possibility wasn't mentioned

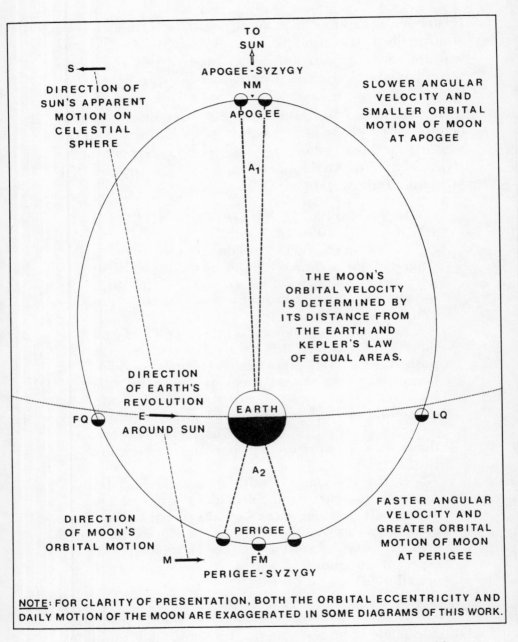

The astronomical positions and motions that determine high tides.

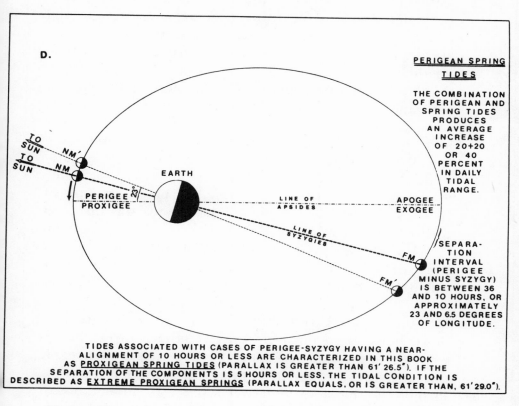

D.

THE COMBINATION
OF PERIGEAN AND
SPRING TIDES
PRODUCES
AN AVERAGE
INCREASE
OF 20+20
OR 40
PERCENT
IN DAILY
TIDAL
RANGE.

TO
SUN
NM'

TO
SUN
NM

EARTH

PERIGEE
PROXIGEE

23

LINE OF
APSIDES

APOGEE
EXOGEE

LINE OF
SYZYGIES

FM

FM'

SEPARA-
TION
INTERVAL
(PERIGEE
MINUS SYZYGY)
IS BETWEEN 36
AND 10 HOURS, OR
APPROXIMATELY
23 AND 6.5 DEGREES
OF LONGITUDE.

TIDES ASSOCIATED WITH CASES OF PERIGEE-SYZYGY HAVING A NEAR-
ALIGNMENT OF 10 HOURS OR LESS ARE CHARACTERIZED IN THIS BOOK
AS PROXIGEAN SPRING TIDES (PARALLAX IS GREATER THAN 61' 26.5"). IF THE
SEPARATION OF THE COMPONENTS IS 5 HOURS OR LESS, THE TIDAL CONDITION IS
DESCRIBED AS EXTREME PROXIGEAN SPRINGS (PARALLAX EQUALS, OR IS GREATER THAN, 61'29.0").

The positions of sun, moon and earth when the highest of tides
create flooding conditions. *(Tidal Dynamics)*

at all in Time or in newspaper articles about the January floodings and barely noted in Newsweek. Fortunately, as I can attest, the tides then weren't accompanied by storms.

After the first edition of Wood's book came out in 1978 with definitive proof of his thesis and a table of "advisories" stretching far into the future, the revelations were still largely ignored by weather watchers and coastal inhabitants alike. So far there have been some thirty-six cases of tidal flooding coincident with onshore wind and perigee-syzygy that could have been anticipated. Typical of the cost of ignorance were results of tidal flooding along the California coast during January 27 to 31 of 1983 when 2,600 homes and 496 businesses were damaged, 1,964 people were forced to flee, the Pacific Coast Highway was blocked at more than four places, and piers collapsed at Seal Beach and Point Arena. To all intents and purposes, accounts of these events were eerie echoes of those Wood dug up about the first recorded tidal disaster in American history in 1635.

"This year the 24 or 25 of August was such a mighty storm of wind and raine as none living in these parts, either English or Indians, ever saw," wrote William Bradford in *History of Plimoth Plantation*. Of the same event Nathaniel Morton reported in *New England Memorial* that it "blew down houses and uncovered divers others; divers vessels were lost at sea in it, and many more in extreme danger. It caused the sea to swell in some places to the southward of Plymouth, as that it arose to twenty feet right up and down, and made many of the Indians to climb into trees for their safety. The mark of it will remain this many years in those parts where it was sorest; the moon suffered a great eclipse two nights after it." In his journal Governor John Winthrop recorded a wind shift at the time from southwest to an onshore northeasterly gale.

The tipoff to Wood that he had found a classic case of his proxigean spring tides turning a wind storm into the kind of flooding that chased Indians into trees was the mention of an eclipse, the ultimate syzygy. In view of the way the world has changed in other respects since then, it seems remarkable that flooding still catches its most sophisticated citizens just as much by surprise. Wood has been trying to spread the word of his discoveries whenever and wherever he can for the last sixteen years, but his personal estimate of the present state of affairs came through when he told me: "About 80 percent of our coastlines are built wall-to-wall with homes that can be destroyed. Out at Malibu they are built over the water, and back in 1974 they were all floating. As Johnny Carson said, 'When somebody goes by floating in a bathtub we know we have a flood.'"

One reason for this is that the offical weather services upon which most people rely don't base predictions on such seemingly esoteric matters as lunisolar cycles—or, in fact, cycles in general. What could happen if they did was demonstrated dramatically in 1987, giving Wood reason to hope for progress in prognostication in the reasonably near future. With scientific caution, Wood always hedged his public statements. He would point out that his long range forecasts of high tides couldn't be considered predictions of flooding since the weather creating the necessary strong onshore winds couldn't be predicted at the same time. So matters stood until Wood got a call one day in 1986 from Irving P. Krick, Ph.D., president of Irving P. Krick Associates, Inc., Weather Engineers of Palm Springs, California.

Krick is a weatherman's weatherman—but not of the variety who become celebrities from cracking jokes on TV. His most legendary feat was advising Eisenhower on the weather for D-Day. For many years head of the meteorological department at California Institute of Technology, he was also in private practice as a forecaster for people who think that knowing the weather far in advance is worth good money. Krick does pay attention to cycles,

93

and on this day he told Wood, "You've got to be careful when you say we can't predict the weather, Fergus. Let's get together on this and see what we can do."

Wood's tables listed a proxigee-syzygy alignment for December 30, 1986. Several weeks before that date—long enough for people on the coasts to take precautions—the Krick organization sent Wood prognostic weather charts for the North American continent from December 29 through January 3, 1987. Weather features to be anticipated along the coasts and offshore were predicted accurately within twelve hours of their occurrence. Centered around the witching hour of New Year's Eve the charts showed probable storms with strong onshore winds along both coasts. Equipped with this information Wood decided to go out on a limb and issue a flooding "advisory" when *USA Today* called him to discuss what they might run in their December 26–28, 1986, weekend edition.

As in 1974, brief excerpts from two newspapers tell the rest of the story. First, the *USA Today* feature: "A triple celestial phenomenon that hasn't occurred in a generation may leave USA coastlines flooded in record tides next week . . . Possible trouble spots: Carolina coasts, Puget Sound, Bay of Maine . . ." Next, a story by Dennis Hevesi in the New York *Times*, January 3, 1987: "A classic northeaster, combined with tides raised unusually high by a rare celestial configuration, sent New Englanders scurrying inland yesterday afternoon after the storm left six people dead and caused at least $14 million in damage along the southeastern coast of the United States . . . In Marshfield, Mass., the tides whipped by winds of up to 60 miles an hour, broke through a sea wall at about noon and trapped hundreds of people. Rescuers used boats and trucks to reach some of the people. People had scrambled onto the roofs of their homes, cars or places of business." Sounds a lot like the Indians in the same state 352 years earlier, doesn't it? In the Puget Sound area, the flooding damage was of less magnitude and shorter duration only because the winds were less severe.

Leaving the rest of the world to catch up with him on tides, Wood is applying his knowledge of lunisolar cycles and gravitational forces to a study of as-yet unexplained vertical movements in the oceans and unexpected drifts of icebergs away from the poles. Both of these phenomena show preliminary evidence of a relationship to proxigee-syzygy events in the heavens. So do earthquakes, an uncontrollable natural force that can be more devastating to human life and property than tides, according to the findings of another scientist who is a student of both gravity and cycles.

John P. Bagby earns a living as a senior scientist and mechanical engineer for Hughes Aircraft in Los Angeles, but he has spent his off-duty time for twenty-five years pondering about, and experimenting with, such matters as why gravity doesn't work precisely according to the gospel of Newton. Together with his scientifically minded wife, Loretta, Bagby has conducted precise and tedious experiments that have led him to conclude, among other things, that planetary cycles are responsible for variations in the effect of gravity, as they are in tides. The gravitational pull the other planets exert on earth is also a factor in earthquakes in Bagby's view.

"What I think about earthquakes," Bagby explained to me, "is that the ground builds up a stress, and the stress is going to release at some time. What happens is that the moon and sun and planets pull on the earth and cause it to prematurely trigger the quake. In other words, the quake is going to happen anyway, but these celestial influences, which most scientists think are ridiculously weak, tease the earthquake into going off ahead of time. Since the earthquake is triggered into going off sooner than it would if it was allowed to build up its stress to the breaking point, we have fours, fives, and sixes on the Richter scale instead of having eights, nines and tens. I look upon the planets and the moon as a beneficial artifact of nature that teases earth into premature quakes. It's amazing how little energy it takes from those bodies, and no one can really say why theoretically this is so. That's where the problem arises. There is no theory to account for this synergetic effect. It is out of all proportion to the mass of the planet or the moon or where it is, but when planets line up at certain angles to each other there is this tendency to release energy."

If much is still unknown about this force, the knowledge that makes tides predictable is nevertheless applicable to earthquakes. "This celestial influence is very predictable, and it repeats," Bagby insists. "Some 33 percent of all earthquakes over 7.3 occur when the moon is new or full or in the quarter—a cardinal phase. But the other 66 percent of large earthquakes are triggered when the moon is half way between, when the moon's tidal force is most rapidly changing from weak to strong." There is a cyclical nature to earthquakes themselves. For instance, Bagby found that the recent quakes in Armenia fit into a historical eleven-year pattern.

Despite his knowledge and convictions, Bagby is even more reluctant to make "predictions" about specific earthquake occurrences than Wood is about tides. "There's a kind of law against it," he says. "The Geophysical Union and the Geological Society of America both put out bulletins requesting that all of us refrain from making predictions." One reason for this may be the potential havoc that earthquake predictions could cause unless they are 100 percent accurate. This is still impossible with the state of the art. Using time series analysis, Bagby can predict when the triggering forces for earthquakes are likely to be present down to the year, month, day and hour, but he can't say where on earth they will happen. Knowing that information is the provence of geology. "Geologists know where the stresses are but don't cooperate much with people predicting time," he says. As in the case of Wood and weathermen, earthquake prediction is badly in need of interdisciplinary attitudes.

There are, however, some hopeful signs that the disciplines are coming together on the common ground of cycles with respect to tides. Recently, Martin Sitch Kokus, assistant professor of physics at Columbia Basin College in Pasco, Washington, and research associate at Redstone Arsenal, wrote an article for Cycles magazine entitled "Earthquakes, Earth Expansion, and Tidal Cycles" in which he provided considerable support for Bagby's contentions. He pointed out that thinkers, notably including Aristotle, have linked earthquakes and volcanic eruptions with lunar cycles from the days of antiquity. Kokus then states flatly that "the solid earth has tides much like ocean tides but much smaller in magnitude. The forces that drive them are the same, and are present whenever two celestial bodies rotate in equilibrium about each other." After discussing various theories about the cause of earthquakes, Kokus concludes: "It is my sincere belief that the study of tidal cycles in earthquakes would yield the greatest improvement in quake prediction."

Like King Canute long before them, the students of the cyclical influences on tides make no pretension to being able to control them. What they do claim is that the time has come to acknowledge the nature and predictability of tides and to act accordingly. In one concrete instance, tidal table and charts could be rewritten right out of Wood's book right now to inform mariners and seaside residents of the coming of very high—and correspondingly very low—tides on specific dates for hundreds of years hence. Whether I might have noted such an entry if it had been there back in 1974 is a factor of fallible human perception and judgment. But I would at least have been given a reasonable warning to set a safer course, and there is little more that we can ask of our prophets.

CHAPTER

7

WILL IT RAIN ON OUR PARADE? . . . WILL WE BE LIVING IN A GREENHOUSE?

WAS IT MARK TWAIN who complained that everybody talks about the weather, but nobody does anything about it? If not, it sounds like him. It certainly was Mark Twain who said on another occasion that the weather in New England where he lived was "always doing something." Even in more equable climates, the weather is busy. In the Virgin Islands, for instance, where I've been privileged to spend a good deal of time, there is almost perpetual sunshine and very little temperature change the year around, but I've seen four or five quick showers in an hour, and there are occasional devastating hurricanes. This busyness of weather is one reason that it remains an inexhaustible topic of conversation. A more compelling reason for its fascination, however, may be the element of surprise in weather. If not, in fact, unpredictable, it is frequently unpredicted. We can't do anything about the weather, because we don't know what it is going to do. Thus, whatever else might be said about it, weather isn't boring.

In spite of weather's proven value as entertainment, human beings have devoted a great deal of mostly frustrated thought, time, effort and expense to turning it into a less mysterious and uncontrollable phenomenon. At the moment of this writing and in a place called the Geophysical Fluid Dynamics Laboratory in Princeton, New Jersey, there are two $25 million supercomputers running around the clock in an attempt to cope with billions of numbers in simulations of global weather and climate. The extent to which these machines are succeeding in making sense out of weather can be judged by the fact that the laboratory's director, Jerry D. Mahlman, still calls weather "a horrendously complicated mess," according to a report by J. I. Merritt in the Princeton Alumni Weekly.

Nevertheless, the team of fifty scientists at G.F.D.L., which is funded by the National Oceanographic and Atmospheric Administration, continues making and testing computer models in an effort to understand the fluid dynamics of the atmosphere and oceans from whence weather comes. A measure of the complexity facing these researchers is that the printout of a single model can be as large as a metropolitan telephone book, contain as many as thirty thousand lines of computer code and take ten years to write. As Merritt explains the process:

"A model divides the atmosphere into a vast three-dimensional grid comprising tens of thousands of rectangular boxes. Each box contains a set of equations representing the laws of motion and thermal dynamics governing fluid systems, and each set of equations includes such meteorological variables as wind speed and direction, temperature, barometric pressure, humidity, and incoming solar radiation. A box reflects the conditions of its particular space, taking into account the effects of latitude, vegetation, topography, and cloud cover. Every box is linked mathematically to its neighbors, so that changes in one affect the solutions to equations in others. A model represents the atmosphere at a point in time. Once the initial conditions are set, the computer can begin solving the model's equations. Like a time-lapse film, a model runs many times faster than reality, in a matter of minutes or hours projecting scenarios for conditions a week, a season, or even decades into the future."

Although this sounds as if weather is about to be put into a box—actually thousands of boxes—it isn't turning out that way so far. Even the best of models is not, in fact, living weather, and the surprises keep coming. One model the G.F.D.L. scientists created to predict the impact of greenhouse warming by the year 2050 called for drier summers in the southeastern Great Lakes and plain states while another concluded that they would be wetter. Such puzzles notwithstanding, computer-assisted analysis of the history of the weather seems to be establishing some reliable natural laws governing weather that could be the basis for a marked improvement in forecasting. To the surprise of nobody in cycleland, one of these laws is the tendency of weather-making factors to recur in cycles.

The enormous value to mankind of better weather forecasting does not have to be spelled out. In a monetary sense alone, the cost of a laboratory such as the one at Princeton is insignificant compared to the damage that unforeseen weather extremes visit upon mankind's works and plans, and no measure exists to evaluate the worth of lives lost in droughts and floods. It would be equally impossible to assess the daily stress upon individuals of weather related frustrations and disappointments ranging from getting stuck in a snow drift to having a picnic washed out or a new hairdo ruined by rain. The scientists in Princeton are using an analysis of one of the more brutal weather assaults on the human race—the 1988 summer drought in middle America—for predictive models based on cycles.

101

In examining weather dynamics, researchers have concluded that both the ocean of air and the oceans of water have to be studied together. One of the strongest forces they have found is a cycle of alternating warm and cold sea surface temperatures in the equatorial Pacific Ocean. This watery cycle has been linked to variations in both the monsoons of the tropics and the rainfall of North America. Because it recurs with regularity around Christmas, the warm phase of this cycle is called El Niño after the Christ child. Searching for a possible cause of the 1988 drought, scientists at the National Center for Atmospheric Research in Boulder, Colorado, noted that sea-surface temperatures during El Niño in 1987 were below normal. From that observation, they postulated that a cold El Niño forced a mass of unstable air northward until it settled southeast of Hawaii like a rock in a stream. There it created eddies of high and low pressure which diverted the winds off the Pacific that usually carry rain to the central part of the United States.

Subscribing to this analysis, Kikuro Myakoda, a senior scientist at G.F.D.L. says, "In principle the probability of drought or rain, or extremes of heat and cold in temperate zones, can be deduced from changes in sea-surface temperatures at the equator. Our strategy is first to figure out what will happen in the tropics, then infer the effect at higher latitudes." Myakoda is making models based on this probability, and he modestly asserts that the models may eventually enable meteorologists to predict rainfall and temperature three months to a year in advance.

Even a quick glance at the history and present status of weather forecasting is enough to suggest the enormous advance in practical knowledge that the Myakoda models will represent if they work. Considering the enduring and pervasive impact of weather on human affairs, it is stupefying to realize how long it took us to develop any systematic study of the weather. Of necessity, human beings have

102

always been acutely aware of weather, and the annals of the race are steeped in references to weather conditions at the time they were inscribed. During the many millennia when travel and communication were limited to the horizon line for the bulk of humanity, people developed an instinctive widsom about the weather around them and passed it on in sayings like "red sky at night sailor's delight; red sky in the morning sailors take warning." But it wasn't until 1743 that Benjamin Franklin became the first person to note that weather moves: on a September day, he reported, a storm he experienced in Philadelphia moved up to Boston. It took more than another century before the U.S. Signal Corps set up the first national weather service in 1870. From then until 1933 when Henry Wallace became Secretary of Agriculture, no government forecast was made more than twenty-four hours in advance. With several generations of farmers in his family, Wallace pressed for at least a forty-eight-hour forecast.

Not only is it a general inconvenience having no idea what the weather will be more than a couple of days in advance, it is a hindrance to scientific research. With little data accumulated over the years, it becomes very difficult to find and authenticate weather cycles. Computer models become extremely valuable in reconstructing the past as well as projecting the future. And even without this most recent advance, the Foundation for the Study of Cycles has adhered to its self-appointed mission of extracting statistically viable cycles from any available data bank and has managed to identify a number of recurring patterns that have an obvious bearing on weather.

Mainly because the records were available, the Foundation studied barometric pressure in New York from 1873 through 1967. The Foundation's founder, Edward R. Dewey, always took the position that the organization's mission was to identify cycles wherever they appeared, regardless of their apparent significance or lack thereof. In this case, the potential usefulness of a barometric cycle was almost self-evident in that barometric pressure is an acknowledged predictor of weather. There are, in Dewey's calculation, about five quadrillion tons of atmosphere bearing down on earth with an air pressure at sea level of 14.7 pounds per square inch, or one ton per square foot. The barometer records this pressure as inches of mercury, and 29.91 such inches equal 14.7 pounds of air pressure per square inch. When the mercury rises, the weather turns fair; when it falls, it turns foul. From the barometer readings in New York, the Foundation plotted a graph that formed a 7.6-year cycle. By the time Dewey wrote about this discovery, he could report that another researcher had found a 7.4-year cycle in barometric pressure at five widely separated weather stations around the world.

Another weather cycle that Dewey reported for meteorologists to ponder was one having to do with what he called "the rhythm of the rain." Working with figures from 1820 to 1960 of recorded rainfall at Philadelphia, the Foundation discovered a 4.33-year cycle in precipitation. Follow-up analyses of data for New York and Baltimore produced exactly the same figure. Less authoritative but very intriguing to Dewey was a finding by one Dr. E. G. Bowen, Chief of the Radiophysics Division of the Commonwealth Scientific and Industrial Research Organization in Australia, that it rained so regularly on January 23 in Brisbane as to be more probable than chance—a finding later corroborated by a U.S. Weather Bureau study showing a recurring high and low rainfall pattern on the same calendar days. Dewey also expressed considerable confidence in the thirty-five-year Brückner cycle of wet oceanic and dry continental European weather, Ellsworth Huntington's 9.66-year cycle of atmospheric ozone as measured in London and Paris from 1877 to 1910, and Raymond H. Wheeler's one hundred-year climatic cycle coinciding with tree rings and the rise and fall of civilizations.

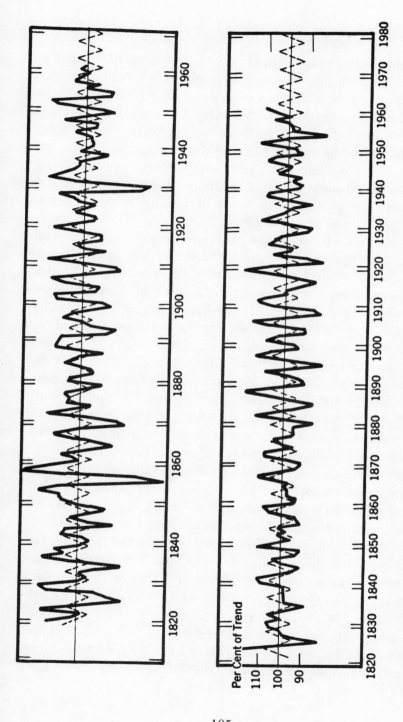

Per Cent of Trend

Studies by the Foundation for the Study of Cycles show the "rhythm of the rain," but weather forecasters have tended to ignore such evidence until very recently. (*Cycles*)

Some twenty years ago, Dewey reported his findings with rueful misgivings. "When meteorologists accept Einstein's famous premise that 'God does not play dice with the universe' and recognize that there are rhythmic behavior patterns in climatology, they may be able to predict weather several years into the future!" he wrote in Cycles. "Yet many of them continue to work with their heads in the sand—or the clouds. Show them the graph, and they will tell you that the obvious 4.33-year cycle in Philadelphia precipitation since 1820 is mere coincidence."

Cycle theory hasn't made much progress toward incorporation into the mainstream of weather forecasting. Private forecasters use cycles in their work, but the current staff of the Foundation for the Study of Cycles and the cycle scientists with whom I talked were unanimous in asserting that the National Weather Service for the most part still shuns cycles. Professor Rhodes Fairbridge, a Columbia University geologist and consultant to NASA's Goddard Institute for Space Studies, believes that this is the result of compartmentalized education. The standard text for meteorology, written a century ago, took the position that the climate of any country was basically set, "chiseled in granite," according to Professor Fairbridge. "Weather was fluctuation around a mean, a God-given mean, and this was held to be a fundamental principle of science. People who talked about climatic fluctuation—cycles going up and down—were considered out of their minds," he says. "A one hundred-year inheritance of that thinking has had the effect on most praticing meteorologists of imbuing them with a kind of Ayatollah conservatism which is alarming." The usual training for meteorology consists of a combination of geography and physics but does not include geology or botany, the disciplines through which the hard evidence of climatic cycles that run through the entire history of earth is being found. Botanists reading tree rings and geologists reading sedimentary characteristics are reading the same story of cycles that have clearly affected weather, but, says Fairbridge, "We're dealing with a dichotomy of training here, a dichotomy of the fundamental principles with which we look at science."

It's interesting to note that the academic interchange between the scientists at the Geophysical Fluid Dynamics Laboratory, where weather cycles are under investigation, and nearby Princeton University is through the university's department of geology—twelve of the laboratory's fifty scientists are visiting professors. They are also basing their models on global weather, which is a concept that Fairbridge claims has been too long lacking in traditional weather thinking. In discussing the subject with me, Professor Fairbridge also cited the effect of El Niño on in the United States weather, a bit of largely neglected knowledge that he attributed to another pioneering climatologist named Reed Bryson at the University of Wisconsin. Studying variations in the Indian monsoon, Bryson came up with an earth-girdling linkage of cycles. Snowfall in the Himalayas in Tibet in winter can give warning as to the strength of rainfall in the summer in India which, in turn, corresponds 80 percent of the time with El Niño which, as the Boulder scientists now theorize, can predict rainfall in the United States another six months into the future.

"These things tend to be interlocked," Professor Fairbridge told me, "and what we desperately need is more information about them. One of the problems with the meteorological services in different countries is that their basic job is to predict the weather in Chicago or Paris or New Delhi, but that's not the right way to go about it. What they should do is look at the global weather and consider the whole world as their study material and then hone in on particular spots. The atmosphere is a continuous medium around the world and it is circulating at a high rate of speed. It's quite impossible to predict what will happen in Washington or San Francisco without thinking about the rest of the world.

"We are now beginning to look at the satellite pictures for areas outside of North America, but it is still rather spotty. It is very good for Europe, of course. There they've had the brains to form a centralized long-term weather prediction group. So they are trying to do this. But I still think that we lack coverage of large areas of the Pacific and South Atlantic, and it's still part of the same machinery. It's both a money situation and a conceptual situation—partly cost and partly attitude. I think there are a lot of hard-nosed Congressmen who would find it difficult to pay for putting a weather station somewhere on an island down in the South Pacific. But we should know the sea water temperature, the air temperature, the upper air velocities down there—a whole series of parameters that should be monitored continuously. We have beautiful computers now, and there is no reason why they shouldn't be fed with this information. We would get a revolutionary picture of weather."

Listening to this plea, I couldn't help thinking about the six—quite possibly seven—figure salary contracts that go routinely to weather entertainers on TV whose product is only as good as the science supporting it. If there's a dichotomy of scientific principles in the weather business, there's an even greater dichotomy of values. But the work at Princeton is encouraging with respect to both money and attitude, and it is reported that the National Weather Service is adapting some of the G.F.D.L. models for forecasting. There is, however, no report I've come across of substantial work outside of cycle circles on the relationship between celestial cycles and earthly weather cycles. This would seem to be a new frontier along which pioneers like Fairbridge and Theodor Landscheidt, director of the Schroeter Institute for Research in Cycles of Solar Activity, are making discoveries that could be as revolutionary in terms of forecasting as in understanding of the dynamics of the earth's atmosphere.

These pioneers are finding evidence that the movements of the moon and sun that control earth's tides also have a correlation with—if not a controlling effect upon—earth's climate. To the extent that these observations can be enlarged upon and proven in practice, both short-term and long-term forecasting can become more accurate. Some heavenly cycles last a century or more, and all of them are more predictable than those in the atmosphere and oceans. They are not, however, entirely regular because there is an elusive dynamics in celestial activity as well as in terrestrial fluids. The sun's planets do what might be described as a form of dance around each other in which their movements are determined by interaction as with partners on a ballroom floor, as noted earlier in a quotation from Fairbridge and Sander.

Following in this train of thought, Dr. Landscheidt uses one cosmic dance step in particular to illustrate this hypothesis that solar events do correlate with weather. It is an alignment of Jupiter, the center of mass, and the sun's center that he calls JU-CM-CS. This alignment is cyclical because it recurs in rhythms that vary from two to sixteen years. Checked against a graph of yearly rainfall in Germany from 1851 to 1983, it developed that JU-CM-CS epochs coincided with peaks in precipitation.

A recent Fairbridge paper, written with Robert Guinn Currie of the State University of New York at Stony Brook and published in Quaternary Science Reviews, used climatic references in China's unique written history to come up with a more than coincidental connection between heavenly happenings and recurring floods and droughts in China. Their conclusion: "Analysis of a drought-flood index for Peking (Beijing) in northeastern China since A.D. 1470 supports evidence for both periodic lunar nodal 18.6-year and solar cyclic 11-year induced drought-flood in the region." The moon's nodal cycle begins and ends at the points where its orbit intersects the elliptic, the plane of the earth's orbit; the sun's 11-year-cycle is the periodic waxing and waning of sunspots.

The importance to Fairbridge and his colleagues of their investigations is that "they may serve perhaps to illustrate what is now beginning to emerge as a great new paradigm of twentieth century science: the exogenic theory of climate." One of those words that sends reporters scampering to the dictionary, exogenic simply means originating from the outside. In this case, it is used to indicate the belief that forces from outside of earth's atmosphere cause changes in climate and associated weather. This represents an even more radical departure from the traditional meteorology that Fairbridge deplores. Thus, it would be the contention of cycle theorists that data on celestial activity ought to be fed into the computer along with that about global atmospheric and oceanic conditions to arrive at forecasts.

In some quarters, the Fairbridge paradigm wouldn't be considered new. Francis J. Socey, a consultant meteorologist of Weems, Virginia, has been making a living forecasting weather for more than fifty years. He conducted his first radio weather program in his hometown of Altoona, Pennsylvania, when he was fifteen, served as an instructor in weather analysis in the Air Corps during World War II, and has since become affiliated with such prestigious organizations as the American Meteorological Society, the American Geophysical Union, the American Association for the Advancement of Science and the Royal Meteorological Society of England. Unlike your local weatherman, Socey has to be possessed of distant vision since he sells his services to the publishers of almanacs in the United States and South America as well as to people in the commodities markets. Properly cautious, as anyone dealing with the complicated subject of weather learns to be, he says, "I don't predict. I don't say what's going to happen. I give an outlook."

If Socey's "outlooks" weren't accurate more often than not he wouldn't have stayed in business this long, and so his extensive use of what might be called celestial-assisted forecasting stands as a form of practical proof of what the cycle theorists are saying. Socey started studying weather at the age of twelve and acknowledges that "cycles never entered my mind at that tender age." But when a natural progression through meteorology, including a stint of upper-air analysis to try to predict weather for the Philippine invasion, led him to think about planetary motion, he became a cycles convert. In the forty-odd years since World War II, he has constructed his own kind of computer—fifty-two thousand three-by-five inch index cards that show the various positions of the planets in relationship to one another.

From Socey's point of view, different planets do different things to earthly weather. "Mercury gives you wind, Venus gives you showers, Mars gives you heat, Jupiter gives you dryness—that is, in a broad sense," he says. "Saturn is changeable; Neptune gives heavy precipitation within narrow limits." Socey finds planetary influence strongest when the celestial bodies are in conjunction with each other—that is, within plus or minus two degrees of longitude. "Take Mercury and the sun," he explains. "Minus two degrees means that Mercury is approaching the sun; plus two degrees means it is going away from the sun. Within the four days it is in that range—Mercury is a fast mover—it affects all the pressure systems on earth to the degree of how close the bodies are to one another. When Mercury and the sun are at perihelion (Mercury closest to the sun), the planet's influence on Earth will be most apparent; when they are at aphelion (Mercury farthest from the sun) it will be less. There is also an effect from a planet's speed of approach to the sun—when it approaches perihelion it speeds up and when it goes away it slows up until it becomes neutral. The same thing happens at aphelion, but the distance reduces the effect."

Even Socey's fifty-two thousand index cards don't contain the wealth of data available to, say, a stock market cycle analyst. Neptune, with a cycle of 165 years, has orbited only once during the time that human beings have really been recording and studying weather, and Uranus scarcely more on its eighty-four-year cycle. Nevertheless, Socey makes use of Neptune. In historical records, ancient astrologers and sages note that precipitation increased whenever Neptune crossed a meridian, and so does Socey. At the time I was talking to him we had just experienced two or three of the worst rain storms that I have encountered, in thirty-seven years of residence in Connecticut. Without any prompting from me, Socey said, "This spring [1989] we have a lot of rain in the east. You'll ask, 'Now why?' Well, if you look at Neptune, you'll see that when it passes a certain meridian, it does enhance or inhibit terrestrial pressure systems. Since Neptune has been in the east with Uranus and Saturn and Jupiter, we've been having quite a time in the eastern part of the continent. We have a certain specific weather that will be with us for a couple of years." All I can say with certainty as of this writing is that Socey has been right for more than thirty intervening days and the two days ahead that the weathermen are willing to call.

Whether celestial cycles are fed into the mainstream of weather forecasting or not, it would seem essential to take them into consideration in the debate now raging on an international level about the "greenhouse effect." The name is most appropriate, according to Professor Fairbridge who says, "If you possess a greenhouse in the back of your home, you know how it warms up in sunshine. If you raise the carbon dioxide, or CO_2 in the atmosphere, the CO_2 tends to raise the water vapor, and the two together raise the heat retaining capacity of atmosphere like the glass over the greenhouse." CO_2 is released into the atmosphere by a number of natural processes, but since the Industrial Revolution and the onrush of modern civilization, unnatural, man-made processes such as the burning of fossil fuels and the release of the kind of chemicals found in spray cans is upsetting the natural atmospheric balance. A very small change in global temperature can result in great changes in climatic characteristics. Since some scientists have detected an abnormally rapid rate of increase in atmospheric CO_2 in recent years, an alarming scenario has been concocted: a greenhouse warming might cause such things as flooding from oceans swelled by melting polar ice caps and/or encroaching desert in the food belts of the world.

Although nobody denies the possibility that this scenario could play itself out, the vagaries of weather and climate that make it so fascinating and frustrating at the same time cause the scientists most directly concerned with the atmosphere to be more cautious than politicians or alarmed environmentalists. If you were to boil down into a phrase all the information I've absorbed about the greenhouse effect from reading and talking to experts, it would be this: just about anything can happen. Remember the different results that the Geophysical Fluid Dynamics Laboratory got from their two models for 2050? There are many, many factors besides carbon dioxide content that influence the heat retaining capacity of the atmosphere. One is clouds. Those fluffy white cumulus clouds of a summer day reflect heat back into space while high-altitude cirrus clouds let sunlight through and trap heat.

"How we treat cloud cover in our models can affect by a factor of two the impact of a doubling in atmospheric carbon dioxide," G.F.D.L. scientist Syukuro Manabe told Princeton Alumni Weekly's Merritt. "There are all kinds of cloud types, and to model them accurately we need to know how their optical qualities would change with increasing

113

levels of carbon dioxide. Our knowledge in this area is deficient, and until we know more and can incorporate this knowledge into the models, we have to be humble in our predictions."

But an even more important—and also quite variable—factor is the sun itself, since the sun is the source of any and all heat. Both Fairbridge and Landscheidt are in full agreement that we are in for a period of minimum solar activity between 1990 and 2013. Professor Fairbridge spelled out for me what this means:

"This prediction is based on a study of planetary alignments made by Shirley [James H. Shirley, a solar physicist] and myself. We came to the conclusion that the sun's orbit around the barycenter of the solar system has a direction of symmetry. When it comes back to a starting point something like once every 178-odd years we find that there is a minimum of solar activity. In the past when that happened we saw 'little ice age' conditions. In the last little ice age, mean winter temperatures in New England and northwest Europe dropped about four degrees celsius, or eight degrees fahrenheit. It was highly noticeable. There were small fluctuations of this sort from 1805 to 1825 approximately, and New York Harbor and the East River froze repeatedly for long periods of time. It was reported that an ox was roasted in the middle of the East River. In Britain during one ice age, they held fairs on the frozen Thames River, and there's a picture of Henry VIII and his entourage riding on horseback from Hampton Court to Westminster down the middle of the Thames."

The arrival of this next ice age should, in theory, counteract the greenhouse warming. But because of all the many variables, Professor Fairbridge won't hazard a guess as to what will actually happen. Like the Princeton scientists, Fairbridge emphasizes the role the oceans play in the atmosphere. Atmospheric CO_2 is in equilibrium with that in the oceans which is always changing. Take Fairbridge's ice age scenario as he outlined it to me: "As you lower temperatures, particularly in high latitudes, it would increase wind velocity which would increase the strength of the jet stream. This would raise the organic activity—the metabolic rate of the organisms living on the surface of the warm waters of the ocean. In the process, these organisms would consume more CO_2 which would tend to cool the earth further. But if the earth gets warmer due to the greenhouse effect, less CO_2 will be consumed by organisms in a sluggish ocean and more will be liberated into the atmosphere, making it warmer still. I have no idea in which direction it will go."

This uncertainty does not cause anyone in the field of atmospheric studies to suggest that human beings slow down on the gathering momentum worldwide to curb manmade pollution, particularly from the burning of fossil fuels like oil and coal. As in other aspects of this cycle story, I'm prompted to make a comparison with medicine which is so often called an art rather than a science. Art can encompass an intuitive wisdom that is lacking in a science pridefully based on so-called absolute proof. I am specifically reminded of a conversation I had with the former Surgeon General of the United States, Dr. C. Everett Koop, when I was working with him on an anti-smoking article. I had just given up the habit myself after more than forty-eight years of smoking something once every waking hour, and I was still looking for a rationale to go back to that craved comfort. Since I had a father who smoked and lived until the age of ninety-two, I asked Dr. Koop if a genetic intolerance for smoke wasn't the real cause of cancer rather than the substance itself. Conceding that this *might* be true, Dr. Koop said, "You could be one of the lucky ones, but from what we know today, to go on smoking is like playing Russian roulette with your life." I haven't drawn a breath of smoke since, and so I am personally inclined to go along with the scientists who advise us to play it safe with the atmosphere.

Meanwhile, I can safely predict that there is no danger of mankind's losing its favorite topic of conversation. Indeed, as with so many other subjects, the more we know, the more interesting it becomes. It can even be hoped that one day TV weathermen might try entertaining their audiences by truly explaining the intricacies of living weather, instead of by cracking feeble inside jokes. It could cause a welcome revolution in both knowledge and values.

CHAPTER

8

OF TIME AND LIGHT AND LIFE

CARL LINNAEUS, a Swedish savant who died in 1778, was one of those all-around men of the eighteenth century. Both physician and botanist, he served as a naval surgeon, taught his sciences at Uppsala University and wrote 180 scholarly works. Now considered the father of systematic botany, he was once offered a royal post by the King of Spain and was granted a patent of nobility by his own sovereign. But his lasting claim to fame may well be a playful creation that he called a "flower clock."

In the northern hemisphere certain flowers open or close at certain of the twelve daylight hours of summer. Drawing upon his close observation of plant life, Linnaeus laid out a clock-faced garden which would display the time through its blooms within a half hour's accuracy. Starting at 6:00 A.M. with the opening of spotted cat's ear (*Hypochoeris maculata*), the clock ran as follows: 7:00 A.M.—African marigold (*Tagetes erecta*) opens; 8:00 A.M.—mouse-ear hawkweed (*Hier-*

117

acrum pilosella) opens; 9:00 A.M.—prickly sowthistle *(Sonchus apser)* closes: 10:00 A.M.—common nipplewort *(Lapsana communis)* closes; 11:00 A.M.—Star of Bethlehem *(Ornithogalum umbellatum)* opens; 12:00 noon—passion flower *(Passiflora caerulea)* opens; 1:00 P.M.—childing pink *(Dianthus sp)* closes: 2:00 P.M.—scarlet pimpernel *(Anagallis arvensis)* closes; 3:00 P.M.—hawkbit *(Leontodon hispidus)* closes; 4:00 P.M.—bindweed *(Convolvulus arvensis)* closes; 5:00 P.M.—white water-lily *(Nymphaea alba)* closes; 6:00 P.M.—evening primose *(Oethera erythrosepala)* opens.

Whether it was Linnaeus's intent or not, he managed to stage a stunning demonstration of the recurring daily rhythms to be found in all forms of life on earth, human beings included. These are cycles as reliable and predictable as the celestial orbits from which they take their cues. Insects, birds, animals and people may not put on as precise and visible a show of the rhythms animating them as Linnaeus's flowers, but they all march to the same drum beat of light. Although there are many cycles of light and time affecting life, the twenty-four-hour cycle of night and day is the most basic. In the parlance of botanay and biology, the rhythms of this cycle are called "circadian" from the Latin for "about a day."

The study of the natural cycles within living things is one of the more rapidly developing scientific specialties of our time. Using the Greek word for time, scientists have coined a new term which I used earlier—chronobiology—for this new branch of an old discipline. The intricacies of what could be called the biological clock and the challenges they present to researchers tinkering with it can be judged from a recent statement by John Burns, a chronobiologist who once headed the Foundation for the Study of Cycles: "About one hundred new biological cycles are described every day, and this makes it humanly impossible to keep track of them all." Nevertheless, chronobiologists—Dr. Burns among them—are encouraged by what they have

118

been able to glean from their reading of the biological clock, and they are already able to give sound scientific advice on how to improve life in matters as diverse as acquiring a better understanding of physical and psychological feelings, organizing work more productively, improving agricultural output, sleeping more soundly, dispensing medicine more effectively, and getting over jet lag. If it prompts Dr. Burns to tell me with scientific caution that "biological clocks aren't really understood yet," the wealth of new material being mined through research is a guarantee of more revelations to come.

Dr. Burns is one of some 350 members of the International Society for Chronobiology, which by its very existence and geographical spread is indicative of the range and growth of the discipline. A glance at only a few of the abstracts of some 213 papers presented at the organization's Nineteenth International Conference in Maryland in June 1989 and published in its house organ, Chronobiologia, shows the scope and variety of the research in progress and its relevancy to the human condition.

— A study group in France looked into "rhythms of stimulated gastric acid secretion in duodenal ulcer" and concluded that there was a four-month ultrannual (less than a year) rhythm involved.

— A University of Texas School of Public Health report on "circannual variation of human mortality in Texas" found that "a six-month period was detected in ischemic heart disease mortality with peaks in January and July. Suicides, in contrast, were most common around May. The etiology of seasonal patterns of human mortality is as yet undetermined: it could involve seasonal variation in environmental conditions as well as circannual rhythms in physiology and behavior."

— A West German investigation of "melatonin treatment of jet lag" came up with what may be good news for world travelers: "In general the results indicate that melatonin [a secretion of the pineal gland that acts as a natural relaxing agent] may be an effective zeitgeber [a common chronobiological term, from the German for "time giver," which means an agent that initiates a biological rhythm] for human subjects. Consequently melatonin may be used to influence the circadian system after time zone transitions to reduce jet lag symptoms."

— Clinical experiments in timing dosages of cancer drugs to circadian rhythms resulted in a report that stated emphatically: "Living organisms are not 'zero-order' in their requirements for or response to drugs. They are predictably resonating dynamic systems which require different amounts of drugs at different times in order to maximize desired and minimize undesired drug effects."

— An Italian group made a systematic study of digestive disturbances in shift workers as compared to non-shift workers and expressed the conviction that "shift work is *per se* responsible for digestive diseases in the workers engaged in it" and that "it is very important to distinguish the kind of shift work which may produce environmental, psychological and motivational differences."

— Authors from the Department of Plant Biology, University of Minnesota; the Department of Agronomy, University of Wisconsin, and the Agricultural Research Service of the U.S. Deaprtment of Agriculture joined in an overview that said: "An awareness of biological oscillations and attempts to understand these phenomena are important to increasing the productivity and efficiency of agriculture, the quality of agricultural products, and environmental quality. The utilization of biological oscillations by manipulating or taking advantage of their characteristics will become increasingly important in animal and plant strategies."

In addition to these very few samples, there were papers from research facilities in China, Japan, Russia, Spain, Israel, Great Britain, Canada and other points east and west along with those from many centers of chronobiological investigation in the United States. Most of these papers were highly technical and focused sharply on a specific aspect or a specific cog in the machinery of the biological clock such as, say, blood pressure that can rise and fall by as much as 20 percent in its circadian cycle. But, by reading through them, even a layman can appreciate their usefulness to scientists trying to piece together the chronobiological puzzle and to health professionals in practical need of better tools for diagnosis and treatment of malfunctions in the human system.

Meanwhile, there seems to be a reliable consensus among chronobiologists, cycle scholars and others concerned with the interlocking rhythms of the universe and terrestrial organisms that both the quality and quantity of life could be enhanced by paying more attention to what is already known for sure about the biological clock. There are a number of truisms in this area that are beyond debate. One of them is that human beings are by nature diurnal animals, which means that they come to life during daylight hours and sleep during the night—a cycle that rolls in reverse for nocturnal creatures like bats. It is possible for human beings to function by night and for bats to fly by day, but either effort amounts to going contrary to the clock. Fortunately, living organisms are astonishingly adaptable to changing circumstances, but adaptation to unnatural conditions almost always exacts a price, as noted in the Italian research on shift workers. With respect to the human animal at least, this price has largely gone unnoted and unmeasured during the short century or so since an explosion in technology gave man what seemed to be the means to bend nature to his will. In this perspective, the new knowledge coming out of chronobiology can be seen as a paradox. On the one hand, it is revealing the high price of resisting the driving cycles of nature; on the other hand, it is suggesting ways to compensate, as noted in the German research on using melatonin to deal with jet lag.

121

Central to the fact that biological clocks aren't "really understood," according to Dr. Burns, is a mystery as to how their oscillations or cycles are produced. "Some people think that they are produced inside the organism and some from the outside," he says, and so far there is good evidence to support either, or both, of these views. A lot of this evidence is accumulating in studies of the effect of light.

Consider some causes for confusion. Seasonal cycles, in which the major factors are duration and warmth of sunlight caused by the tilt of the earth with respect to the sun, are self-evident in the migrations and matings of the animal kingdom, and germination and flowering among the plants. This has led to logical postulations. Small mammals, like the hare and ferret, are called long-day breeders since the lengthening of days at the end of winter seems to result in a mating that will produce young by spring. Like the circadian cycle itself, the theory about bats runs in reverse: the early twilight of September days presaging longer, livelier nights, is their mating cue. But nature is a signal switcher. For instance, sheep kept under constant light for some three years went right on breeding in the same old cycle, giving rise to the distinct possibility of an endogenous sexual rhythm. An even more thought-provoking indication that living things have a built-in circannual clock is seen in the fact that European trees transplanted by nineteenth century colonists to the tropics came into leaf on their northern cycle.

When it comes to human beings, it has been said facetiously that Thomas Edison did away with circadian rhythms by inventing the electric light. If so, he was the right man for the job since he personally scorned wasting time on a night's sleep and made up for the loss by catnapping throughout the day. In any event, there is no doubt that Edison's invention is one of the major devices that gives modern man the feeling of having gained control over nature. Some recent chronobiological investigations are supportive of this view. Nobody needs a psychiatrist to diagnose or describe the winter blues that can accompany short, dark days. But in some people they can become a form of clinical depression known as Seasonal Affective Disorder or SAD. This affliction is apparently caused by oversensitivity or overreaction to melatonin, that pineal hormone which is the natural relaxer that flows into the system at dusk to ready the body for sleep. Researchers have discovered recently that SAD victims exposed to thirty minutes daily of high levels of wide-spectrum illumination are able to shake off the winter blues.

"If we can do with light what we have been trying to do with drugs or motivation, we are vastly better off," Dr. David F. Dinges, a biological psychologist at the Institute of Pennsylvania Hospital told the New York *Times* in commenting on the latest experiments in which human body clocks were reset by artificial light. The work was announced in the journal Science by Dr. Charles A. Czeisler of Harvard Medical School and Dr. Richard E. Kronauer, a Harvard mathematician. In forty-five laboratory attempts to readjust the biological clocks of fourteen men aged eighteen to twenty-four they achieved "uniform success." As distinct and easily measurable as the ticks of a mantle clock are the circadian biological rhythms that show up in body temperature, hormone levels and kidney function. To reset the clocks the researchers exposed their subjects to five hours of bright light when their body temperature was lowest. The result: one application made the circadian rhythm irregular, a second reduced it and a third restarted the clock in the way that dawn lifts the temperature to induce waking.

The ramifications of this research are obviously many and have yet to be put to the test. Researchers suggest that one of these could be tried by anyone who flies across time zones. If, for example, a person arriving in Sydney, Australia, from New York would spend part of the first two days outdoors to absorb the equivalent of the first two doses of light, he or she would find the internal clock reset to local time by dawn of the third day. This contrasts with other research showing that people can take up to eight days to reset their body clocks on a westbound flight and eighteen days on an eastbound flight through six time zones. Other possibilities raised by the Harvard work are using light to reset the clocks of shift workers—some 2.2 million Americans alone—who are more prone to accident in the middle of the night when their temperatures are low; and using knowledge of light's effect to help insomniacs who often aggravate their problem by turning on lights to read or drive away the dark.

Over recent years there have been innumerable studies as to how photoperiodism—the effect of alternating periods of light and darkness on living organisms—relates to the rhythms in human beings. In general, they keep revealing new bodily links with light. Often these experiments on volunteers involve isolation from normal light and time as in the case of Josy Laures, a Parisian midwife, who spent eighty-eight days in a deep cave with only a dim miner's lamp for light. Cooperating with Dr. Alain Reinberg and his associates, she took her daily temperature and timed her menstrual cycle for a year before and after the experiment. In the cave, Josy lived a 24.6-hour day, a *statistically* significant departure from the 24-hour day she lived by the clock above ground; her monthly cycle of rectal temperature was 29.4 days; her menstrual cycle changed from 29 days to 25.7 days. This last effect was a surprise to Dr. Reinberg who searched the literature and found studies showing that first menstruation in six hundred young girls in northern Germany occurred most frequently in winter, that girls born blind reached menarche earlier than sighted girls. All this raised the real possibility that dim light, or lack of light, might stimulate reproductive hormones in women. When

Josy came out into natural light again, all of her cycles returned to normal.

Regardless of what may turn up in further chrono-biological research, enough is now known about circadian rhythms to provide guidance for more effective living within the natural cycle of light and dark. Most importantly, all now agree that individual human beings are, to a greater or lesser extent, either "larks," who feel and function better early in the day, or "owls," whose vitality rises as the day goes on. For owls who have been haunted for centuries by the kind of sentiment expressed in Benjamin Franklin's homily, "Early to bed and early to rise, makes a man healthy, wealthy and wise," it must have come as a godsend when science could prove that the lark/owl distinction is not a matter of character: it depends on that measurable ticking of the inner clock. Body temperature declines at night and rises during the day for all of us on a normal schedule, but, according to Dr. Czeisler, the exact timing of the low point and high point within any individual is what separates a lark from an owl. This inner temperature cycle is as much a part of a person's makeup as eye color of fingerprints, and learning how to live with it rather than wishing it were different is the way of wisdom.

Without losing sight of individual differences, researchers have been able to discern averages across the broad spectrum of circadian rhythms that enable them to make very practical suggestions for scheduling a day's activities. In evaluating these, keep in mind that even extreme early morning people and extreme evening people have cycles that are only two hours apart. Low points in everybody's twenty-four-hour day are between 2:00 A.M. and 4:00 A.M. and after lunch, or approximately the same time twelve hours later. Sleep is definitely indicated as the appropriate activity for the early morning lag, and the siesta habit in Latin countries would seem to have been grounded in

125

physical realities. From the scientific point of view, the early afternoon low is not attributable to the two-martini lunch or its equivalent in past eras since everybody experiences it. Then there are high times for certain activities. Morning generally—late morning particularly—is best for important mental tasks such as composition, analyzing problems, engaging in creative meetings. Mid-afternoon hours, following the post-luncheon lag, are best for repetitive tasks like filing and sorting or those requirimg manual skill like typing or practicing the piano. Late afternoon into early evening is the optimum time for sports. One fascinating finding is that all of the senses—taste, sight, hearing, touch and smell—are at their most acute in the evening which no doubt accounts for the fact that those hours are universally preferred for dining and dalliance. The science of chronobiology is largely concerned with rooting out the causes of these phenomena, but it may be years before enough data has been collected and thoroughly analyzed and any cogent theories are formulated.

In today's so-called advanced civilizations, where time is determined by mechanical or electronic clocks and where electricity has done away with the absolute need for light, human beings (much like laboratory animals) are routinely called upon to perform activities that do violence to the inner clock. Take two common instances: an owl is confronted with a very important examination in the very early morning because it is convenient or essential in terms of a school's computerized scheduling; a lark, compelled to work nine to five by the logistics of the marketplace, can only find time to deal with the intellectual challenge of working out his or her income tax in the evening. Fortunately, human history is star-studded with instances of people "rising to the occasion." While acknowledging that this is the case, chronobiologists advise being aware of the unintended consequences. Performing out of time with your inner clock can cause digestive disturbances, emotional outbursts, loss of appetite, errors in judgment. If these reactions can be anticipated and their nature understood, they can be accepted and handled with more grace by all concerned.

The power of the rhythms within us is evident in this passage from *The Rhythms of Life,* edited by Edward S. Ayensu and Dr. Philip Whitfield, one of the most comprehensive reports on current biological research: "It is a basic assumption that circadian rhythmicity evolved in step with primitive life, and hence that it is an essential property of all cells. Certainly single-celled algae and protozoa, that is, the very simplest of plants and animals, have circadian rhythms, and so do isolated culture cells taken from higher plants and animals . . . The body of an animal or plant, thus, consists of a panoply of clocks at many levels of organization—in cell, tissue and organ—and in the whole organism that must all tick together." But there is a dominant, or driving, clock that dictates overt behavior. It is the part of the organism that responds to light—in the higher animals and human beings, the eye and brain. Animals in the wild instinctively time their behavior in all areas of living from migration to sexual performance to sleep to feeding by this driving clock. Only human beings turn deaf ears to the ticking of this infinitely intricate system of inner clocks, and it is small wonder that great strain results. In this light, an awareness of cycles cries out for a re-examination of our thinking about the nature of time itself.

The extent and nature of suffering imposed upon the human animal by the logical, linear, mathematical, mechanical, economically profitable, man-made measure of time is beyond calculation. There are, however, welcome signs that this form of unnatural servitude to arbitrary time may be coming to an end as a result of more knowledge about the variable, cyclical, dynamic nature of every entity in the universe. These signs range from calls for new scientific and philosophical concepts about time to hard-headed industrial experiments with flextime, instead of the nine-to-five regimen, to elicit more production, and hence more profits, out of employees. In *The Third Wave*, futurist Alvin Toffler uses these signs of new thinking about time as one of his strongest arguments for the thesis that a new form of civilization is in the making.

"Each emerging civilization brings with it not merely changes in how people handle time in daily life but also changes in their mental maps of time," Toffler writes. "Second Wave civilization, from Newton on, assumed that time ran along a single line from the mists of the past into the most distant future. It pictured time as absolute, uniform throughout all parts of the universe, and independent of matter and space. It assumed that each moment, or chunk of time was the same as the next. Today, according to John Gribbin, an astrophysicist-turned-science-writer, 'Sober scientists with impeccable academic credentials and years of research experience calmly inform us that . . . time isn't something that flows inexorably forward at the steady pace indicated by our clocks and calendars, but that it can be warped and distorted in nature, with the end product being different depending on just where you are measuring it from. At the ultimate extreme, super-collapsed objects— black holes—can negate time altogether making it stand still in their vicinity.' "

Toffler cites Einstein's proof of the relativity of time as a turning point in our understanding of this dimension's nature. In Einstein's illustration, a man standing beside a railroad track sees two bolts of lightning strike the earth at the same time—one in front of a high speed train heading north, the other behind it. A passenger on the train sees both bolts of lightning, too, but to his eye they don't strike simultaneously. The one to the north toward which the train is speeding appears to hit first. Thus, the chronology of events—which comes first, second and so on—depends upon the velocity of the observer. As physics goes beyond

Einstein, more questions about the structure of time are raised. Columbia University's Dr. Gerald Feinberg hypothesized the existence of microscopic particles called tachyons for which time moves backward because they move faster than light, according to Toffler who quotes another physicist, Fritjof Capta, as saying that time is "flowing at different rates in different parts of the universe."

A different concept of the nature of time would be nothing new in human history. In the Chinese philosophy of Taoism dating back to the seventh century before Christ, time was conceived of as cyclical and related to the life cycles of living organisms. This was true, too, of Buddhism with its wheel of life and Hinduism with its recurrent *kalpas* of four thousand million years that comprised a single Brahma day of re-creation, dissolution, re-creation again. Cyclical time predominated in pre-Christian Greek thinking. Pythagoras, for instance, who first heard the "music of the spheres," taught a doctrine of the eternal recurrence of time.

In *Time and Eastern Man,* Joseph Needham presents the argument that the linear view of time is a natural outgrowth of Judeo-Christian thought. "For Christian thought the whole of history was structured around the centre, a temporal mid-point, the historicity of the life of Christ, and extended from the creation through . . . the covenent of Abraham to . . . the messianic millennium and the end of the world," Needham writes. "In this world-outlook the recurring present was always unique, unrepeatable, decisive, with an open future before it, which could or would be affected by the action of the individual who might assist or hinder the irreversible meaningful directedness of the whole . . . The world process, in sum, was a divine drama enacted on a single stage, with no repeat performances."

The extent to which this linear, progressive view of time accounts for the rapid development of modern science in Western civiliztion is still debatable, according to Needham.

Measurable time is an essential dimension in scientific experiments and mathematical calculations, and Needham suggests that the concept of time as linear and infinitely progressive is a psychological spur to scientific striving. "For if the sum of human scientific effort were to be doomed beforehand to ineluctable dissolution, only to be reformed with endless toil aeon after aeon one might as well seek radical escape in religious meditation or Stoic detachment rather than wearing oneself out like a coral-building polyp engaged with its colleagues in blindly constructing a reef on the rim of a live volcano," he argues. Scientists would certainly not be so strongly motivated if they thought that the knowledge system they were building up could perish in some cyclical turn of civilization. It's notable that time in the form of units of duration is essential in today's statistical analysis of cycles. But it is also notable that science's measurement of those units of duration is based entirely on the cycles of earth with reference to the sun and other stars.

In the development of cycle theory there is a suggestion that any new concept of time will represent a compromise between these two historical views. There can be no doubt that time as we experience and measure it derives from celestial and biological cycles. But the more these cycles are studied the more apparent it is that they are not fixed. The orbit of the supposedly steady sun, for example, is now known to vary in response to the gravitational pull of the various planets in their differing alignments. In addition, the shape of a cycle is more likely to be descibed these days as a spiral—a shape that can accommodate change and progress within recurrence.

The practical importance of how we view time lies in what we do with it. To acknowledge the relationships through cycles between time, light and life is to acknowledge the interdependence of all natural systems, an interdependence from which man is not exempt. More flexibility in adapting human plans and enterprises to the realities of time is certainly in order, and the flexibility in thinking about time that Toffler explores is essential to that end. In space, where astronauts see a new day dawning every ninety minutes instead of every twenty-four hours, the current solution to keeping their bodies from getting out of synchrony with environmental time is for them to schedule functions like eating and resting in accordance with Houston time throughout a flight. There is irony in the promise of freeing human beings from time by experiments using artificial light to reset the inner time clocks of time defiers like shift workers, international travelers and astronauts. If it works, is is simply a confirmation of the power of the cycle of light within the interlocking cycles of time, light and life, rather than any dominance by man.

One of the deep thinkers about time whose words have stood the test of time is "Ecclesiastes, Or The Preacher," as the Revised Standard Version of the Holy Bible identifies the author of an Old Testament book. Since he was a poet of cyclical thinking—"What has been is what will be, and what has been done is what will be done; and there is nothing new under the sun"—there is another irony in the preservation of his words within the Hebrew culture that time historian Needham credits with first introducing the linear view of time to world thought. Evidently, it wasn't possible to exclude Ecclesiastes from the pantheon of prophets, philosophers and poets, because what he said corresponded so closely with the experience of even unthinking people and because it has yet to be contradicted in any significant way by science. Consider again the words of that preacher:

"For everything there is a season, and a time for every matter under heaven:

> a time to be born, and a time to die;
> a time to plant, and a time to pluck up what is planted;

131

a time to kill, and a time to heal;
a time to break down, and a time to build up;
a time to weep, and a time to laugh;
a time to mourn, and a time to dance;
a time to cast away stones, and a time to gather stones together;
a time to embrace, and a time to refrain from embracing;
a time to seek, and a time to lose;
a time to keep, and a time to cast away;
a time to rend, and a time to sew;
a time to keep silence, and a time to speak;
a time to love, and a time to hate;
a time for war, and a time for peace."

If he had carried Ecclestiastes' litany into the world of livng plants, Linnaeus would certainly have added that there is a time to open and a time to close. Nobody knows yet why this is so, but is would be hard to argue that it isn't so. I am no kind of flower, but I have found that I "open"— at least in alertness and creativity—early in the morning and start closing along about the end of TV's evening news. Being married to an owl, I have had to summon support for my arguments that my timing was neither peculiar nor the result of some sort of character deficiency, from the memoirs of great literary lights who expressed marked preference for working in the morning hours. In researching cycles I have not only discovered hard evidence that these writers were instinctively picking the best hours for mental labor but also that I and my owl, like Linnaeus's flowers, have all along been doing what comes naturally. Thus, in my personal dealings with time, as in so many other matters, knowledge has, as the saying goes, made all the difference.

CHAPTER

9

CAN CYCLES BE CALLED A SCIENCE?

SCIENCE IS SOMETHING of a buzzword of our times. Like other reporters, I tend to use it and its associated adjective and adverb too often and too loosely. The intent is an innocent one—a shortcut to saying that whatever is being discussed is real, definitive, reliable, believable without recourse to faith. This is understood since the scientist, as putative master of mystery and purveyor of truth, has long been Western civilization's most universally acknowledged priest. Collectively and mostly anonymously, scientists have delivered into the hands of human beings an understanding and control of natural power that allows man to step on the moon, fly routinely faster than sound, lengthen the span of human life, view from his easy chair simultaneous happenings in any part of the globe, destroy a city—and possibly earth itself—with a bomb. It would take an act of faith *not* to stand in awe of science unless, perhaps, you are a scientist.

One of the more revealing aspects of a foray into scientific territory by a layman like myself is to observe the extent of humility and doubt that the best of scientists exhibit. According to the testimony that comes through their words and work thus far in history, the so-called scientific solution to a problem is more likely to raise questions than to provide answers. This is what makes for the excitement and challenge in research. It should also make for a degree of caution and skepticism on the part of laymen in assessing claims on truth by reason of something's being "scientific."

With this caveat, it has to be admitted that science could not have wrought its miracles without a structure and discipline that distinguishes it from other forms of learning and knowledge. The best short definition of the word itself that I've run across is this one from the *Encyclopeida Britannica:* "For our purpose, science may be defined as ordered knowledge of natural phenomena and of the relations between them." *Webster's* employs, significantly, the words study, practice, method, system in its several definitions of science. These are elements in any form of learning that can properly be called a branch of science, and it is the presence of one or all of them that accounts for the popular perception of science as grounded in provable fact instead of fancy.

It was this common understanding of what science is that Edward R. Dewey, the founder of the Foundation for the Study of Cycles, had in mind when he devoted his director's letter in the August 1960 issue of the Cycles to the question: "Are cycle students cranks or scientists?" Dewey's answer is worth repeating since it is still valid after thirty years. First quoting a Dr. L. J. Lafleur who charged in Scientific Monthly that cranks "propose and dogmatically affirm to be true propositions which the scientist recognizes as preposterous, and contrary to all the recognized truths of his science," Dewey wrote:

"This comes rather close to the place where the cycle student lives, especially when he ventures to study rhythmic cycles in economic phenomena. One economist told me, 'If the things you say are true, all I have ever learned is wrong.' Workers in certain other fields doubtless feel the same way.

"Now let us see what the cycle student says.

"He says that *some* of the rhythmic ups and downs visible in *some* of the series of figures representing natural and social phenomena cannot possibly be random and that rhythmic phenomena are therefore worthy of further study.

"He is not dogmatic. He does not say that they *cannot* be random; he just says that the smart thing to do is to find out.

"He does not contend that *all* the regularities *are* significant. He just says that *some* of them *may* be. He says that it would be hard for *all* of them to come about through the operations of the laws of chance.

"Moreover—canny fellow that he is—he does not assert that any particular rhythm is significant. He merely says that out of all the observed rhythms, some of them, reasonably, are significant. To prove against him that any one rhythm is the result of chance is like shooting out one leg from underneath a centipede; he still has ninety-nine feet left to stand on!

"Dr. Lafleur goes on to say, 'It is typical of the crank theories that they contradict many established laws rather than one . . . Not once in a generation is there an innovation so important that it changes many laws, and can truly be called revolutionary for some branch of science. Cranks propose such innovations every day, and happily assume that they are not merely scientists, but members of that highly restricted group fortunate enough to discover revolutionary new laws . . . The odds favor the assumption that anyone proposing a revolutionary doctrine is a crank, rather than a scientist, but this does not settle the issue for any individual case.'

"These comments hit even closer home, for the cycle student and his ideas do cut across many branches of science. However, cycle concepts do not *contradict* established laws. The cycle students attempt to introduce law into areas where, hitherto, law has been unrecognized and unsuspected.

"Dr. Lafleur continues, 'There is another characteristic of a revolutionary scientific principle in which it differs from the typical crank theory; no matter how widespread its implications, no matter how many previously accepted laws must be modified, all the changes fit into one thoroughly integrated pattern. The scientist respects nature and its laws insofar as they are already known to man.'

"Here the cycle student fares better. The ideas proposed do, at least potentially, fit into one pattern. The force, whatever it is, which creates rhythmic fluctuation in one phenomenon may be the cause of similar rhythmic fluctuations in another.

"Dr. Lafleur again: 'In attempting to defend the divergences from currently accepted view, the crank may be led to excessive reliance upon minority opinions and the authority of individuals. As a corollary to this, he may also attempt to discredit majority opinion, scientific method, or scientists in general.'

"Here again cycle students are absolved. The cycle student rests upon no authority except the facts themselves. He does not discredit scientists. But he does deplore closed minds."

Dewey's words reflect both a becoming humility and an understandable exasperation. He candidly admitted that he had often been called a crank, but he continued steadfastly onward in what he considered to be the pursuit of a science. Steadfastly may be too weak a word for the actions of a man who, as his son told me, was "a workaholic—no golf, no tennis, no dancing, no drinking." He was an overachiever who was equally demanding of his associates, according to his longtime research director, Gertrude Shirk, who recalls, "He couldn't understand people who would take an hour and ten minutes for a lunch they could eat in twenty minutes." But Shirk found him to be "an interesting man, more or less a man of the world" with whom she had never-ending discussions and arguments about their mutual interest in what they were learning. Despite his fierce dedication to the cause of cycles, Dewey retained that open mind he admired into his eighties.

"Dewey was slowing down physically, but up to the week he died he was full of ideas," Ms. Shirk told me. "For example, we had an astronomer on staff—a Ph.D. candidate in astronomy. He pointed out that if you want to make a comparison of timing in planets and timing on earth, you have to be aware of the fact that planets do not move at a constant speed. So Dewey said, 'Give me the varying speeds of the planets so that I will know when they are going faster and slower.' He was working with a 5.9-year cycle in cotton prices and a 5.9-year astronomical cycle. What he was looking for was to see whether, if an anomaly developed in cotton prices, a counterpart anomaly occurred in astronomy."

Dewey didn't have time to finish this project; he died in 1978, eighteen years after his defense of cycle students cited above, and he was full of confidence in the future of his science. According to his son, Edward S. Dewey, "He was very pleased with what he had done with his life. Toward the end he was getting some recognition. He was, for instance, one of the few American members of the World Academy of Arts and Sciences. He was very happy, and he went out like a rocket. He visualized himself as the man before Copernicus—that is, after he had finished all the work he could do the next man would come along in twenty or so years and tie up all the knots."

All the knots are not yet tied. Indeed, in keeping with the whole story of scientific endeavor, they may never be. But Dewey's confidence that cycles would take an appropriate place in the scientific world seems to have been well placed. One reliable measure of this growing acceptance is that an increasing number of people whose backgrounds and systematic methods of research are certifiably "scientific" are allying themselves directly with the Foundation or indirectly supporting its thesis that cycles are an important determinant factor in the workings of the universe. The research that validates cycle theory is in no sense frivolous, and it is coming out of all sorts of disciplines—cutting across many branches of science, as Dewey foresaw that it would. Although seemingly unrelated in specific focus, the following examples of studies in progress are each related to cycles, and the manner in which they are being pursued shows a common devotion to scientific discipline.

Typical of one type of scientist who believes in cycles is Fergus J. Wood, trained in astronomy but famed as an authority on tides. Wood's work on tides is reported in Chapter 6, but when I talked to him about this book he wanted me to make it crystal clear that his discovery of the role that a cyclical configuration of celestial bodies plays in extremely high or low tides is based on the most painstaking and systematic study.

"We have established for the first time that there are definite astronomical cycles," he told me. "We call them luni-solar cycles, a combination of the moon's action and the sun's action. Because they do exist in nature, we've been able to do what we've done in terms of putting down when these things will happen and what they will do.

"I made a large number of tests of this sort of thing because in science we cannot be content on the basis of one particular circumstance. I did this for one hundred events or more. We not only take many events, but we twist them around to try to show that they're wrong so that we know they are right if they work out. One test is to take something that is absolutely devoid of any meaning in terms of what it is that you are doing and use that as a parameter on which to base the systematic work that you are doing.

"An example is that I took six different coastal towns of the same name throughout the world. The selection had nothing whatsoever to do with the physical law that I was exploring. If you take six remote places joined only by the circumstances of name and the hypothesis still works out, you believe you are on the right track.

"I took six towns with the name of Newport—Newport, Oregon; Newport Beach, California; Newport, Rhode Island; Newport News, Virginia; and two Newports in England on different coasts. I took tidal flooding at these places all the way back in time—in some cases to A.D. 1099. I associated them only through mathematical luni-solar relationships. The numerical value is determined by what the moon and sun are doing at the time, and simple multiples of these values will work out to the distance in time between events. In this case, the celestial circumstances that should have produced coastal flooding did produce coastal flooding in the Newports back through history."

A different type of scientist in cycleland is John P. Bagby whose research is as detailed and disciplined as Wood's and whose range of interest has the interdisciplinary character of cycles itself. A mechanical engineer at Hughes Aircraft in Los Angeles, Bagby got his education in that discipline at Cornell, Drexel, Oklahoma A. & M., Chrysler Institute in Detroit and Lake Forest College. What he remembers most from his education is a professor who told him that once a person is trained in one subject, he can train himself in others. For the last thirty years, Bagby has done just that in and out of working hours and with the enthusiastic help and encouragement of his scientifically minded wife. Trained as a medical technician in junior college, Loretta Bagby took further work in medicine and chemistry in hospitals and at Wayne State University. While rearing three children, she has collaborated with her hhusband in studies and experiments in astronomy and physics that are now shaking one of the pillars of modern scientific thought—the law of gravity.

The law of gravity was passed, as it were, more than three hundred years ago as the result of discoveries by Galileo Galilei and Sir Isaac Newton. Galileo "proved" that the acceleration of any falling body is constant and has the same value for all bodies; Newton "proved" that any two bodies in the universe attract each other in proportion to the product of their masses and inversely as the square of their distances apart. In all the intervening time, the law of gravity has served man well in the development of science and engineering, but increasingly such inquiring minds as those of the Bagbys have been questioning the assumption that gravity is the uniformly steady force described by Galileo and Newton. Because of anomalies detected in gravity's action, there is even talk of a fifth or sixth force in addition to the already acknowledged four forces supposedly holding the universe together—gravity, electromagnetism, and the so-called strong and weak forces binding atomic nuclei.

The background of how and why the Bagbys developed the interest and temerity to challenge an iron rule of a science not their own has a bearing on any determination of what is, or isn't, a science. Their story begins in the 1950s when John Bagby sought work at Bell & Howell, the Illinois camera maker. "They said my work had all been with large mechanisms and pipes and forgings and castings—a forty-inch pipe isn't a camera," he recalls, "and I said, 'Well, an engineer is an engineer, and I should be able to work with small things, too.'" Although he was hired, Bagby soon discovered that he would have to work outside the system. Discouraged by the company's engineering department when he came up with an idea for an automatic focus mechanism for cameras, he and Loretta worked together on it at home, assembling experimental models on the kitchen table. Evidently operating on what Bagby calls the "NIH factor—Not Invented Here," the engineering vice-president rejected Bagby's request to put the camera into development at the company.

In retrospect, this became an important turning point in Bagby's development as an experimental scientist. In talking to me, he credited Loretta with giving him the heart to pursue these interests outside of his regular job. "Her thought is that, if you are afraid to make mistakes, you will never take risks," he says. "She encouraged me to take more risks than they were allowing. When the vice-president of engineering and the chief engineer went on vacation, I took the camera to a business manager named Bill Roberts who immediately arranged funding for the experiment. The result wasn't all pleasant. I didn't get a raise for two and a half years, wasn't promoted, was taken out of my job and in general was really roughed up. But we got the camera."

Today Bagby shares eight patents on solar-powered automatic focus cameras and has developed a much thicker skin with respect to rejection by orthodox thinkers—a rejection that wasn't limited to the industrial world. Possibly because he was writing about subjects for which he had no standard academic or career credentials, it took Bagby thirteen years and innumerable revisions before his first scientific paper was finally published in the prestigious journal Nature. But the persistence that enabled Bagby to be published at all was an essential ingredient of the Bagbys' investigation into the law of gravity. For a long time, Bagby had wondered whether it was really true that bodies of different weight and composition fell at the same velocity and whether bodies weighed the same at different times. He and Loretta concocted an experiment in which they weighed objects on a balance and observed how their weights changed relative to each other over a span of time. It was tedious and meticulous work. When John Bagby left Illinois for a job in California in 1978, Loretta stayed behind to keep the children in school and sell their home. It turned out to be a separation of fourteen months during which each filled the lonely hours by conducting experiments that they discussed by phone. Using one empty weekend for intensive work, Bagby set an alarm to wake himself every twenty minutes over a period of forty-eight hours in order to measure bits of lead, brass, copper, aluminum, water and ice on a scale. As a result of such efforts, the Bagbys decided that there were more variations in weights than allowable under Newton's law, and that they were cyclical in character.

"We couldn't make sense of it at first. Sometimes we saw a force that was positive and sometimes a force that was negative and sometimes none at all," he told me. "Then suddenly we saw this pattern. It was irregular but cyclic, periodic. We analyzed it and found that there were two main cycles involved—at 2.66 and 4 hours." Convinced that there was an outside, cyclical force involved in recurrent weight changes of the same object, the Bagbys reasoned that, as he explained to Shari Roan of the Orange County Register, "the moon or stars or planets were acting in gravitational enhancement. We felt it was due to their alignment. We were convinced that the law of gravity was wrong. How could something be the same and change its weight? We were frightened. I thought these were sacred laws. But I couldn't accept them."

Attempting to interest others in these insights was as frustrating as attempting to sell the concept of an automatic focus camera, and, until 1986, the Bagbys turned to studies of the relationship between celestial gravitational forces and earthquakes. In that year, a physicist with the proper academic credentials—Ephriam Fischbach of Purdue University—joined the challengers of the law of gravity by announcing that all bodies do not fall at the same rate and postulating that the attraction between two bodies had as much to do with their chemical composition as with their mass alone. Hearing this supportive fire from the right quarters, the Bagbys went back into battle against the impregnable scientific citadel of gravity. In the two-story foyer of their home in Anaheim, they loaded one paper cup with wood and another with pennies of equal weight, dropped them simultaneously from a height of eight feet and filmed the descent with a camcorder. The cups interchanged positions like runners on a race track with one gaining as much as 1.5 inches on the other and falling back again, and they didn't always land at the same time. This happened in cyclical patterns over and over again in repeated experiments.

In another experiment, Bagby constructed a horizontal balsa wood pendulum and put equally weighted but different size disks of silicon and molybdenum at either end. Setting the pendulum to swing horizontally, Bagby took the elapsed time of eight swings, divided by eight to get an average and repeated the exepriment eight more times; then repeated the entire experiment at twenty minute intervals; then changed the disks to opposite ends of the pendulum and went through the entire experiment once more; then rotated the balance 180 degrees and repeated the experiment for a third time. The upshot? More cyclical patterns that suggest an outside force in the form of gravitational waves from the planets.

It was 1987 before John Bagby heard of the Foundation for the Study of Cycles, located almost in his own backyard at Irvine. He attended a spring symposium staged by the Foundation and found himself among like-minded mavericks in the sciences. "I learned that other people have worked in other fields with a lot of the same abuse as we've had, but they all have the same bias that we do—that there is this influence from the planets," he says. But Bagby is

143

under no illusion that his postulations will find their way into the scientific mainstream any faster than those of Dewey or, for that matter, of Newtown whose ideas were in circulation for twenty years before they brought about a scientific revolution.

The synchrony in timing between celestial and terrestrial cycles, or between cycles in unrelated phenomena on earth, was one of the findings of the Foundation that caused Dewey to lay claim to the name of science. "We began to look more closely at all the cycles with the same length, and what we discovered convinced not only me but a large body of previously doubting scientists that cycles are a reality," he wrote in his book *Cycles*. "We discovered that all cycles of the same length tend to turn at the same time! Now if it is difficult to find cycles with identical lengths in unrelated phenomena by chance alone, think how much more diffi- cult it is to find cycles with identical lengths that also turn at or about the same calendar time. What amazed us even more was to learn that all cycles of the same length behave this same way. This was unusually powerful evidence that we were dealing with real and not random behavior." Dewey's evidence that there is a synchrony in cycles is im- pressive, and the association of phenomena through these cycles is fascinating. Here are a few samples:

— Among some thirty-seven cycles of 9.6 or 9.7 years in length are those of colored fox abundance in Canada, salmon abundance in England, tent caterpillar abundance in New Jersey, ozone content of the atmosphere in London and Paris, heart disease in New England, international battles in wars.

— Among ten cycles turning every 5.91 years are business failures since 1857, combined stock prices since 1871, grouse abundance since 1848, sunspots since 1749.

— Among twelve cycles with an 18.2-year period are mar- riages in the United States, real estate activity since 1851, flood stages of the Nile River since 641, and Java tree rings since 1514.

Dewey was quite frank in admitting that the reason for the interrelation of certain cycles remained a mystery, but he was sure that there was a reason to be found. The strength of his conviction emerges from Gertrude Shirk's story about the puzzle he was trying to solve in the last weeks of his life. Today the scientists working with cycles seem less hesitant in asserting definite and predictable connections between, say, luni-solar cycles, climate and the abundance of various forms of life. They also remain as intrigued as Dewey was by the statistical evidence of synchrony between such logically linked natural cycles and those that appear in collective and individual human behavior such as the battles in the 9.6-year cycles, the waves in stock prices in the 5.91-year series, the ups and down of marriages every 18.2 years. There is a consensus that the force, or forces, behind cycles in everything else could well be the same that drive cycles in the human psyche.

Although he remained appropriately cautious and tentative in public statements, Dewey was evidently quite certain as to where his science was leading. "Toward the end my father felt very sure that he had put it together—in other words, the cause was extraterrestrial in some way," Edward S. Dewey says. "He talked about such things as latitudinal variations in the abundance of animals that could be accounted for only by extraterrestrial forces—forces such as gravity and the relations of planets. He used magnetic force as the kind of force that could affect us en masse." It's not hard to imagine the excitement that Dewey would have felt in learning of the unfolding work of scientists like Wood and Bagby, and he would surely have kept a sharp eye on research that was reported in a recent book highly recommended by his successors at the Foundation—*The Body Elec-*

tric: Electromagnetism and the Foundation of Life by Robert O. Becker, M.D., and Gary Selden.

Becker and Selden hint that discoveries as to the function of electricity in the human body suggest a physical mechanism for the effect of celestial cycles on those in the human body, including the nervous system, which is responsible for both thought and feeling. To attempt any kind of summary of the argument and rich supportive detail in the Becker and Selden book would be gross oversimplification. But the book's own summary of current knowledge about earth's electromagnetic field is enough to indicate the growing importance of cycles in scientific thinking:

"At the end of the nineteenth century, geophysicists found that the earth's magnetic field varied as the moon revolved around it. In the same period, anthropologists were learning that most preliterate cultures reckoned their calendar time primarily by the moon. These discoveries led Svante Arrhenius, the Swedish natural philosopher and father of ion chemistry, to suggest that his tidal magnetic rhythm was an innate timekeeper regulating the few obvious biocycles then known.

"Since then we've learned of many other cyclic changes in the energy structure around us:

- The earth's electromagnetic field is largely a result of interaction between the magnetic field per se, emanating from the planet's molten iron-nickel core, and the charged gas of the ionosphere. It varies with the lunar day and month, and there's also a yearly change as we revolve around the sun.

- A cycle of several centuries is driven from somewhere in the galactic center.

- The earth's surface and the ionosphere form an electrodynamic resonating cavity that produces micropulsations in the magnetic field at extremely low frequencies, from about twenty-five per second down to one every ten seconds. Most of the micropulsation energy is concentrated at about ten hertz (cycles per second).

- Solar flares spew charged particles into the earth's field, causing magnetic storms. The particles join those already in the outer reaches of the field (the Van Allen belts), which protect us by absorbing these and other high-energy rays.

- Every flash of lightning releases a burst of radio energy at kilocycle frequencies, which travels parallel to the magnetic field's lines of force and bounces back and forth between the north and south poles many times before fading out.

- The surface and ionosphere act as the charged plates of a condenser (a charge storage device), producing an electrostatic field of hundreds of thousands of volts per foot. This electric field continually ionizes many of the molecules of the air's gases, and it, too, pulses in the ELF (extremely low frequency) range.

- There are also large direct currents continually flowing within the ionosphere and as telluric (within-the-earth) currents, generating their own subsidiary electromagnetic fields.

- In the 1970s we learned that the sun's magnetic field is divided from pole to pole into sectors, like the sections of an orange, and the field in each sector is oriented in the direction opposite to adjacent sectors. About every eight days the sun's rotation brings a new region of the interplanetary (solar) magnetic field opposite us, and the earth's field is slightly changed in response to the flip-flop in polarity. The sector boundary's passage also induces a day or two of turbulence.

"The potential interactions among all these electromagnetic phenomena and life are almost infinitely complex."

That there are such interactions is proved by the many animal and human experiments the authors cite. One of the most convincing involved hundreds of volunteers who spent several months in bunkers that isolated them from all clues of time. One group wasn't shielded from electromagnetic fields; the other was. "Persons in both rooms soon developed irregular rhythms," Dr. Becker reports, "but those in the completely shielded room had significantly longer ones. Those still exposed to the earth's field kept to a rhythm close to twenty-four hours. In some of these people, a few variables wandered from the circadian rate, but they always stabilized at some new rate in harmony with the basic one—two days instead of one, for example. People kept from contact with the earth's field, on the other hand, became thoroughly desynchronized." When a very weak electric field (0.025 volts per centimeter) pulsing at ten hertz was reintroduced into the shielded bunker, a normal cycle returned to most of the subjects' biological rhythms.

Research that is scientific by any definition continues to reveal the cyclical nature of the universe and make its exact functioning an ever more important subject for study. Recognizing this, the Dewey family set aside a sizable fund in 1989 to create the Edward R. Dewey Institute for Cycle Research, a nonprofit Pennsylvania corporation that will operate independently of the Foundation. With an international scientific advisory board, the Institute's main function will be to award grants and prizes to stimulate work on cycles within the academic world—to encourage new research as well as to recognize research that is already being done. It will be interdisciplinary as well as international, and Dewey's son hopes that it will at last close the gap between the study of cycles and the study of "science." For Dewey himself, according to his son, "the intellectual ballgame was over, and he didn't worry about when other people would catch up with him." Certainly Dewey would be most gratified to find a memorial designed to help others along the path he pioneered.

10

THE WORLD ACCORDING TO WHEELER

FEW THINKERS HAVE the mental energy and courage to tackle the whole of human history in search of an organizing principle. But there is something in the air of cycleland that attracts more than its share of these few. Among them the most intriguing figure is that of Raymond H. Wheeler. Part of that intrigue derives from the fact that Wheeler, who died at sixty-nine in 1961, found himself outside the normal parameters of the academic and publishing establishments. As a result, much of his work remains unknown to the intellectual mainstream. It's probable that the question, "Who is Raymond Wheeler?" would be greeted with blank expressions and total silence in any gathering of erudite citizens beyond the boundaries of cycleland.

So massive and absorbing were the studies to which Wheeler dedicated himself that he never had time to complete them or to turn them into a final, comprehensive published work. Although he held positions of distinction, he was not the sort of scholarly or popular celebrity that appeals to biographers. Leading a quiet thinker's life, he nevertheless yearned to have word of his discoveries spread. Diane Epperson, managing editor of Cycles magazine, who looked into Wheeler's life for a profile early last spring says, "Wheeler died in the process of getting his data together, and supposedly he asked his wife to burn his material because he wasn't recognized."

Fortunately, Wheeler's papers weren't burned. They went instead to a former student, S. Howard Bartley, who had become Distinguished Research Professor in Psychology at the University of Memphis, Tennessee. Eventually Bartley passed them along to a friend, Michael Zahorchak, an executive director of the Foundation for the Study of Cycles, who turned one set of Wheeler notebooks into a volume entitled *Climate: The Key to Understanding Business Cycles.* When Zahorchak died in 1987, the rich lode of the Wheeler research and thought went to the Foundation's headquarters in Irvine, California, where it is likely to be mined for years to come. In an introduction to the Zahorchak book, Bartley provided this revealing glimpse into Wheeler, the man:

"I knew Dr. Wheeler, for he was one of my university teachers and mentor for my advanced degrees. He was so devoted to this long study, and particularly to the basic philosophy of scientific reasoning, that he seemed too serious at the time. But the value of his insights and his endeavors are not surpassed by anyone my education has made me aware of."

The route by which Raymond Holder Wheeler arrived at being a "too serious" man began in Berlin, Massachusetts, in 1892. Attracted by the study of psychology, he attended Clark College in Worcester and earned a doctorate from Clark University where he studied under John Wallace Baird, an early leader in the field. In 1915, he became a faculty member of the University of Oregon, but his academic career was soon interrupted by World War I. He left Oregon to act as chief of psychological services at Camp Bowie, Texas, and he served on a special committee established by the Surgeon General to study intelligence testing. Back at Oregon, Wheeler became director of the psychology laboratory. In 1924, he went to the University of Kansas as chairman of the psychology department, a post he held for twenty-two years. Wheeler moved on from Kansas to Erskine College in South Carolina and then to Babson Institute of Business Administration in Wellesley, Massachusetts, thus completing a personal geographical cycle. While he was at Babson, he also spent summers as chief of staff for climatic research at the Weather Science Foundation in Crystal Lake, Illinois, and published for two years the Journal of Human Ecology to provide an outlet for his unorthodox views.

Until 1938 when fascination with the big picture of human affairs seems to have overtaken him, Wheeler followed a fairly conventional academic path. One of the rules of getting anywhere along that road, then as now, is "publish or perish," and the publishing is generally expected to reflect growing expertise in the scholar's discipline. Wheeler's rise through the ranks was notably accompanied by nearly thirty published papers on various aspects of psychology. "Wheeler was a proponent of the Gestalt school," Ms. Epperson told me. "He was trying to figure out why people were resisting new therapy based on Gestalt theory, and on his own he looked back through history to see that every so many years people tended to go with this theory or that one. From that he came up with the idea of cycles in human behavior, and it mushroomed out."

But it may have been more than that. The Gestalt school takes its name from a German word that can variously be translated as shape, pattern or structure. It maintains that the whole is greater than—or different from—the sum of its parts. The genesis of Gestalt thinking was work on sensory perception by Austrian psychologist Christian von Ehrenfels in the late nineteenth century and it was being expanded during Wheeler's time by the German scholars W. Kökle and M. Wertheimer. An example of the Gestalt view of reality with respect to perception is that a major or minor mode in a musical melody is a characteristic of the melody itself and not of its individual notes. Again and again this kind of holistic thinking emerges in the study of cycles, and it's to be presumed that it provided the foundation of Wheeler's desire and ability to find the grand patterns in history.

Wheeler's own description of his mental odyssey, set forth in a speech at the Kansas Academy of Science, coincides with that given by Ms. Epperson: "It began over ten years ago, not as a problem in human ecology but as a study of fluctuations in human thought and attitude stumbled upon by accident and confined at first to fluctuations in points of view in the histories of psychology, biology, and philosophy. It seemed hardly explainable that these three subjects fluctuated by chance together from one point of view to its opposite and back again down through history. The problem became even more fascinating when upon an examination of the other sciences it was found that they were varying in the same manner. This coincidence suggested looking still further into the history of human achievement, into art, literature, music, and even into political history. The same pattern was repeated in so many ways, in so many countries and cultures, in so amazingly a precise and objective manner, that the results seemed almost uncanny. Forthwith a rough curve was drawn of these see-saw movements, actions and reactions, characteristic of entire culture patterns, north and south, east and west, covering every known country in the world upon which historical information could be obtained."

As uncanny as the emergence of that curve which Wheeler called a cultural cycle was the incident that next enlarged his view. A colleague at the University of Kansas, H. H. Lane, who headed the zoology department, looked at Wheeler's curve and remarked casually that it resembled a curve that he had seen of California sequoia tree growth. The latter curve was developed by a Dr. Andrew E. Douglass who used measurements of the rings in 3,300-year-old trees to chart climatic fluctuations over the millennia. Trees grown slowly during dry periods and rapidly during wet ones. When Wheeler saw the tree ring curves, he recognized at once that "the peaks and valleys in the culture curve corresponded with the fifty-year smoothed tree-growth curve in a fashion that chance could not possibly explain." Although it seemed obvious that the cycles in human behavior were mirror images of the cycles in nature, Wheeler, as a disciplined scholar, knew that he had simply come upon a proposition in need of proof. He would spend the rest of his life accumulating that proof.

The logistics of the Wheeler effort are nearly as impressive as the results. As an original thinker, Wheeler had no model to follow in accumulating the data necessary to arrive at objective, "scientific" conclusions. There was no possibility of examining or measuring his vast subject in the narrow confines of a laboratory (although he did once conduct a controlled experiment on rats to measure the effects of temperature), nor would it be possible for one person to do the job. To get the project under way Wheeler himself read some 250 volumes of history and, with the help of faculty colleagues, undertook a self-instructed course in climatology, meteorology, geography. With an overall view of what he needed, he assembled a staff of typists, file clerks, draftsmen, statisticians, and graduate students in various disciplines to collect his data. Over the years, he had two hundred assistants, working in groups of about forty at a time. It being the Depression era, he was assisted with funds from the National Youth Administration as well as the university.

The task to which Wheeler set himself and his helpers was filling the blank pages of a ledger book made to his order by the World Company of Lawrence, Kansas. Each of the book's two thousand pages measures eighteen by forty-five inches, and the opened book spans seven and a half feet. The pages are ruled into forty-six vertical columns with headings such as *History, Mathematics, Medicine/Pharmacy, Music, Inventions, Religion/Church,* under which are recorded events and developments during the time period designated in the far left column. Thus, it is possible by just glancing from left to right across the horizontal stretch of the book to see what the human race was doing at any given period. The entries are handwritten in the many individual scripts of the assistants and color-coded red for "warm" or green for "cold" as designated by Wheeler who determined these to be the major weather cycles of earth. Over a time period that begins with the geological history of earth and continues until 1936, there are 700,000 items recorded. Because the availability of data increased, the time period on each two page spread narrows. The years between 600 B.C. and A.D. 900 are covered in twenty-year bites, for instance, while the years between 1800 and 1936 are one-year segments.

Wheeler's ledger can be viewed as a laboriously hand-crafted computer. In it a mind-boggling amount of raw data is stored and reorganized into usable form. The Wheeler researchers went through five thousand literary selections and ten thousands titles in science. They examined more than fifty thousand samples of painting, sculpture, architecture, costumes and other works of art from all the world cultures. Their historical studies encompassed approximately eighteen thousand battles in civil and international conflicts. Possibly because the money ran out, the ledger ends in 1936, but 1936 represents only the beginning of Wheeler's long struggle to use his "computer" to reshape world history into new patterns that would be logical, predictable and challenging to some of the most cherished concepts about human life and destiny.

In this overview of cycleland, I can present only a summary—with all the risks attendant upon oversimplification—of the Wheeler findings scattered through unpublished manuscripts, articles, notes and speeches. Whether everything Wheeler believed will prove out in the final analysis is less important than the scope his work gives to cycles as a system of thought. Compared with cycles in most areas under scrutiny, his cycles were long—five-hundred and one thousand-year historical epochs; twenty-five-year and one hundred-year climatic fluctuations. The effect of the cycles he saw is to govern the way people, both as individuals and in the mass, feel, think and act. He argues persuasively that certain kinds of human attitudes and activities in every facet of life from artistic creativity to war correlate with certain climatic conditions over and over again across the millennia.

Essential to accepting Wheeler's view is an acknowledgement of the various effects that climate can have on human beings. In his writings, he offers all sorts of proof for this thesis, from historical anecdote and statistical analysis to biological and psychological laboratory experiments. The major mood-and-mind-affecting element in climate is temperature. Wheeler's research yielded convincing maps, graphs, charts and statistics to show that what he calls "dynamic civilization," as defined by the location of the world's major cities and the density of human population, is to be found in belts around both hemispheres with a yearly range of average temperature from forty-seven to fifty-two degrees fahrenheit and an average daily temperature range of ten to thirty degrees. Areas in these temperature ranges also enjoy a type of rainfall favorable to human activity that Wheeler calls "the cyclonic storm," which brings with it wind, moderate to strong changes in temperature and moderate to strong changes in barometric pressure. Generally cooler climates with frequent fluctuations in rainfall and temperature have demonstrably brought out the best in people, according to Wheeler who summons to his side other witnesses of this phenomenon down through history, beginning with a number of Chinese sages and the great Greek physician Hippocrates.

The reason for this state of affairs is that a temperate climate imparts more energy and vitality to the individual human being than either tropical heat or arctic cold. As only one of many proofs, Wheeler cites facts that go against the grain of the popular myth that tropical peoples are more sexually active and fertile than those in the temperate zones. "This is a fallacy due, first, to a misunderstanding of the marriage customs and sexual behavior of tropical peoples, and second, to the fact that tropical people look much younger than they are," he writes. "Actually, fertility develops later in life in the tropics than in the temperate zones, and many marriages are consummated long before childbearing can begin. The average Philippine girl, for example, begins to menstruate a year and a half later than the average girl in Minnesota, and she will not bear children until she is about twenty-one years of age." These observations are supported by animal experiments, including Wheeler's own with white rats in which he learned that litters born in a room kept at ninety degrees matured ten to fourteen days later than those born in a room at fifty-five degrees.

While I was studying Wheeler's works, I had a curious and convincing demonstration of the palpable biological effect of heat on human energy. In a usually temperate part of the country, we were into the second day of heat in excess of ninety-five degrees. Not unnaturally, my wife, Dorrie, complained that she didn't feel like doing anything and added, "It's the strangest thing, but I have the sensation that my heart is beating too slowly. I just know it, and it's scary."

It *was* scary. I didn't have the same sensation but then I wasn't trying to do anything more strenuous than move my eyes across a page. But minutes after Dorrie told me how she felt, I came across this passage in Wheeler's *Climate: The Key to Understanding Cycles* that I rushed out to read aloud to her: "It is one of the provisions of a 'wise' nature that, when temperatures external to the body are high, combustion processes within the body slow down. The heart beats more slowly (heat is generated with each heart beat), breathing becomes more shallow, and one's appetite lessens, causing a reduction in digestive work for the body."

Operating on the premise that climate is destiny, Wheeler used tree rings and human accounts of climate at corresponding times to establish four major conditions that could be correlated with human activity: warm-wet, warm-dry, cold-wet and cold-dry. "These combinations were found to follow one another more or less regularly in the order named and to repeat themselves in cycles of varying lengths," he said. "Tree growth, in general, registers these four sequences in a synthetic manner, putting in a maximum during the warm-wet climatic phase, a minimum during the subsequent hot drought (usually of lesser duration), a second recovery during the next revival of rainfall while it is turning cold, and another, usually a longer and lower minimum during the cold-dry phase in which both variables, temperature and rainfall, operate against rapid growth."

With the cycles of climate worked out, Wheeler was able to go into his ledger cum computer and come up with significant relationships between weather and human behavior. During warm times, state control prevailed in politics, classical themes in the arts, aristocracy in society, dogmatism in religion. During cold times, individual freedom dominated the political scene, romanticism was favored in the arts, the proletariat was exulted in society, and

Warm-Cold Culture Patterns

Wheeler identified hundreds of characteristics that he distinguished as either predominantly "warm" or "cold." This abridged list gives some of the major attributes he defined in each category.

WARM	COLD

Politics/Government

WARM	COLD
STATE CONTROL	INDIVIDUAL FREEDOM
Dictatorship	Democracy
Autocratic	Constitutional
Centralized	Decentralized
International	National
Socialism; communism	Individualism
Conservative	Liberal
Benevolent rulers	Reformers
International wars	Civil wars; social reform

Economics

WARM	COLD
COOPERATION	COMPETITION
Public works	Private interest
Urban development	Suburban development
Manufacturing	Agriculture
Monopoly	Small business
Rising prices	Falling prices
Federal regulation	Free Enterprise

Society

WARM	COLD
ARISTOCRACY	PROLETARIAT
Austerity	Indulgence
Refined tastes	Vulgar attitudes
Moral decadence	Wholesomeness
Sexual excess; promiscuity	Modesty
State institutions	Secular schools
Team sports	Individual sports
Simple, dignified dress	Frivolous, garrish costume
Introversion	Extroversion
Creative insight	Blind instinct
Learn by discovery	Learn by repetition
Derived	Innate
Lethargic	Energetic; alert
Declining health	Improving health

Philosophy/Religion

WARM	COLD
UNIFIED WHOLE	RANDOM PARTS
Subjective	Objective
Rational	Empirical
Deductive reasoning;	Inductive reasoning
Profound ideas	Superficial; mundane
Pessimism	Optimism
Transcendentalism	Materialism
Abstract theology	Personal faith
State religion	Evangelism; reform movements
Monotheism	Polytheism
Mysticism	Naturalism

	WARM	COLD

Art/Architecture

WARM	COLD
CLASSICAL	ROMANTIC
Creative	Imitative
Sophisticated	Primitive
Symbolic; stylized; abstract	Pictorial; concrete
Fantasy; surrealism	Realism
Impressionism	Expressionism
Gods, human subjects	Humble subjects; nature
Subdued colors	Garrish colors; polychromes
Streamlined	Ornate; rococo
Functional	Decorative

Music

WARM	COLD
CLASSICAL	ROMANTIC
Formal	Informal
Harmonious	Chaotic
Total composition	Individual notes
Complex harmony	Simple melody
Masses; symphonies	Hymns (to sing)
Grand opera	Comic opera
Big bands; orchestras	Soloists; small groups

Literature

WARM	COLD
INTELLECTUAL	EMOTIONAL
Philosophical	Sentimental
Fate	Chance
Tragedy	Comedy
Historical	Contemporary
Free verse	Lyric poetry
Dramatic	Poetic
Profound themes	Simple, everyday themes

The Sciences

WARM	COLD
THEORY	FACT
Relative; generalizations	Absolute; specifics
Equilibrium	Chaos
Field theory	Particles theory
Functional; dynamic	Structural; mechanical
Organic	Atomic
Epigenesis	Preformation
Gradient theory	Cell theory
Physiology	Morphology; taxonomy
Psychiatry	Pathology
Geometry	Algebra; statistics
Universal laws	Applied science; inventions

159

personal faith had a religious revival. A table that accompanied Diane Epperson's Cycles article shows the Wheeler
analysis in more detail:

One of Wheeler's most important findings is that human
social organization swings back and forth between au-
thoritarian and democratic ideas and actions in accordance
with the recurring climatic conditions. He illustrates this
point with many concrete examples through all the years
from 600 B.C. to the time of his writing. Two passages from
Climate: The Key to Understanding Business Cycles are typical of
the kind of argument he makes. The first is in support of
his observation that hot drought phases of climate promote
a tendency toward social control over the individual, including absolute dictatorship, and it would be hard for
anyone with memories of the "dust bowl" years and World
War II not to be intrigued by this view:

"In 1816, England during a hot drought repealed the
Habeas Corpus Act. In Germany liberal ideas were suppressed. In Poland the liberty of the press was completely
nullified. Massacres were committed on both sides by the
Egyptians and Sudanese. In 1821, the Turks massacred
Greeks at Smyrna. This was also a period of commercial
depression throughout the world.

"The most recent hot drought era occurred in the 1930s,
when an epidemic of dictatorships broke out all over the
world. Of the more than twenty republics organized after
World War I, only Czechoslovakia survived. Fanaticism,
persecution of minorities, and decadent nationalistic movements along with swings toward socialism and communism
became the order of the day. The birth rate declined, health
suffered, and economic systems all but collapsed during
one of the most severe economic collapses in history."

Cooler periods present a brighter picture. Wheeler identified the most favorable conditions as those during a transition from cold to early warm. They produced what he

called the "Golden Ages" of history. One fascinating bit of Wheeler data in this regard: of fifty-three rulers entitled "The Great" by a consensus of authoritative historical sources, 91.7 percent reigned during one of these climatic periods. But the following passage from his book gives a more general picture of the contrast in social organization during cold periods with that in warm ones:

"In the cold 1640s, the first written constitution of modern times was drawn up during the war between Parliament and the Crown at the time of Cromwell. Later, during a short cold period in the 1680s, the British Bill of Rights was signed. At about the same time in the colonies, the Quakers of Pennsylvania voluntarily emancipated their Negro slaves.

"During the cold decades of the eighteenth century, labor troubles developed almost everywhere. In one of the first strikes in history, bakers and journeymen left their work in protest for higher wages in New York. They were arrested, tried and convicted, but there is no record that they were sentenced. Slave riots developed at this same time in New York and New Jersey. The American Revolution was paralleled throughout the world. In France the third estate usurped power in the National Assembly on behalf of the common people. Egypt declared herself independent of the Turks, while Austria abolished serfdom."

In Wheeler's understanding of cycles, there are cycles within cycles, all in harmonic relationship with each other. His longest cycle is one thousand years, and we are now just beyond the middle of the third of these cycles for which he accumulated data. The next harmonic is the five hundred-year cycle. Both of these cycles are not only cycles in long range weather trends but in human affairs since at their turning points there is always, according to Wheeler, "the decline and fall of civilizations the world over and the birth of a new era." Each turning point occurred during an exceptionally cold period. As of this writing, earth is again

161

in transition to a cold period, and another turning in Wheeler's five hundred-year cycle is due about the year 2000.

Since cold produces creativity and individualism among human beings, Wheeler cheerfully predicts a new Renaissance and "a finer and greater democracy than the world has yet known." But he also calls for a shift in the balance of power and influence from Western to Eastern civilization. This cycle in the Wheeler analysis is as regular as a sine wave with every other five hundred-year period in history dominated by West or East. "The next five hundred years will belong to Asia," Wheeler stated flatly in 1951. It's a prophecy that might make all kinds of sense to anyone working in a Nissan plant in Tennessee or living in a Connecticut suburb where the priciest homes are selling to Japanese or pondering Japan's offers to bail third world countries out of debt. In addition, both the emergence of China as a potential economic power and the internal struggles for more democracy fit well into the Wheeler scheme of things.

Although Wheeler exhibits a wider vision and greater daring in prediction than most of the others, he does not stand alone in his conviction that human history is controlled by the natural cycles of the universe. One of the others was a Wheeler contemporary, Ellsworth Huntington, a Yale University geographer. Huntington was better known than Wheeler since he published prolifically. His books were used as geography texts in American schools, and his masterwork, *Mainsprings of Civilization,* is still considered a classic of bold, interdisciplinary thought. In that book, Huntington wrote grandly that "the whole history of life is a record of cycles."

Not surprisingly, Huntington was friend and collaborator to both Edward R. Dewey, founder of the Foundation for the Study of Cycles, and Raymond Wheeler. Huntington once devoted three weeks to fine-combing a one thousand-

In his book, Huntington told the story of a specific cycle's effect in much more recent history to demonstrate how climate can determine human destiny. This cycle was first noted by Sir Francis Bacon who wrote in the seventeenth century: "They say it is observed in the Low Countries (I know not what part), that in every five and thirty years the same kind and suit of years and weathers come about again; as great frosts, great wet, great drought, warm winters, summers with little heat, and the like, and they call it prime; it is a thing I do rather mention, because, computing backwards, I have found some concurrence." The cycle finally got a name—Brückner—in the late nineteenth century when a German analyst of data made up of such facts as the dates of wheat harvest and wine making, the freezing of rivers and the rise and fall of lakes came up with a cycle of European weather averaging thirty-five years. The swing was from an oceanic climate with wet, cool summers and mild, moist winters, to a continental climate of dry, sunny, warm summers and cold, clear winters. It was, according to Huntington, oceanic phases of this Brückner cycle that caused two of history's greatest migrations—the flights of millions of Irish to America in 1846–48 and again in 1881– page Wheeler manuscript that was never published, but which earned from Huntington this encouraging judgment: "I believe you have hold of one of the great contributions of human knowledge." In turn, Wheeler was one of the few people whom Huntington sought out when he wanted criticism of his own manuscript. Huntington recognized the truths in Wheeler's arguments as a result of difficult and sometimes dangerous personal experience. An explorer who trekked the wastes of Central Asia, he came upon evidences of towns and agricultural lands that had been overwhelmed by advancing desert and concluded that the great invasions of western Europe by the Mongol hordes were primarily caused by a cycle in climate that made their homelands unlivable.

91 when the failure of potato crops caused widespread starvation.

One natural cycle that both Wheeler and Huntington consider to be very influential in human affairs is the eleven-year sunspot cycle. This is because the amount of heat or energy the sun delivers to earth varies with the number and size of sunspots. Sunspots, which are storms in the sun's gaseous atmosphere, reach what is known as a maxima on the average of once every eleven years. Occasionally, they are more severe than normal, last as long as two years, and become visible to the human eye on earth. Wheeler claimed that evidence of a correlation between sunspot maxima and the onset of cold climatic phases goes back to A.D. 51 when sunspots and the aurora often associated with them were seen just a year after reports of extreme cold in Britain.

Very recently another cycle scholar has confirmed and surpassed Wheeler's work in identifying solar activity as one of the keys to history. But Dr. Theodor Landscheidt, director of the Schroeter Institute for Research in Cycles of Solar Activity, argues that, although sunspots have received great attention because they are so spectacular and well documented, "flares are the most powerful and explosive of all forms of solar eruption and the most important in terrestrial effect." Because flares couldn't be observed systematically until the invention of the spectrohelioscope in 1926, not enough data has been collected to establish a cycle. But then, as Dr. Landscheidt points out, it took two hundred years to discover the eleven-year sunspot cycle.

Dr. Landscheidt has, nevertheless, been able to compare solar eruptions, regardless of flares, with human activity and come up with some conclusions strikingly like those of Wheeler. Claiming that the energy from these solar eruptions which, in turn, are related to planetary cycles, stimulates creativity in human beings, Dr. Landscheidt finds what he calls "borderline phenomena" when an old cycle meshes with a new one. This is a state of instability and change that is characterized by both revolution and renaissance in the affairs of men.

"When the sun is very active, as it is now, people are very active," Dr. Landscheidt told me. "You can see it now in China and Eastern Europe. When the sun is in the eleven-year maximum—and it is there now [1989] or near it and will be next year, you get revolutions. Those revolutions that were successful were made when the sun was in the maximum. That was true in 1789 with the French Revolution and in 1948 when Mao was successful in China. If you didn't observe the sun and looked only at revolutions, you could predict that there must be an eleven-year maximum in solar activity. The next maximum is coming up, and if you are a revolutionary, I could advise you to prepare your revolution for 2002 and be successful in 2004 or 2005."

Especially since Dr. Landscheidt also foresees a period of creativity in which there will be new inventions and new ideas as people come out of a cycle of inertia in 2002, his vision comes quite close to that of Dr. Wheeler about what will take place during the turning point of a five hundred-year climatic cycle. Although Dr. Landscheidt's impressive background has been described elsewhere in this book, it is important to recall it here. Like Wheeler and Huntington before him, he is a serious and disciplined man who is not afraid to make the great leap of looking at creation as a living and interactive whole rather than the sum of isolated and independent parts. I submit that respect must be paid to men like this. When they reach such similar conclusions coming from such dissimilar scholarly disciplines and personal experiences, the odds in favor of their closing in on the truth are highly enhanced. At the very least, it is fascinating to contemplate the world according to Wheeler & Co. because it becomes a world in which the shape of events to come is discernable on the mind's horizon.

11

CYCLES, CYCLES EVERYWHERE

WHEN SHAKESPEARE HAD Hamlet cry out in exasperation, "There are more things in heaven and earth, Horatio, than are dreamt of in your philosophy," he might have been speaking for cycle researchers. Despite fifty years of effort, the undermanned, underfunded Foundation for the Study of Cycles hasn't been able to track down many of the intriguing clues as to cycles at work in human belief and behavior that crop up in its files. The data is less readily available and more difficult to translate into mathematical formulae for analysis than that to be found in such areas as bodily functions or celestial orbits. Nevertheless, Foundation members have followed leads far and have enough respect for cyclical thinkers in other fields to subscribe to the Shakespearean view. As Dr. Jeffrey Horovitz, the director of the Foundation when I visited it, put it to me, "We are just kicking the top of icebergs."

One of those icebergs could be the cycle of sin. Although Edward R. Dewey, the Foundation's founder, took a serious view of cycle study as a science, he liked to leaven the subject with humor whenever possible. Presumably he had this intent in passing along the gist of a conversation he had once with Dr. Alvin Johnson, then head of the New School for Social Research in New York. Serving on a New York City commission on the spread of venereal disease, Dr. Johnson took a look at a system of segregating prostitutes in Berlin that had apparently made significant inroads on the disease in that city. Then he made a comparative study of the problem in other European cities and came up with a nine-year cycle in venereal disease in each place. The Berlin experiment coincided with the down swing of the cycle elsewhere, and the decline in cases during the same period was as great in the cities where nothing had been done as in Berlin. New York was spared what was deemed to be a fruitless effort, but Dewey was given another "hint" of a cycle for future investigation.

When it comes to seeking salvation, however, the evidence of cyclical involvement is more impressive. Dewey first began to suspect something of the sort in 1950 when a Harold Martin, pastor of the First Congregational Church in Norwalk, Connecticut, came to see him with an interesting compilation of figures and set of charts. In studying the record over a century of new membership enrollment in his own denomination and in the Methodist, Episcopal and Presbyterian churches for comparison, pastor Martin had made some unsettling discoveries. Contrary to his belief that new members were drawn to a church by local factors such as a fine facility, a friendly congregation or fiery preaching, he found the figures to be the same for the same dates for Congregational churches all over the country. In addition, they were the same for all of the denominations he studied, and there was no newsworthy national or international catastrophe, charismatic leader or wave of evangelism to account for the peaks. But there was a cycle of approximately nine-years. Dewey confirmed the existence of Pastor Martin's cycle by statistical analysis and began keeping an eye out for other data. He saw what he had anticipated in a 1967 Gallup poll that reported an increase in church attendance to 45 percent of the adult population, the highest peak since a 49-percent attendance was recorded in the year 1958.

With his eyes opened to a new area for cycle research, it's not surprising that Dewey opened the pages of his magazine Cycles to a historical analysis by Arthus Louis Joquel II on the cycle of the world's great religions. Joquel spotted a 625-year cycle in the rise of important religious movements beginning at approximately 1275 B.C. He describes six cyclic peaks, each with a secondary harmonic peak half-way between:

— 1275 B.C.: an averaged date for the times of Akhnaton, the Egyptian pharaoh whose futile efforts to establish monotheism led him to be called "the first man who truly saw God," and of Moses who led the children of Israel out of Egypt. The secondary peak around 937 B.C. was characterized by the coming of Elijah, the first of the great line of Hebrew prophets.

— 625 B.C.: on or about this date there was Zoroaster in Iran, famed as the founder of the wisdom of the Magi; Lao-tzu, the father of Taoism, and Confucius, the sage, in China; Gautama Buddha in India. Very close to the harmonic about 312 B.C., Meng-tzu was restating Confucianism in China and King Asoka, a convert, was spreading Buddhism in India.

— 4 B.C. or A.D. 6: depending upon a reading of Matthew or Luke in the gospels one of these dates saw the birth of Jesus of Nazareth. By the harmonic in the fourth century, the Ante-Nicene Fathers and Saint Augustine were refining the doctrines of the religion founded in his name, Christianity.

— A.D. 625: the work of Muhammad, prophet of Islam and author of the Koran, who died in 632. Although not precise as

169

to the harmonic of 938, "the most glorious epoch in the history of the caliphate" is the way the ninth century reigns of Muhammad's earthly successors Harun ar-Rashid and Mamun the Great have been described.

— A.D. 1250: the lives and writings of the Christian saints, Thomas Aquinas and Francis of Assisi, add inspiration to the faith; Quetzalcoatl appears in Central America. Around the secondary peak of 1562 are clustered the Christian reformers like Martin Luther and John Calvin who brought Protestantism into being.

— A.D. 1875: the rise of Christian Science, Mormonism, the Oxford Movement. The harmonic to this cycle peak will not arrive until A.D. 2187.

Dewey offered the Joquel thesis as tempting food for thought rather than the solid sustenance of science. Tossed out by Dewey as mere morsels for mental gestation were studies that hinted at the presence of cycles in the quality as well as the quantity of human concern for righteousness. One was what he called a curve of conscience derived from an analysis of voluntary tax payments by British citizens, which are carried on the Chancellor of Exchequer's ledger as "conscience money, remitted by sundry persons for conscience' sake." Transcribed to a graph covering the period from 1923 to 1954, the figures produced a cycle with peaks at three and one-half year intervals. An even more tantalizing tidbit was served up to Dewey by Carle Brawner, a member of the Orange Grove Friends Meeting in Pasadena, California. It was the kind of Quaker meeting where there was no planned service; members just rose and spoke when they were "moved by the spirit." For more than three years, Brawner kept a record of the number of people who rose to speak each Sunday. When he charted the data, there was a rhythmic wave that peaked every April, September, December. Bemused by the look of this line, Dewey compared it to one created by Ellsworth Huntington to show the seasonal cycles of intellectual activity as expressed through non-fiction withdrawals from the Honolulu Public Library and found remarkable similarities.

Whatever the extent of cyclical religious fervor might be, there is no question in the mind of one cycle analyst that the Bible itself is loaded with references to cycles. He is E. T. Garrett, a retired U.S. Air Force colonel and former professor at the Air Force Academy in Colorado. As a hobby, Garrett and some engineering associates used a computer program developed to analyze the Consumer Price Index to have a look at numbers in the Bible—especially those in the Book of Numbers. It turned out that the numbers given as a head count of the tribes of Israel were a code for cycles. "Take the tribe of Judah—74,600," Garrett says. "A number that big is a day rather than a cycle count—number of days. But when you run it through the program, it says that 74,600 mean solar days is equal to thirty-two orbital periods of Venus, and the accuracy is one part in ten million. Basically, there are twelve numbers given for the twelve tribes of Israel, and every one of those can be traced back to a cycle that was important to ancient astrologers."

Analysis of other numbers in the Bible also reveals a code. The intent, according to Garrett, was to disguise the knowledge that the scribes used for prophecy. "A really classic example is Chapter V of Genesis," he told me. "That's where we have all these patriarchs living to these ridiculous ages. All of those are the same sorts of numbers. You take the numbers out of genesis V and run them through the program, and you find them looking at cycles. In there is the ratio of the lunar year to the solar year; in there also is the ratio of the sidereal day to the solar day. All those guys were astronomers. If you read the Bible, anybody who was anybody ended up sojourning in Egypt to learn from the Egyptian priests. I think Joseph might have done that. One reason for secrecy was that they were forecasting things of political importance like famines, as Joseph did with his seven fat and seven lean years."

It would take a considerable degree of computer literacy to read the Bible as Garrett does. Judging from his testimony, the experience can result in a new respect for both the venerability and viability of cycles. "I would hazard a guess that there isn't a cycle that we know in modern times that wasn't known to the Hebrews and their predecessors. They implicitly believed as the result of many hundreds, if not thousands, of years of observation that life on earth is terribly affected by cycles," says Garrett, who, as a result of his studies comparing the Consumer Price Index with celestial activity, couldn't agree with them more. "The Consumer Price Index involves two hundred million people—everybody who makes purchasing decisions. When you see the timing of the actions of two hundred million people being driven by these planetary and lunar cycles, you begin to appreciate their power. I think the majority of biological cycles start with lunar cycles, and earthquakes tend to run with lunar cycles combined with planetary."

There are a number of perceived cycles on earth that haven't yet been analyzed by computers or linked to the heavens but that are nevertheless regarded as hints or hunches worthy of more exploration in cycle circles. Both Raymond Wheeler, the psychologist turned generalist, and Ellsworth Huntington saw cycles revolving in the arts down through history. Wheeler asked two experts to examine their artistic specialties in the light of his overall theory that the state of civilization corresponds to long climatic cycles turning from hot to cold, wet to dry. Cleta Olmstead Boughton, Ph.D., archaeologist and art historian associated with the universities of Rochester and Florida State, took on painting and architecture; Warren D. Allen, Ph.D., a musical historian associated with the universities of Stanford and Florida State, took on music. When Wheeler published the conclusions of Boughton and Allen in his Journal of Human Ecology in the early 1950s he noted, "Both [articles] will doubtless be received with the mixed feelings typical of reactions to pioneer endeavor." Feelings upon encountering this work today are still likely to be mixed since establishing the existence of cycles in art remains in a pioneering stage.

Dr. Boughton did identify climatic cycles in both architecture and painting. In general, she concluded that buildings designed in the warm periods of history or for warm climates emphasize exterior appearance because they don't have to comply with as many practical demands for shelter; buildings influenced by cold are more functional on the outside with ornamentation reserved for the interior. To give only one example of her supporting argument: "Obviously the early Gothic is of the warm-wet style. On the elaborated exterior soaring towers touch the skies. Buttresses fly into space; everywhere air and light dance through the form in complete disregard for functionalism. To Abbé Suger (c. 1081–1151) is attributed the beginning of the Gothic style. That the second half of the twelfth century was predominantly cold might explain why the new style did not quickly flower."

In painting, Dr. Boughton also found hot-cold, wet-dry styles. For illustration she chose fourteen paintings from different periods in nineteenth century French art and related them to the possible influence of climate on their creation. Especially interesting in the light of Wheeler's assertion that the classical style in art thrives in warm periods is her analysis of a painting by Jean Auguste Ingres: "After 1800 when Ingres began painting, the weather turned warm and dry. His *Valpinçon Bather* is concerned only with the luscious formal style of a closed composition in which the obvious space is filled with the spherical volume of one solid nude. She is the idealistic classical type so

173

without individuality that she is viewed impersonally from her expansive back, and to further obliterate her personality, her face is hidden. She resembles the fully ripened fruit of a calm summer time. Her skin, thin and smooth, appears enameled; her body is intensely golden, the sheets are pure white with full light, and the curtain is richly green like summer foliage."

To introduce a note of objectivity into the study, Wheeler asked hundreds of people to look at reproductions of the paintings Dr. Boughton used as examples and pick which they considered to be warm-phase paintings and which cold-phase paintings. There was a consistency of 80 to 90 percent in their judgment as compared with Dr. Boughton's, according to Wheeler. He discovered a similar agreement as to the music Dr. Allen chose to illustrate his thesis that there have been five 500-year cycles in that art dating from the time of Athenian drama in 576 B.C. Dr. Allen found that, like Wheeler's 500-year cycle of civilizations, the great musical periods were defined by cataclysmic changes in weather and culture. A small taste gives the flavor of the Allen argument:

"The great Greek playwrights lived through the glory of Athenian victory over the Persians only to see Athens turn from democracy to tyranny within one 100-year cycle. All their passionate plays were sung or chanted. As long as the warm period lasted, the plays were veritable operas, or at least great oratorios, with choruses, soloists, and dancers in common measures. As it turned colder, the Greeks could see the comic side of life, even with disaster threatening. Aristophanes was the father of comic opera; his verses are in the same lilting, dancing, popular meters that we find in Gilbert and Sullivan. Aristophanes in *The Knights*, Gilbert in *Iolanthe* and the *Pirates*, [Penzance] and Offenbach in *The Grand Duchess* all ridicule generals, even when the life of the nation is at stake. All did so during the same phases of a one

174

hundred-year cycle, even though 2,300 years apart. This, according to Wheeler, is due to the higher level of vitality in cold eras."

In one branch of the arts—fashion—periodic changes in style have usually been attributed to the whim of woman rather than to some natural phenomenon like cycles. True, Vermont Royster of the *Wall Street Journal* once claimed to have detected a relationship between hemlines and bust-lines and the Gross National Product. In the soaring 1960s, Royster noted, hemlines also rose; bustlines reached their lowest level during a peak in the prosperity of Crete. If there are cycles in economics, then it follows that there must be cycles in fashion. Neither the popular view nor Royster's playful conceit would be acceptable to a man who made a grimly serious study of the matter in the late 1930s—A. B. Young, author of *Recurring Cycles of Fashion*.

The "data" Young used for his study consisted of illustrations from fashion magazines back to 1760, the first ever issued in Britain and France. He then took long sheets of paper ruled into squares, each row of which represented a year. Drawings of skirts from the illustrations (he used only street dresses) were entered into the squares, one for each new style up to fifty a year. The same process was repeated for sleeves, collars, cuffs, belts. It was then possible, according to Young, to see at a glance the dominant style features for each year and to combine them into a composite costume. Photostats were made of these 178 composites covering the years of the study. Young then arranged the photostats in rows on six card tables set against a wall in his Ohio home. As he walked back and forth in front of the tables, he was able to see clearly those recurring cycles.

Although they phased in and out of each other in a gradual manner, there were three main cycles as shown by the shape, not the length, of the skirts—bustle or back-fullness, 1760–1795; body or tubular, 1796–1829; bell,

1830–1867; bustle again, 1868–1899; body again, 1900–1937. Young was unequivocal about his conclusions: "There has never been a truly new fashion. Everything that fashion does is a modification of something that has been done before. By tracing changes underway at any given time we can find remarkably reliable clues to what fashion is going to do next. A scientific analysis of the changes that have taken place in every year during almost two centuries shows that they follow cycles which almost resemble in regularity and reliability the recurring cycles of the tides and seasons."

Young did not, however, think that fashion cycles bore any relationship to business cycles. Whether they have continued in his pattern may depend upon the eye of the beholder. One cycle believer pointed out to me that the dirndls and other fullish skirts of the 1940s and 1950s could qualify as "bells" and that there was certainly a lot of "body" in the minis and tight jeans from the 1960s on. This same observer suggested that the cheeky display made unavoidable by the most recent style in bathing suits may signal a transition to an emphasis on the same part of the anatomy to which the bustle drew the eye.

The extent to which cycles control fashion may be of little importance, but the same can't be said about those aspects of human existence that can be covered by the broadest interpretation of the term "life cycle." Although it can't be seen or measured like the transit of a star or the beat of a pulse, and can't be reduced to statistics and mathematical models, the life cycle exists by consensus of the human experience. It is essentially the birth, growth and death of any living organism, man included. But it is also applied to the collective life of organisms from the cycles of wildlife abundance to those of the social systems and civilizations of human beings. Once again the spiral rather than the circle allows for a more accurate visualization of what is meant by life cycle in all of its contexts, because the spiral can picture change and direction rather than a simple return to the same starting point.

To apply the concept of cycles to the individual human life is to note the significance of a recurring rhythm and predictability in that life. Those who see cycles in human lives—and the list of such sages goes back 2,500 years—are in remarkable agreement as to what they are and when they occur. The Hebrew Talmud, the sayings of Confucius, the writings of the Greek poet Solon—all mention cycles that are still prevalent in today's thinking: from zero to fifteen to twenty, the formative years of childhood; from twenty to forty, the years of young adulthood when, according to Confucius, a person should "plant his feet firmly on the ground"; from forty to sixty, middle adulthood, when Solon claimed that "the tongue and the mind are now at their best"; from sixty on, a period which the Talmud viewed neutrally as the time for "becoming an elder," Solon viewed negatively as "the time to depart on the ebb-tide of death," and Confucius viewed positively as an age during which to enter a new relation to heaven.

Considering their relevance to every person's life, it seems surprising that these philosophical, poetical musings about the life cycle, in which the likes of Ecclesiastes and Shakespeare—remember Shakespeare's seven ages of man from the "mewling and puking" infant to the oldster "sans teeth, sans eyes, sans taste, sans everything"—joined, have been the subject of little in the way of systematic, scientific research until recently. First, there was some attention of this sort paid to the childhood years when psychiatry, then and now a relatively new branch of science, attributed the shape of personality largely to events during early nurture. Much of what was learned was useful and tended to confirm Pope's insightful line from "Epistle I" of his *Moral Essays,* "Just as the twig is bent the tree's inclined." In the

177

1970s, the focus began shifting finally to the last three quarters of life.

Although the subject was popularized by Gail Sheehy's lively, anecdotal, best-selling book *Passages: Predictable Crises of Adult Life,* it was Daniel J. Levinson, Yale University psychologist who conducted the basic scientific study that firmly established the existence and nature of adult life cycles. For his book *The Seasons of a Man's Life,* Levinson and his research associates followed the lives of forty men for ten years. Perhaps the most important of their discoveries was that, although the lives were quite varied in detail, all of the men went through similar crises at about the same time in their lives. As with biological rhythms, it was almost as if there were an exogenous or endogenous time device in place—a calendar instead of a clock.

The main turning points in the lives of Levinson's people coincided remarkably with those in the writings of the ancients, but the systematic research turned up some refinements. Although there was an average age for the beginning and end of each cycle, there was also a variation of about five years around that average. In addition, the transition between each stage could take as much as five years. "Though pre-adulthood ends at roughly age twenty-two, early adulthood begins several years earlier, usually at seventeen," Levinson writes. "The span from seventeen to twenty-two is thus a 'zone of overlap,' a period in which the old era is being completed and the new one is starting. This period is the Early Adult Transition. It bridges the two eras and is part of both. Likewise, the Mid-Life Transition extends from roughly forty to forty-five. It serves to terminate early adulthood and to initiate middle adulthood. There is a subsequent transition in the early sixties, we believe, and perhaps another at about eighty."

In Levinson's view the cycles are alternating periods of what he calls "structure building" that are relatively stable and last about seven years, and periods of "structure changing" that can last four or five years. In each period, the individual is presented with a task which is roughly the same task every other individual faces. During Early Adult Transition, for example, the job is to move from the dependence of childhood to the relative independence of adulthood. In the next seven or eight stable years, the common tasks are to establish a family and start a career. Then comes the Age Thirty Transition when the structure built in the stable years is reexamined and extended or sometimes torn down as indicated by the high divorce rates at this age. And so it goes. Since this book is about cycles *per se,* it would be inappropriate and a disservice to Levinson's ground-breaking work to try to delve further into the extensive psychological ramifications of his theory.

It is appropriate, however, to pass along Levinson's hypothesis about the life cycle based on his study. Like any good scientist, he issues a caveat to the effect that none of his insights and generalizations are given as "fully demonstrated truths." Experience has taught him, he claims, to be cautious about calling any features of human life, such as the eras and periods he outlines in the life cycle, universal or enduring. The caveats acknowledged, Levinson's statement is one of the strongest I have come across in my own research:

"This sequence of eras and periods exists is all societies, throughout the human species, at the present stage in human evolution. The eras and periods are grounded in the nature of man as a biological, psychological and social organism, and in the nature of society as a complex enterprise extending over many generations. They represent the life cycle of the species. Individuals go through the periods in infinitely varied ways, but the periods themselves are universal. These eras and periods have governed human development for the past five or ten thousand years—since the beginning of more complex, stable societies.

"In posting a *combined* biological, psychological and social

179

basis for this developmental sequence, we are saying that none of these bases is sufficient in itself. No evidence now exists that the eras and periods stem simply from an unfolding of a biological, genetic program in the individual. Nor do they follow directly from a timetable established universally by social institutions or cultures. If this developmental sequence does hold to some degree for the species, its origins must be found in the interaction of all these influences as they operate during a particular phase in man's evolution."

Leaning strongly on the work of Levinson, a number of family therapists have begun to identify generational cycles at work in families. In a book titled *Family Life Cycles*, editors Elizabeth A. Carter of Family Institute of Westchester and Monica McGoldrick of Rutgers Medical School and Community Mental Health Center, collected papers from colleagues along these lines. In their editorial summary, Carter and McGoldrick defined three main cycles in self-explanatory terms: Unattached Young Adult, the period of the individual's coming to terms with his or her family origin; The Family With Young Children, the years of establishing a new family; and Launching Children and Moving On, the "empty nest" years that now constitute the longest cycle of all.

There are many others who subscribe to variations on the life cycle concept. One is Kelly R. Bennett, managing director of Veltona Versani International in Mosman, New South Wales, Australia. Bennett uses his own hypothesis of an eighty-four-year cycle/spiral, subdivided into twelve harmonics of seven years each, for psychological counseling. The time span is of special interest in the light of the kind of folk wisdom implied in sayings like "the seven-year itch." In any case, according to his article in Cycles, Bennett echoes Levinson in seeing a first cycle rebirth at twenty-eight, a second cycle rebirth at fifty-six, and a third cycle

rebirth at eight-four. Furthermore, the tasks Bennett as-
cribes to these cycles are virtually the same as those identified by Levinson.

Another advocate of the seven-year cycle, Alexander
Ruperti, author of *Cycles of Becoming,* offered some supporting evidence that, as in instances I've reported elsewhere,
brought the study of cycles very much alive for me. Ruperti
called the appearance of the first permanent teeth at about
the age of seven a sign of the first cyclical turning. I have a
grandson living in Austria who had such trouble sitting still
in school that we were all alarmed and began looking into
the causes and treatment of hyperactivity. With no real
conviction, my daughter passed along the opinion of an old
Austrian friend that we ought to be patient—according to
that country's folk lore, children change when they get their
second teeth. Sure enough, as soon as new teeth sprouted
to fill the gap in the front of his mouth, the boy's whole
attitude about school took a 180-degree turn. Not then
informed by cycle research, I checked with a psychologist
friend of mine who had a daughter the same age as my
grandson, and discovered that she, too, had undergone a
personality change that coincided with the emergence of a
new set of teeth.

The degree to which there's a connection between natural and psychological cycles is vast, largely unexplored territory. But in his *Stages of Life,* one of the true greats of
psychology, the Swiss savant Carl Jung, couldn't resist a
powerful, poetic analogy to describe the course of life:

"In order to characterize it I must take for comparison
the daily course of the sun—but a sun that is endowed with
human feeling and man's limited consciousness. In the
morning it rises from the nocturnal sea of unconsciousness
and looks upon the wide, bright world which lies before it
in an expanse that steadily widens the higher it climbs in the
firmament. In this extension of its field of action caused by

its own rising, the sun will discover its significance; it will see the attainment of the greatest possible height, and the widest possible dissemination of its blessings, as its goal. In this conviction, the sun pursues its course to the unforeseen zenith—unforeseen, because its career is unique and individual, and the culminating point could not be calculated in advance. At the stroke of noon the descent begins. And the descent means the reversal of all the ideals and values that were cherished in the morning. The sun falls into contradiction with itself. It is as though it should draw in its rays instead of emitting them. Light and warmth decline and are at last extinguished.

"Fortunately, we are not rising and setting suns, for then it would fare badly with our cultural values. But there is something sunlike within us, and to speak of the morning and spring, of the evening and autumn of life is not mere sentimental jargon."

In the area of mass psychology, cycle enthusiasts are more likely to postulate some connection between the events in nature and human behavior. Wheeler and Huntington related their long cycles in human history directly to climate and environment; hard-headed economists like Paul Volcker, former head of the Federal Reserve, attribute business cycles to mass psychology which, in turn, is increasingly linked with celestial cycles. Although these linkages have yet to be proved beyond doubt, there are so many believable witnesses to cycles operating in the communal affairs of men as they do in nature that their testimony has to be taken seriously. In addition to avowed cycle proponents like Wheeler and Huntington, historians of the stature of Oswald Spengler and Arnold Toynbee sketched the rise and fall of civilizations in terms not unlike those used to describe the individual human life cycle. An optimist who believed in progressive evolution, Toynbee was troubled by the possibility that people might see his recurrent rhythms in history in the common circular image of a cycle, and he came up with a metaphor in his *Study of History* that deserves a place in any form of cycle thinking:

"The metaphor of the wheel . . . offers an illustration of recurrence being concurrent with progress. The movement of the wheel is admittedly repetitive in relation to the wheel's own axle, but the wheel has only been made and fitted to its axle in order to give mobility to a vehicle of which the wheel is merely a part, and the fact that the vehicle, which is the wheel's *raison d'être,* can only move in virtue of the wheel's circular movement round its axle does not compel the vehicle itself to travel like a merry-go-round in a circular track. This harmony on the wings of minor repetitive movement—is perhaps the essence of what we mean by rhythm; and we can discern this play of forces not only in vehicular traction and in modern machinery but likewise in the organic rhythm of life."

If the cycles of world history are something of a grand hypothesis, the cycles in American history—and probably in the specific history of any other country—are measurable and testable in the caldron of practical politics. Credited with spotting these cycles is Harvard historian Arthur M. Schlesinger who first mentioned them in 1924 and outlined them in *Paths to the Present* in 1949. Schlesinger saw them as tides averaging 16.55 years apart that alternated between periods of "concern for the rights of the few" and "concern for the wrongs of the many." His first cycle from 1765 to 1787 involved the colonists' resistance to the British imperialism and "an excess of democracy" under the Articles of Confederation; his second cycle from 1787 to 1801 was a period of constitutional government and dominance by the commercial classes; his third cycle from 1801 to 1816 featured Jeffersonian accent on popular rights. And so it continued through eleven cycles. A supreme test for cyclical theory is its ability to make accurate predictions.

Schlesinger saw another rise in the conservative tide "around 1978"—just two years before the Reagan revolution.

Schlesinger's son, Arthur M. Schlesinger, Jr., has carried his father's thesis forward in his recent book, *The Cycles of American History.* His differences with his father include seeing the length of the cycles as thirty years and defining the cycles as "a continuing shift in national involvement between public purpose and private interest." He goes further, too, in trying to explain the working cycles:

"A true cycle . . . is self-generating. It cannot be determined, short of catastrophe, by external events. War, depressions, inflations, may heighten or complicate moods, but the cycle itself rolls on, self-contained, self-sufficient and autonomous. The independence of the political cycle is confirmed by the absence of correlation with even something so potent in impact as the business cycle. The Depression ushered in the New Deal, but the Progressive era began in a time of general prosperity, and two grinding depressions took place in the 1869–1901 period without reversing the ground swell of conservatism.

"The roots of this cyclical self-sufficiency doubtless lie deep in the natural life of humanity. There is a cyclical pattern in the systole and diastole of the human heart. The physiologist Walter B. Canon half a century ago demonstrated that automatic corrective reactions take place in the human body when a shift from the stable state is threatened and thereafter speculated that a similar 'homeostasis' may be at work in the social organism.

"There is also a cyclical basis in the very psychology of modernity. With the acceleration in the rate of social change, humans become creatures characterized by inextinguishable discontent. Wishes are boundless and therefore can never be fully satisfied. Adam Smith celebrated 'the desire of bettering our condition, a desire which . . . comes with us from the womb, and never leaves us till we go into the grave. In the whole interval which separates those two moments, there is scarce perhaps a single instant in which any man is so perfectly and completely satisfied with his situation, as to be without any wish of alteration or improvement' . . . Disappointment is the universal human malady. It is also the basic spring of political change. People can never be fulfilled for long either in the public or in the private sphere. We try one, then the other, and frustration compels a change in course."

In agreement with Schlesinger is Lee Iacocca whose belief in historical cycles presumably comes more from the automobile marketplace than the library. Certainly his language does. "As far back as I can remember, I've always been a strong believer in the importance of cycles," he writes in *Talking Straight.* "You'd better try to understand them, because all of your timing and often your luck is tied up in them. I've even formulated a little theory of my own about them, which I call 'Twenty and Eight.' In a nutshell, the theory is that the country tends to stagger through twenty years of havoc and activism and then to settle into eight years of relative calm. After catching its breath for eight years, it goes through the wringer again for another twenty years. And so on and so on." One example fitting neatly into his theory is the social activism that began with Franklin Roosevelt's capture of the White House in 1932 and ended in the quiet conservatism that Dwight Eisenhower brought with him in 1952. There's a somewhat raucous echo of the Schlesinger thesis in the conclusion Iacocca draws from this example: "My theory is that in a democracy people finally get worn out from too much activism. They can endure only about twenty years of it at a stretch and then they need some time to reorient themselves and figure out whether they're going nuts or not."

Whatever cycles may tell us about history, the history of cycles tells us that they are likely to turn up anywhere and everywhere if the observer's eye is trained to spot them. For the inquiring mind, the fact that new cycles tend to create new mysteries is only a source of enticement. It's a fairly safe bet that any man alive today with the vision of a Shakespeare would advise his Horatio to keep an open mind as to the undreamt of things that cycles might reveal.

CHAPTER

12

CYCLES AS A CRYSTAL BALL

WHEN I WAS researching in the offices of the Foundation for the Study of Cycles in the spring of 1989, the mail brought a handwritten postcard from far out in cycleland that warned of an earthquake in a few days. It was not thrown into the waste basket. As people who work with cycles and live in California, the staff takes both predictions and earthquakes seriously. I really didn't know what to make of it.

The next evening my wife, Dorrie, and I were dining at the Laguna Beach home of the Foundation's then director, Dr. Jeffrey Horovitz. Suddenly there was a loud report as the panes in a wall of sliding glass doors facing the ocean visibly bulged and snapped back into place. By some miracle nothing broke. Dorrie, who hadn't heard about the postcard, thought that we had been hit by the kind of unexpected wind gust we call a "door slammer" in the northeast. The only native Californian among us claimed that it had been an earthquake, an opinion immediately confirmed by an announcer on the local radio station.

Since we had escaped unharmed and there were no reports of other damage over the car radio as we drove back to our Irvine hotel—strangely, no other reports of any kind—I said to Dorrie, "Isn't this serendipity? You didn't know it, but a card came into the office yesterday predicting an earthquake. What a great example of the value of cycles for the book!" By morning, however, the media silence about our "earthquake" was, as they say, deafening. In the Foundation offices, it was concluded that we and some others all the way down the coast to San Diego had been treated to the fallout from naval target practice offshore, a not infrequent happening in those parts.

As a result of the incident, a feeling of skepticism—and, yes, disappointment—rode home with me to Connecticut. But only a few weeks later there *was* an earthquake in California of sufficient magnitude to make the network news. Thus, when my interest in cycles began to draw predictions to my door, too, I put them in the active rather than the circular file. One of the first of these was that an unusual spell of wet weather we were having in my area would be around for some seventy-three days. As I write these words, the prediction has been true for seventy-seven days, but this very morning a dry, cold air mass from Canada has driven away a long summer's damp for the forecast future. It's almost eerie.

Unfortunately, I won't be able to report on the others before this book has to go to press. One was a phone call informing me of the probability of dangerous flood tides along the east coast several months hence. A note as to the dates of that event isn't in my file but propped right up on my desk where I stare at it daily, because I have a small boat moored safely for ordinary conditions that could be set adrift or swamped in such a flood. Another prediction that's hard to put out of mind was scrawled as an afterthought on the back of an envelope containing a letter about different matters: "Prepare for the fall crash of 1989 & the depression of 1990."

The ability to predict future happenings or at least to recognize their character when they come along is, of course, the practical payoff from the study and use of cycles. The people who believe in cycles have a horror of being lumped together with the people who believe in horoscopes, crystal-ball gazing, palm reading, card cutting and the like. The cycle prophets arrive at their conclusions through what they consider scientific methods, and they tend to be as cautious and tentative as other scientists in announcing them. In the following words from a book written with Edwin F. Dakin and significantly titled *Cycles: The Science of Prediction,* Edward R. Dewey set the tone that his followers still adhere to:

"The student of periodic rhythms in human affairs has a tool which the law of averages itself puts into his hands. If trends have continued for decades, or if the oscillations of cycles around the trend have repeated themselves so many times and so regularly that the rhythm cannot reasonably be the result of chance, it is unwise to ignore the probability that these behaviors will continue.

"The result is not prediction, in the sense in which the word is ordinarily understood. If the reader nevertheless wishes to regard essential parts of this book as prediction, then it should be emphasized that the 'forecasts' are written by the data themselves. They emerge as tendencies in the organisms being studied. They do not rest on the opinion of any man, or men. They are, in effect, the *probabilities* of tomorrow."

Since Dewey wrote those words nearly fifty years ago, the computer has made possible an estimation of those probabilities in affairs where sufficient data is available, such as the financial markets. Dewey's most recent successor as director of the Foundation for the Study of Cycles, Richard

189

Mogey, told me that the "batting average" of cycles as a predictive device is turning out to be between 80 and 90 percent, and Dr. Anthony F. Herbst, of the University of Texas, who designed the Foundation's software, put it in the range of 70 to 90 percent. Any gambler presented with such probabilities would think he had died and gone to heaven. In broader areas of human affairs, like politics and wars, that may not lend themselves to such precise statistical analysis, observable events have tended to give cyclical prophecy the same high level of probability.

Nevertheless, most of today's cycle enthusiasts remain as cautious as Dewey for very good reasons. The more they learn about cycles the more they realize that they are dealing with a highly complex, interactive system. In any given context there may be hundreds of cycles of various lengths and strengths, each affecting the others. For predictive purposes, it is usually possible to isolate dominant cycles— the longer, the stronger in most cases—but it is never possible to be certain that other cycles won't gang up and take over under certain circumstances. Nor is it possible to foresee exactly how a cycle will react to cataclysmic external forces such as war. A demonstrably regular cycle of swings between Democratic and Republican critical in American history, for example, was drastically shortened by the Civil War and lengthened by its aftermath.

In this light, the earthquake coming a few weeks instead of a few days after the postcard, and the wet spell lasting a few days longer than anticipated, represent amazingly accurate predictions and are probably typical of what to expect from cycles. In any case, the record chalked up by predictions based on cycles has been so good so far that, as Dewey said, it is unwise to ignore them. I didn't press people for predictions during my research, but they seemed to come along naturally or to show up regularly in the reading. In selecting a few for 1990 and beyond to pass along, I have tried to stick to those of general importance on which there seems to be some consensus. In most cases, I have identified the sources and discussed their participation in particular phases of the cycle story elsewhere in the book. At the very least, it is fascinating to look at the future through their eyes; at most, the exercise could save some of us from trouble or disaster.

Since economic forecasts have been more or less the backbone of cycle research, it might be appropriate to begin with them. The warning I got on the back of that envelope gets some support from others although not precisely as to time and in gentler terms. Closest to this scenario is that of Dr. Theodor Landscheidt who finds that from 1968 onward bottoms in the cycle of stock prices have coincided with conjunctions of Jupiter. In *Sun-Earth-Man* he writes:

"This pattern will be preserved until 2002, the epoch of the start of the next major instability event. Thus, the epoch of the next minor instability event, the conjunction of Jupiter with the center of mass in 1990.3 (April 20, 1990), points to the coming turning point where stock prices reach their bottom and begin to rise again. Such turning points indicate a global trend that affects all important stock exchanges such that the average of their indices is a good match. The indices of individual stock markets may fall several months behind the exact date of the turning point or show a premature release. Thorough knowledge of the state of the special market of interest remains a necessary condition of making appropriate use of the fundamental tool offered here. Chart techniques alone are not sufficient to foresee major change. Black Monday, the stock market crash on October 19, 1987, is evidence of this. A combination of expertise, chart techniques, and a general survey of the fundamental turning points will yield more satisfying results than less holistic attempts in the past." Certainly there is no empirical evidence of a causal relationship between these celestial events and the market, but, again, that is not to say that somewhere in the myriad, complex web of electromagnetic, energy and planetary systems that such a relationship does not exist.

Foundation director Mogey, a trading consultant by background, told me, "The stock market should be down somewhere in '91 or '92 with a slowing of the business cycle. I would anticipate that it will be mild, more like the slowdown we had in 1985." Weighing the influence of the so-called long waves—the Elliott and Kondratieff waves—on commodities in a Cycles article, Dan Ascani, editor of Elliott Wave Commodity Forecast, wrote:

"The K-wave points down hard into 2003, when the next inflationary cycle is due to begin. Like the 1930s, however, stock and commodity prices should begin their next Supercycle advance ahead of that low. If the amount of time needed to complete the deflationary phase is similar to the last cycle, then the period from peak inflation to peak deflation should be about thirteen years. A bottom in commodity prices is therefore expected circa 1993."

In one economic area that touches more lives than the markets—residential real estate—there has been curiously little analysis by the Foundation. At one point Dewey did identify an 18.2-year cycle in real estate transfers between 1795 and 1958 and in residential building construction between 1856 and 1950. He was bemused by the synchrony with a similar cycle in U.S. marriages and opined that the start of new families might have something to do with the start of new homes. Running the available data through his computer, Mogey recently confirmed a seventeen- to eighteen-year rhythm in real estate. Using a mix of five cycles that have dominated real estate values for forty years, Mogey felt confident in making the following forecast in a May/June 1989 Cycles article:

"For the most part, these cycles have been very accurate, the only aberration being the great postwar boom of the early 1950s. Real estate values bottomed in the last quarter of 1951, and the projected cycles bottomed in the next quarter. The next major top in the value of real estate occurred in the second quarter of 1955, with the cycles having projected the first quarter of that year. The next actual low came simultaneously with the cycle projection low in the first quarter of 1967. The next major high occurred in the first quarter of 1973, with the cycles projecting a top in the third quarter. The 1975 low came in the first quarter of 1975 whereas the cycles had projected the second quarter. Since 1975, the cycles have projected the subsequent turns exactly, beginning with the high in 1978 and the low in 1982. Currently the cycles project a top in real estate values in the first quarter of 1994 . . . Based on cycle projections, the value of real estate should continue to outpace the growth in GNP until late 1993–early 1994."

In short, if you own a house or a condo, you might want to think of holding onto it for at least another three or four years.

But what about an even more pervasive influence on human life within the purview of cycles—climate? Here the grounding for prediction is very solid in terms of natural phenomena, and the implications of the far-reaching forecasts are profound. The data for determining climatic cycles would seem to be various and reliable—ranging from prehistoric tree rings and sediment deposits through human historical records of weather to the massive detail fed into modern computers. Recently, a body of reputable scientists had concluded that measurable celestial cycles are a determinant of earthly weather. Since the equations they have worked out produce the right results when they go backward in time, it must be presumed that they are reliable going forward as well.

There is more consensus and more certitude in predictions about climate than about economic affairs. This may be because the predictions are based on observations over extremely long time periods. Columbia University geologist Rhodes Fairbridge and his colleague James Shirley, for instance, use a study of solar activity for thirteen centuries to arrive at a "tentative prediction" of a minimum of solar activity that will cause a pronounced drop in temperatures during the years 1990 to 2013. Also from his reading of solar activity, Landscheidt agrees. This could produce, in Fairbridge's words, "a little ice age" during which rivers and harbors would freeze in the northern reaches of the American continent and Europe while heating costs would soar. It's possible that the cooling will be mitigated by the much discussed "greenhouse" warming caused by man-made pollution. Nobody knows for sure.

A cold-wet period beginning in 1990 was also prophesied by the late Raymond H. Wheeler on the basis of his massive study of earthly data going back to prehistoric times. Wheeler used the coincidence of tree rings and historical accounts of weather to arrive at his five hundred-year and one hundred-year cycles. It should warm up a bit about 1997, according to the notes Wheeler left behind when he died, but there will be another cold-wet period starting in 2015 and an abnormally hot sequence of years in the 2030s equalling those of the 1930s and producing similar agricultural "dust bowl" and market depression conditions. Michael Zahorchak, who published the Wheeler notes in 1983, cites many instances of uncanny accuracy as to weather in the intervening years. Consider just one example: Wheeler had forecast a drop in rainfall between 1980 and 1984; at the very time Zahorchak was sending his material to the printers, New York City and the suburbs in which he lived were on drought alert because of low levels in the reservoirs.

As with climate, there is increasing evidence that cycles will render predictable the dangerous and destructive natural events—volcanic eruptions, earthquakes, droughts, tidal flooding. While expressing the usual scientific caveats, some cycle students are going on record in these areas. Hughes Aircraft scientist John Bagby has been studying earthquakes in his spare moments since 1971. Bagby postulates that they are triggered by gravitational forces controlled by planetary cycles. Interestingly, one of the highest tides in a decade occurred the weekend before the San Francisco earthquake of October 19, 1989. Bagby told me, "Based on history, the months of January in 1990, 1991 and 1996 are going to be peak points in triggering. We should have eight times the normal earthquakes released." Bagby stays away from more specific predictions because he doesn't know where on earth a quake might hit, but he is confident of the timing somewhere. For instance, he says, "No hospital should change shifts at three, six, nine or twelve o'clock standard time anywhere in the world. That's just a stupid thing to do because those are the times when earthquake triggering takes place and they could be needed for emergency medical service." Bagby's personal response to his knowledge of earthquakes was to find a home site on a block of rock in the Anaheim Hills when he moved to California from Illinois even though it is an inconveniently long commute to work.

Jack Sauers, a Seattle, Washington, geologist, is another scientist with enough confidence in cycles to make predictions in this area. In a letter to me in the spring of 1989, he wrote:

"In 1989, we will see the onset of astronomical and astrophysical forces, producing geophysical effects on the earth related to some long cycles, which peak close together. We will have the beginning effects of a cycle related to the retrograde motion of the sun, relative to the barycenter, or center of mass of the solar system, wherein the sun actually goes backwards, as it loops outside the center of mass. Historically, in the past, this has produced an increase in the number and size of earthquakes, and volcanic eruptions. It also has resulted in greater extremes of climate, producing colder winters, hotter summers and droughts worldwide. Being a long cycle, which last had similar peaking condi-

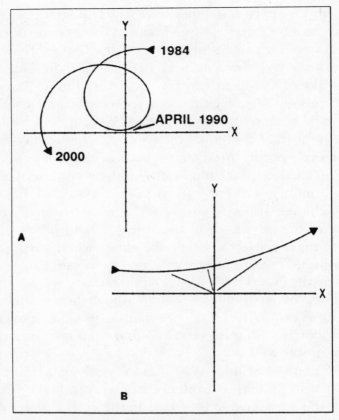

(A) Path of the center of the Sun, relative to the solar system
center of mass, for the years 1984-2000.
(B) Enlarged version of (A), showing that the sense of the motion
is clockwise here (left to right, relative to the origin) during 1990.

More and more cycle scholars are connecting celestial phenomena
with cycles observable in earthly affairs. The retrograde motion of
the sun, shown in this diagram, has been associated with an increase
in earthquakes, volcanic eruptions and climate extremes, which, in
turn, have social and economic effects. This pattern is one basis for
forecasts of "a little ice age" in the making. *(Cycle Magazine)*

tions around 1810–1820, we have had a gradual onset already of colder midcontinent climatic conditions, which push outward, and hotter midsummer drought conditions, that likewise push outward.

"In addition, as lunar declination increases, with the sun going further north and south of the equator, as we approach the peak of the lunar nodal tidal cycle in 1991, we should have greater earth strain produced, giving greater tidal forces and amplitudes. There should thus be a greater chance of volcanic eruptions and earthquakes related to that cycle. Historically, that cycle, too, has been a drought cycle, with greater droughts in the past being reflected in crop production and in tree ring records.

"The solar sunspot numbers have been in a rising trend on solar sunspot cycle number twenty-two, since their low in September of 1986. That was a low of three, and interest rates bottomed then, too, since interest rates for the past three solar sunspot cycles have roughly followed solar sunspot cycles up and down, like inflation. In addition, both the number and size of earthquakes has followed this cycle in the past. I won't give here the voluminous documentation possible for these assertions. Solar sunspot numbers are high already in 1989. The peak is not known, but they will be high while the other two large cycles are high. The solar sunspot cycle has also been a drought cycle, and it peaked last with the lunar nodal tidal cycle in 1936, at the time of the midwest dust bowl. I therefore forecast midcontinent droughts and climatic extremes related to these long cycles, and greater chances of earthquakes and volcanic eruptions."

From the work of Fergus Wood which I've already detailed, it would appear that tides are a truly predictable force. In his book *Tidal Dynamics,* Wood has tables listing every amplified tide through the year 2164. It would be tedious to list these dates here. Until they are incorporated in standard tide tables and forecasts, however, it could well pay anyone living near the oceans to consult the book. Like the other scientists, Wood warns against generalizing about tides and prefers to call his forecasts "advisories" rather than predictions. A high tide *per se* might wet some feet and basements, but it generally won't result in disaster unless accompanied by strong onshore winds—a weather condition that cannot be predicted that far in advance. In fact, it's only in the last year or so that Wood, in cooperation with weather expert Irving P. Krick, has experimented in issuing flood advisories about three months ahead, with astonishingly good results.

If the cycles crystal ball seems a trifle cloudy at times, it is a tribute to the integrity of the people gazing into it. Along with insisting on thinking in terms of probabilities instead of predictions, Edward R. Dewey, the man who virtually invented cycles as a usable tool, always contended, according to his son, that cycle information was only one factor to take into consideration before acting. In discussing stocks, Landscheidt issues the same sort of advice, and so does Wood in talking about tides. In many ways, Dewey seemed to be more confident of the role of cycles in the longer, larger context of human history. In his son's view it was the promise that such cycles offered of a better, saner life for the mass of humanity that interested Dewey most toward the end. "The most important thing for him was the war cycle," Edward S. Dewey says.

Dewey used the massive research of Raymond H. Wheeler to extract the data for his analysis of the war cycles. In the course of their work covering virtually all of recorded history, Wheeler and his staff created indexes of International War Battles and Civil War Battles. The amount of entries can be judged by the fact that there have only been two hundred years of absolute peace in the world during a span of 3,400 years. Wheeler rated wars on a scale of one for a light engagement to three for a heavy battle. By adding the ratings over twelve months he would obtain a figure to assign to each year. Subjecting the Wheeler index of International War Battles to analysis, Dewey came up with cycles of 142, 57, 22⅕, and 11⅕ years.

In 1952, combining these four cycles, Dewey worked out a graph from which he hazarded a forecast of international conflict through 1975. By the time he died a few years later that forecast was still holding true as can be judged by what he wrote about it: "Of course, this forecast was very crude. It used very few cycles. It used no cycles shorter than eleven years, which is like trying to paint a portrait with the foot of an elephant for a brush. All the forecast really said is that times would be rough the world over, in the 1960s, with the possibility that there would be a double peak, the first one in the early sixties and the second one at the end of the decade. The middle 1970s should be reasonably peaceful."

On the basis of this record, Dewey's reading of the 142-year cycle in war gives pause for thought: "This 142-year pattern calls for a more than average number of battles for the seventy-one-year period from 1914 to 1985 and a less than average number of battles for the seventy-one-year period form 1985 to 2056." In this prediction Dewey found himself in agreement with the Wheeler thesis that the cycles of war correspond with the cycles of climate. Wheeler concluded that international wars as well as dictatorships occur most frequently in warm periods while civil wars crop up in cold ones. Therefore, Wheeler predicted that the cold period starting in 1990 would also be a period with a low level of international conflict.

In my personal experience in cycleland, I've found nothing quite as intriguing as the reflection of the vision of Dewey, Wheeler, Landscheidt, et al., in every day's news. What they see in cycles is a time, starting as of *now*, of a decline in international conflicts but a rise in civil strife, a time of democracy and individualism as opposed to authoritarianism and collectivism, a time when world dominance shifts from Western to Eastern civilization. It's almost

impossible in the light of current events not to be impressed
by the broad outlines of cycle prophecy.

As an international, interdisciplinary, holistic-minded figure, Dr. Landscheidt is the epitome of today's cycle thinker.
It is, therefore, appropriate to give him the last word on
cycle prophecy. His outline of history is based on what he
calls instability events, periods of change and revolution
that take place at the turning of cycles when "the special
constellation of Sun and planets that makes the center of
mass and the Sun's surface coalesce." To appreciate his look
ahead, it's best to start with his description of two of these
periods that most of us will recognize or recall:

"About 1933 to 1937: Great economic depression, col-
lapse of the world market; Stalin's dictatorship, forced col-
lectivisation of agriculture; start of Japan's Far Eastern
expansion; breakthrough of Hitler's national socialism;
Goedel's revolution in logic; discovery of neutron, positron,
meson and heavy hydrogen; creation of electron-positron
pairs from energy and vice versa; discovery of nucleic acid
in cell nuclei; invention of television, jet engine and electron microscope.

"About 1968 to 1972: Upheavals and rebellions of students all over the world; spread of hippies' cultural revolution in China; six-day Arab Israeli war; new economic
structures in Czechoslovakia, suppressed by Russian invasion; turning point in Vietnam; space travel; astronauts on
the Moon; Glomar Challenger expedition, plate tectonics;
first AIDS infections; ecological movement; Gnostics of
Princeton; Pop art.

"The next major instability event will start about 2002
and last till 2011. This is an exceptionally long period. It is
impossible to predict the details of its historic effects. But
the basic quality of all boundary functions will be evident:
the years past 2002 will prove to be another turning point, a
period of instability, upheaval, agitation, and revolution,

that ruins traditional structures, but favours the emergence of new patterns in society, economy, art, and science."

If it doesn't sound like the brave, new world of most visionaries, this scenario is equally lacking in the characteristics of chaos and catastrophe so often foreseen in this era of pollution and The Bomb. Because so many of the cycles on which they base their thinking have remained nearly constant for so many millions of years, students of cycles almost to a man or woman display a great deal of faith in the proposition that the future, however it may differ in details, will retain the same general shape as the past and present. Their message is, in fact, that the future as seen in cycles is so reliable that a wise person will search out the probabilities, accept them and prepare for them instead of worrying about, or hoping for, the impossible to occur. Not bad advice, and I am going to take it when it comes to doing something about that boat.

CHAPTER
13

HAS THE DAY OF THE CYCLE COME?

WHAT MIGHT BE CALLED a cyclical view of the universe is still not at all common despite half a century of dogged work and persuasive argument on the part of its proponents. Why? Among the people to whom I addressed this question was Gertrude Shirk, recently retired after more than forty years of service as research director of the Foundation for the Study of Cycles and editor of its magazine. Ms. Shirk has a knack for being straightforward and succinct. "A lot of people are very turned off by the concept of rhythmic behavior," she said. "It's the twentieth century hubris: we control things."

Hubris, which is defined as overweening pride, self-confidence or arrogance, has been building in the human psyche for centuries. It is the natural result of a Judeo-Christian religion that implies a man-centered universe and a mechanistic science that promises to deliver nature into man's hand. In both of these traditions, time is viewed as linear, unrepeatable, angled upward in the direction of something called progress or salvation. Matter is measurable and malleable in accordance with determinable causes and effects. There may be cycles, to be sure, but they would be cogs in the machine rather than the sources of its power or its determining factors.

The fact that the basis for man's hubris is now being undermined by the very science that helped to put it in place can be seen as a cycle in itself. Cycles of doubt, discovery, conviction and doubt again are clearly observable in the history of science. The current doubt cycle that began with Einstein's challenge to the fervent faith placed in Newtonian physics is still rolling along, and the science of cycles is one of its motivating forces. In fact, the students of cycles might well contend that, in their particular phase of science in general, they have rolled through doubt into discovery and are approaching conviction. What cycles people are saying to shake the tower of hubris is that the natural universe operates in a dynamic but rhythmic way; that man, whose inner rhythms are related to outer rhythms, is an integral part of this natural universe; that man is, therefore, controlled rather than controlling; that the end of wisdom is to seek a greater understanding of natural forces in order to work with them instead of defying them.

It is clear that getting hooked on cycles is more than a matter of finding a way of thinking about which stock to buy or what mood you are likely to be in next week. It's a matter of rethinking everything. Edward S. Dewey said, "If those people who believe in cycle theory are correct, the world operates differently from what most people think. If my father was correct, for instance, every economist is wrong—and that's just for openers. They are cause and effect people, and he thought that was wrong." Cycle enthusiasts, like basic researchers in other forms of science, tend to describe their change in thinking in terms reminiscent of religious conversion. Listen to Dr. Jeffrey Horovitz who gave up medical practice to work for the Foundation: "There's just a feeling that some of us get that we are touching something far beyond what we have been aware of or conscious of. It's that feeling of making discoveries like in second grade when you realize you can read. The hair starts to stand up on the back of your neck. You get a different sense of what *everything* is about."

One reason that learning about cycles changes everything is that they are seen to be in everything. Cycles as a science is necessarily interdisciplinary, encompassing not only what are usually thought of as sciences—physics, chemistry, biology, etc.—but also other branches of knowledge such as mathematics, medicine, history, economics, psychology. This means that the study of cycles is isolated from the ordinary academic channels of thought transmission. Scholars in separate disciplines may never even run across cycles as a factor to take into account, and neither will the practitioners trained by these scholars. Added to hubris, this isolation could account for the general lack of understanding and appreciation for the roles that cycles play in the drama of natural and human life.

Given this background, the welcome that cycle believers extend to fellow apostates is to be expected. The first thing you see when you walk into the California headquarters of the Foundation for the Study of Cycles is a shelf of freshly minted books that are advertised and sold to members at a discount and that deal with the new frontiers in science. Although cycles are not specifically considered in many of these works, a lot of common ground is discernible in a shared attitude about the need for interdisciplinary approaches and holistic thinking. Since cycles are likely to come into their own as part of a larger movement, if at all, it's important to have a look at some of these other thinkers who are deemed to be allies. Because of my own self-confessed limitation in scientific training and the scope of this book, I make no pretense of doing justice to the brilliant arguments and depth of research in any of the works I cite. My only intent is to show that there is a new wind rising—or a new cycle turning, if you like—in the scientific realm, of which we all should be aware.

Even though some of these books have been cited in support of various aspects of cycle theory, let's skim the Foundation shelves to get a feeling for the metaphysical climate surrounding the subject of cycles:

— *Entropy: A New World View* by Jeremy Rifkin with Ted Howard:

Entropy is a corollary to the second law of thermodynamics. The first law of thermodynamics states that there is a fixed amount of energy which can be transformed from one form to another to accomplish work—as in electricity turned into heat or heat turned into steam; the second law states that, in the transformation process, some energy will be rendered useless for performing future work. Entropy is the measure of this loss of utility. Another way of stating the second law of thermodynamics is to say that everything has a tendency to move from order to disorder, and entropy is the measure of disorder. In this book, the authors make an impassioned case for the proposition that what they call the Entropy Law "remains the only law of science that seems to make common sense out of the world we live in and provides an explanation of how to survive within it."

In their view the jury is still out on the case for cyclical theory, which they define as a belief that when an expanding universe reaches maximum entropy it will contract itself back to a more ordered state and then re-explode to create another expanding universe and continue the process in endless waves. This, of course, is not necessarily the belief of cycle students who are more concerned with cycles as a functioning characteristic of the universe as we experience it than an answer to those ultimate questions of its beginning and end. But where the authors of *Entropy* are in agreement with cycle people is evident from the following assertion:

"The old Newtonian view that treats all phenomena as isolated components of matter, or fixed stocks, has given away to the idea that everything is part of a dynamic flow. Classical physics, which recognized only two kinds of classifications, things that exist and things that don't exist, has been challenged and overthrown. Things don't just 'exist' as some kind of isolated fixed stock. This static view of the world has been replaced by the view that everything in the world is always in the process of becoming. Even nonliving phenomena are continually changing . . . How different this scientific view is from Newtonian physics with its simple matter in motion, its fixed forces acting against other fixed forces in precise and predictable ways. It's no accident that a science based on manipulating fixed stocks is being replaced by a science based on understanding dynamic flows."

Another point of agreement is that the authors find a form of hubris standing in the way of seeing the truth. In their case, the hubris is pride in technology. Those still imbued with the belief that everything can be reduced to mechanics look to ever-increasing feats of technology to repeal the Law of Entropy—that is, to control the tendency toward the kind of disorder that can be observed, say, in the spread of pollution. What they forget, argue the authors, is the enormous entropy involved in the energy transfer demanded by technology. This is especially true with respect to fossil fuels. In fact, the book illustrates the Law of Entropy in terms of burning a piece of coal. No energy is "lost"; the heat is used for work, and the rest is transformed into sulfur dioxide and other gases. These dissipate in space and add to entropy, or disorder, since the gases cannot be returned to the ordered, usable state of the piece of coal.

Thus, the technology in which we take such pride is killing the earth through entropy at an ever increasing rate. The reverse side of entropy can be seen in living things. Energy, mostly from the sun, creates order out of disorder in the process of developing plants, animals, people. Although entropy is created in this process, too, more energy remains in a usable form, and that form is renewable through reproduction. The idea that usable energy is saved as the result of machines doing work that a man could do is totally wrong in this view.

The case for entropy sounds very much like the case for cycles when the authors write, "Our survival and the survival of all other forms of life now depend on our willingness to make peace with nature and begin to live cooperatively with the rest of our ecosystem. If we do so, and allow the natural recycling process the time it needs to heal the wounds we have inflicted on earth, then we and all other forms of life can expect a long and healthy sojourn on this planet." It is not a case that is likely to be more popular or more readily accepted than acknowledging uncontrollable rhythms since it demands a rejection of the popular concept of progress as an increase in technical expertise and material wealth.

— *Global Mind Change* by Willis Harman:

The relevance of this thought-provoking book to cycle thinking is that it constitutes a strong plea for a more holistic science. The author, whose background includes a professorship in Engineering-Economic Systems at Stanford University, also argues that the mechanistic science of the last several hundred years is no longer acceptable. He, too, sees the attitude that it creates as self-defeating hubris. "Our exuberant Western attitude that all of nature is here to be exploited for our ends may have to be replaced by a far more humble stance if we are to learn from the universe what it would teach us," he writes.

Harman claims that "science has a long history of defending the bulwarks against the persistent reports of phenomena and experiences that 'don't fit in'—such as the spiritual and religious, the exceptionally creative and intuitive, the 'miraculous' in healing and regeneration, the paranormal, seemingly teleologically motivated instinctual patterns, etc." But now he would like to see science "assume the validity of any type of human experience or extraordinary ability which is consistently reported down through the ages, or across cultures, and adapt science in such a way as to accommodate all of these."

Like cycle students, Harman sees a connectedness in everything in the universe. He calls for "an awareness of the finiteness and multiple-interconnectedness of the planetary ecosystem, the inextricable interdependence of all human communities and dependence on the planetary life-support systems." Probably for much the same reason that Edward R. Dewey wanted to see cycles incorporated in the body of scientific study, Harman feels that the mind change to the holistic view he advocates—"the whole is qualitatively different form the sum of its parts"—should take place among scientists.

"We in modern society give tremendous prestige and power to our official, publicly validated knowledge system, namely science. It is unique in this position; none of the coexisting knowledge systems—not any system of philosophy or theology, nor philosophy or theology as a whole—is in a comparable position," Harman writes. "It is impossible to create a well-working society on a knowledge base which is fundamentally inadequate, seriously incomplete, and mistaken in basic assumptions. Yet that is precisely what the modern world has been trying to do."

— *Chaos: Making a New Science* by James Gleick:

As with entropy, the science of chaos—if it yet exists—does not endorse cycles specifically. Since, by definition, it is concerned with the irregularities that keep cropping up in every system, it would seem to constitute a rejection of the cyclical view. Indeed, there's almost a sneering tone about cycles in this passage from the Gleick book: "Why do investors insist on the existence of cycles in gold and silver prices? Because periodicity is the most complicated orderly behavior they can imagine. When they see a complicated pattern of prices, they look for some periodicity wrapped in a little random noise. And scientific experimenters, in physics or chemistry or biology, are no different."

But believers in chaos and believers in cycles would be on the same side in arguing that the concept of a nature made up of static linear systems has got to go. Gleick quotes atomic scientist Enrico Fermi as saying, "It does not say in the Bible that all laws of nature are expressible linearly!" In addition to subscribing to a conviction that all systems are dynamic, both sets of believers recognize the global nature of systems and the need for an interdisciplinary approach to understand them. As Gleick says of chaos believers, "They feel that they are turning back a trend in science toward reductionism, the analysis of systems in terms of their constituent parts: quarks, chromosomes, or neurons. They believe that they are looking for a whole."

But the book is probably on the shelf at the Foundation for the Study of Cycles because Dr. Horovitz sees an affinity between the two approaches to truth that may have escaped others. One definition of cycles is patterns, and, paradoxically, the science of chaos is discerning its own kind of patterns in the universe. As Dr. Horovitz explained to me:

"Fractal relationships from this new science called chaos are related to what we are doing. It's kind of our domain. A fractal is a dimensional relationship. If you take a map of

210

Long Island, for example, and reduce it in size by one thousand you would still have the same edge to it. It's recurring patterns at dimensional leaps. An electron spinning around the nucleus of an atom is an orbital fractal dimension. The next level up is the moon spinning around the earth, the next fractal dimension. The next level up is the planet spinning around the sun, and then you have the solar system spinning around the center of a galaxy, and then you have all these galaxies spinning around the center of what we believe is a super galaxy. Then we think the super galaxy spins with other galaxies around a hub. Also the science of chaos helps you develop probabilities for things that we used to think were random. Science is saying there is less randomness."

— *The Ages of Gaia* by James Lovelock:

"Because of the tribalism that isolates the denizens of the scientific disciplines, biologists who made models of the competitive growth of the species chose to ignore the physical and chemical environment. Geochemists who made models of the cycles of the elements, and geophysicists who modeled the climate, chose to ignore the dynamic interactions of the species. As a result, their models, no matter how detailed, are incomplete."

Those words of Lovelock, a British generalist in the sciences, should sound familiar. He is obviously a member of the growing group of thinkers in revolt against the parochialism of the sciences as they are still generally taught and practiced. From my reading of him, Lovelock's new look at the workings of the universe does not preclude a significant role for cycles. His concern is to get across the concept that what he calls "Gaia"—the earth and its surrounding atmosphere—is a single living entity. A sense of his vision comes through in the following passage:

"Gaia as the largest manifestation of life differs from

other living organisms of Earth in the way that you or I differ from our population of living cells. At some early time in the Earth's history before life existed, the solid Earth, the atmosphere, and oceans were still evolving by the laws of physics and chemistry alone. It was careening, downhill, to the lifeless steady state of a planet almost at equilibrium. Briefly, in its headlong flight through the ranges of chemical and physical states, it entered a stage favorable for life. At some special time in that stage, the newly formed living cells grew until their presence so affected the Earth's environment as to halt the headlong dive towards equilibrium. At that instant, the living things, the rocks, the air, and the oceans merged to form the new entity, Gaia. Just as when the sperm merges with the egg, new life was conceived."

This life within Gaia has acted as an automatic regulator—analogous to a household heating system governed by a thermostat—to keep the environment livable by curbing extremes. All forms of life modify the environment. For example, animals change the atmosphere by breathing, taking in oxygen and letting out carbon dioxide, while plants do the reverse. This has counteracted or at least delayed the buildup of entropy which ultimately results in equilibrium, or death. Since the life cycle *is* a cycle and the home heating analogy is often used to describe the function of cycles, the concept of a Gaia goes well with that of cycles.

— *The Body Electric: Electromagnetism and the Foundation of Life* by Robert O. Becker, M.D. and Gary Selden:

Dr. Becker, a surgeon, started out with a theory that the electrical current in wounds—what he calls the "current of injury"—stimulated regeneration and healing. In the process of investigating and testing this theory he crossed all the boundary lines of scientific specialties to develop a much broader view of the function of electricity in animating the universe. Although he doesn't deal with cycles *per se*, I did cite some of Dr. Becker's discoveries in support of the theory among some cycle students that electromagnetism might be the crossover force that accounts for such phenomena as identical rhythms in celestial bodies and human activities.

Whether this turns out to be true or not, Dr. Becker's thinking is certainly in according with that of cycle proponents. Like them, he takes the position that the dynamic, interrelated systems of the universe can be understood only through a holistic approach. He summons a potent witness for his case in the form of Albert Szent-Györgyi, winner of a Nobel prize for work on oxidation and vitamin C. Speaking at a meeting of the Budapest Academy of Science in 1941, Szent-Györgyi deplored the mechanistic approach of biochemistry on the grounds that, when experimenters broke things down into component parts, life slipped through their fingers and left them staring at dead matter. "It looks as if some basic fact about life were still missing, without which any real understanding is impossible," said the Nobel laureate, according to Dr. Becker. Szent-Györgyi thought that the salient fact might be electricity, but his realization that something was missing in much of scientific thinking also makes his remarks relevant to the claims of cycle advocates.

It seems impossible to stand on the frontier of science without seeing a beckoning vision. Dr. Becker's vision incorporates elements of many of the others, and it has the advantage of being grounded, so to speak, in electricity—a force that most of us understand from daily experience. Here it is in his own words:

"Over and over again biology has found that the whole is more than the sum of its parts. We should expect that the same is true of bioelectromagnetic fields. All life on earth can be considered a unit, a glaze of sentience spread thinly over the crust. *In toto* its field would be a hollow, invisible sphere inscribed with a tracery of all the thoughts and emotions of all creatures. The Jesuit priest and paleontologist-philosopher Pierre Teilhard de Chardin postulated the same thing, a noosphere, or ocean of mind, arising from the biosphere like a spume. Given a biological communications channel that can circle the whole earth in an instant, possibly based on life's very mode of origin, it would be a wonder if each creature had not retained a link with some such aggregate mind. If so, the perineural DC system [current in the nerves] could lead us to the great reservoir of image and dream variously called the collective unconscious, intuition, the pool of archetypes, higher intelligences deific or satanic, the Muse herself."

Even if the shaking of the scientific foundation under the tower of hubris brings it crashing down, the idea that cycles are in control of human affairs will run into heavy resistance. What about mankind's supposed free will, for instance? Cycle proponents argue that there is no greater limit on freedom in acknowledging the existence and function of cycles than there is in acknowledging the authority of the law of gravity by not jumping from a ten-story window. The use of free will comes into play in making the right choices when confronted with probabilities presented by a knowledge of cycles. John Bagby, for example, wasn't *forced* by his belief in a rhythmic return of earthquakes in California to build his house on a rock and undergo the rigors of a long commute instead of easing life by taking the risk of living elsewhere. Nor were the members of the Foundation who chanced a loss by taking money out of what looked like an ever rising stock market in 1987 *forced* to do so by the way they interpreted the cycles. Not even the wildest enthusiast argues that cycles *per se* are overwhelming. Although a cycle may be beyond human control, the consequences of its rhythmic recurrence are not. Take tides, for instance. Because they are controlled by celestial cycles, Fergus Wood can forecast potentially dangerous

214

high tides a century in advance, and no man can change that script. The tide will surely arrive almost to the minute, but the engineering ingenuity of man is such that shoreline facilities could be built in such a way as to make its arrival of no consequence.

The determinism implicit in cyclical thinking has many theological and philosophical overtones. Geologist Rhodes Fairbridge thinks that a tendency to shy away from determinism goes back in history to a rejection of the concept that everything is determined by God—a concept that understandably lost ground with scholars when the church tried to enforce its actions like having the Inquisition sentence Galileo to house arrest for life. "But to substitute nature for God is not a leap that most people with that attitude are prepared to make," Fairbridge says. Except for those few who still cling to a man-centered view of the universe, there would appear to be ample room these days for both God and nature in a universe of cycles. In the interval since scholarship finally broke free of religious control and censorship, most theologians have accepted the continuing discoveries of science as an unfolding of knowledge about how God's creation works. In that sense, cycles would be just another manifestation of the mysterious ways in which God performs his wonders.

There is wide room for doubt and an open mind in cycleland, too. Like all other scientific theories postulated so far, the theory that cycles might be the clue to solving the ultimate mystery of creation is far from proven. The test for the validity of a scientific theory is the ability to make predictions that hold up under experimentation and/or observation. As we have seen, cycle theory does well on this test. But its score is so far from perfect that the users of cycles prefer to speak of advisories and probabilities instead of forecasts and predictions. In this, too, they would appear to be on the cutting edge of science in general. Talk of calling a whole new science "chaos"—"a state of things in which chance is supreme," according to *Webster's*—is enough to indicate how a new humility is gaining ground as unpredictable irregularities keep surfacing in supposedly smooth systems when they are subjected to ever closer scrutiny.

A book not on the Foundation's shelf when I was there but deserving of a place is *A Brief History of Time* by Stephen W. Hawking. Considered by many to be the greatest theoretical physicist since Einstein, Hawking occupies the same chair as did Isaac Newton as Lucasian Professor of Mathematics at Cambridge University in England—something of an irony in view of the challenge his thinking poses to Newtonian law. Much of his book, which became an astonishing bestseller, is devoted to showing how inadequate various theories developed throughout history, including some of his own, have proved to be, and still are, in giving a complete picture of the universe. That the study of cycles might eventually provide such a theory was the hope of Edward R. Dewey, and is the hope of many of his followers today. They would certainly subscribe to Hawking's credo, which he summarizes as follows:

"Because the partial theories that we already have are sufficient to make accurate predictions in all but the most extreme situations, the search for the ultimate theory of the universe seems difficult to justify on practical grounds. (It is worth noting, though, that similar arguments could have been used against both relativity and quantum mechanics, and these theories have given us both nuclear energy and the microelectronics revolution!) The discovery of a complete unified theory, therefore, may not aid the survival of our species. It may not even affect our life-style. But ever since the dawn of civilization, people have not been content to see events as unconnected and inexplicable. They have craved an understanding of the underlying order in the world. Today we still yearn to know why we are here and where we came from. Humanity's deepest desire for knowledge is justification enough for our continuing quest. And our goal is nothing less than a complete description of the universe we live in."

Even if this goal is reached, we are unlikely ever to go beyond dealing in probabilities, according to Hawking. This is because of the uncertainty principle, which he calls "a fundamental, inescapable property of the world." Enunciated by German scientist Werner Heisenberg in 1926, this principle is based on the impossibility of accurately measuring both the position and velocity of a particle at the same time. "The uncertainty principle signaled an end to . . . a model of the universe that would be completely deterministic: one certainly cannot predict future events exactly if one cannot even measure the present state of the universe precisely!" Hawking writes. Quantum mechanics was revised in the light of this principle to use a combination of position and velocity to predict a number of possible likely outcomes instead of a single sure result—in other words, probabilities.

For all practical purposes, the uncertainty principle means that man will have to live by the probabilities he can determine, and the study of cycles already is making an important contribution in that sense. Einstein, also in search of a unified theory, was not fond of the uncertainty principle because it ran counter to his famous statement that "God does not play dice with the universe." On the other hand, the uncertainty principle seen from a theological or philosophical point of view allows God to intervene in the clockwork operation of his creation in the form of irregularities. A theorist of chaos, Joseph Ford, responded to Einstein by saying, "God plays dice with the universe, but they're loaded dice. And the main objective of physics now is to find out by what rules were they loaded and how can we use them for our own ends." It sounds a lot like what the cycle people are trying to do with some success through their own discipline.

Despite the fact that his theory of relativity changed humanity's relationship to the universe for all time, Einstein could be wrong, and one of his endearing traits was that he was often the first to admit it. Nobody knew more than he how little we really know. Einstein was as humble in person as in mind. I used to see him wandering through the campus of Princeton University, sockless feet in tennis shoes, sweat-shirted, white hair in windblown disarray, licking an ice cream cone and obviously lost in thought. With that vision in mind, it didn't surprise me to come upon this prayer-like acknowledgement of awe in contemplation of the universe in Einstein's *The World As I See It*. The Einstein meditation now seems to me the only proper ending to a book exploring any branch of science, cycles included:

"The fairest thing we can experience is the mysterious. It is the fundamental emotion which stands at the cradle of true art and true science. He who knows it not and can no longer wonder, no longer feels amazement, is as good as dead, a snuffed-out candle. It was the experience of mystery—even if mixed with fear—that engendered religion. A knowledge of the existence of something we cannot penetrate, of the manifestations of the profoundest reason and the most radiant beauty, which are only accessible to our reason in their most elementary forms—it is this knowledge and this emotion that constitute the truly religious attitude; in this sense and in this alone, I am a deeply religious man . . . Enough for me the mystery of the eternity of life, and the inkling of the marvellous structure of reality, together with the single-hearted endeavor to comprehend a portion, be it ever so tiny, of the reason that manifests itself in nature."

BIBLIOGRAPHY

IN RESEARCHING THIS BOOK, the author read numerous other books, searched periodical files for all references to cycles over the past decade, reviewed the entire fifty-year run of the magazine Cycles, corresponded with and interviewed more than a dozen current cycle scholars and practitioners. An overall look at a sprawling subject like cycles can only catch the high spots. For readers who would like to follow-up and examine in depth any aspect of the subject, recommended books and articles are listed below. Book references are in alphabetical order according to author; periodical references in alphabetical order according to title of the article, which in most cases is self-explanatory as to subject matter. In addition to the listed references, such standard works as *Encyclopaedia Britannica, The New Funk & Wagnalls Encyclopaedia, Webster's Seventh New Collegiate Dictionary* and the Holy Bible, Revised Standard Version, were consulted. As to personal letters and interviews cited in the text, interested readers who would like to contact the source are invited to send *written* requests to the author.

Bibliography

BOOKS

— Ayensu, Edward S. and Whitfield, Dr. Philip, eds., *The Rhythms of Life,* 1981, Crown Publishers, Inc.

— Becker, Robert O., M.D. and Selden, Gary, *The Body Electric,* 1987, William Morrow & Co., Inc.

— Boslough, John, *Stephen Hawking's Universe,* 1985, William Morrow & Co., Inc.

— Carter, Elizabeth A. and McGoldrick, Monica, eds., *The Family Life Cycle,* 1980, Gardner Press, Inc.

— Collingwood, R. G., *Essays in the Philosophy of History,* 1965, University of Texas Press.

— Cooley, Donald G., *Predict Your Own Future,* 1950, Wilfred Funk, Inc.

— Dewey, Edward R. with Mandino, Og, *Cycles,* 1971, Hawthorn Books.

— Dewey, Edward R., and Dakin, Edwin F., *Cycles: The Science of Prediction,* Foundation for the Study of Cycles, Inc.

— Einstein, Albert, *The World As I See It,* 1949, Philosophical Library.

— Fairbridge, Rhodes, *Planetary Periodicities and Terrestrial Climate Stress,* 1984, D. Reidel Publishing Company.

— Gleick, James, *Chaos,* 1987, Viking.

— Harman, Willis, *Global Mind Change,* 1988, Knowledge Systems, Inc.

— Hawking, Stephen W., *A Brief History of Time,* 1988, Bantam Books.

— Hungtington, Ellsworth, *Mainsprings of Civilization,* 1945, John Wiley and Sons, Inc.

— Huntington, Ellsworth, *Season of Birth,* 1938, John Wiley and Sons, Inc.

— Iacocca, Lee, *Talking Straight,* 1988, Bantam Books.

— Jung, C. W., *The Stages of Life,* The Portable Jung, 1971, Viking.

— Landscheidt, Theodor, *Sun-Earth-Man,* 1989, Urania Trust.

— Levinson, Daniel J., et al., *The Seasons of a Man's Life,* 1978, Alfred A. Knopf.

— Lovelock, James, *The Ages of Gaia,* 1988, W. W. Norton & Co.

— Luce, Gay Gaer, *Biological Rhythms in Psychiatry and Medicine,* 1970, U.S. Department of Health, Education and Welfare, National Institute of Mental Health.

— Martin, Geoffrey J., *Ellsworth Hungtington,* 1973, Archon Books.

— Miller, James Grier, *Living Systems,* 1978, McGraw-Hill Book Company.

— Moore-Ede, Martin C.; Sulzman, Frank M.; and Fuller, Charles A., *The Clocks That Time Us,* 1982, Harvard University Press.

— Needham, Joseph, *Time and Eastern Man,* 1964, Royal Anthropological Institute of Great Britain & Ireland.

— Perry, Susan and Dawson, Jim, *Secrets Our Body Clocks Reveal,* 1988, Rawson Associates.

— Rampino, Michael R.; Sanders, John E.; Newman, Walter S.; Konigsson, L. K., eds., *Climate History, Periodicity, and Predictability,* 1987, Van Nostrand Reinhold Company.

— Rifkin, Jeremy with Howard, Ted, *Entropy: A New World View,* 1986, The Viking Press.

— Ruperti, Alexander, *Cycles of Becoming,* 1978, CRUCS Publications.

— Schlesinger, Arthur M., *Paths to the Present,* 1949, Macmillan Co.

— Schlesinger, Arthur M., Jr., *The Cycles of American History,* 1986, Houghton Mifflin Company.

— Schumpeter, Joseph A., *Business Cycles,* 1939, McGraw-Hill Book Company, Inc.

— Sheehy, Gail, *Passages,* 1974, E. P. Dutton & Co.

— Smith, Edgar Lawrence, *Tides in the Affairs of Men,* 1939, The Macmillan Co.

— Spiller, Robert E., *The Cycle of American Literature,* 1965, The Macmillan Co.

— Sze, William C., ed., *Human Life Cycle,* 1975, Jason Aronson, Inc.

— Thorneycroft, Dr. Terry, *Seasonal Patterns in Business and Everyday Life,* 1987, Gower.

— Toffler, Alvin, *The Third Wave,* 1980, William Morrow & Company, Inc.

— Toynbee, Arnold J., *A Study of History,* 1947, Oxford University Press.

— Volcker, Paul A., *Rediscovery of the Business Cycle,* 1978, The Free Press, Macmillan Publishing Co.

— Wasserman, Harvey, *America Born and Reborn,* 1983, Macmillan Publishing Co.

— Williams, William Appleman, *The Contours of American History,* 1966, Quadrangle Books.

— Wood, Fergus J., *Tidal Dynamics,* 1986, Kluwer Academic Publishers.

— Young, A. B., *Recurring Cycles of Fashion,* 1937.

— Zahorchak, Michael, ed., *Climate: The Key to Understanding Business Cycles,* the Raymond H. Wheeler Papers, 1983, Tide Press.

PERIODICALS

— "A Bundle of Worms" by Dorothy Swiss, Cycles, May/June 1976.

— "A Light in Time" Psychology Today, January 1987.

— "A New Approach to Fighting Cancer: Chronochemotherapy" an interview by Martha Harty, Cycles, June 1982.

— "A 7-Day Cycle in Human Moods" by Nancy B. Brinker, Cycles, April 1973.

— "Abstracts" from Chronobiologia, organ of the International Society for Chronobiology, XIX International Conference, April/June 1989.

— "An Inca Stonehenge?" Cycles, September 1966.

— ". . .As the Classic Business Cycle Changes Its Course" Business Week, April 4, 1988.

— "Beyond Night and Day" by Isabel S. Abrams, Space World, December 1986.

— "Biological Rhythm and Cosmose: The One Commands, The Other Obeys" from Journal de Geneve, Cycles, May 1970.

— "Coffee Break" by Dr. Samuel Lee, Tea & Coffee Trade Journal, September 1982.

— "Commodities in the Perspective of the Elliott and the Kondratieff Waves" by Dan Ascani, Cycles, March/April 1989.

— "Congregational Church Membership" by James E. Vaux, Cycles, February 1971.

— "Cycles" by Neil Spitzer, The Atlantic, February 1988.

— "Cycles: Beating to the Same Pulse?" by Richard Lipkin, Insight Magazine, March 14, 1988.

— "Cycles in Book Publication" by James E. Vaux, Cycles, April 1971.

— "Cycles in Religion" by Arthus Louis Joquel II, Cycles, August 1959.

— "Cycles in Stock Prices—The 40.68-Month Cycle" by Gertrude Shirk, Cycles, March 1987.

— "Cycles in the Birth of Eminent Humans" by Andis Kaulins, Cycles Vol. 30, No. 1, 1979.

— "Cycle Semantics" by Ruth Lynne O'Malley, Executive Report.

— "Cycling Through U.S. History," U.S. News & World Report, December 1, 1986.

— "Defying Gravity" by Shari Roan, The Orange County *Register,* April 6, 1988.

— "Dialogue With a New Member" by Gertrude Shirk, Cycles, November 1966.

— "Director's Letter" by E. R. Dewey, Cycles, August 1960.

— "Earthquakes, Earth Expansion, and Tidal Cycles" by Martin Sitch Kokus, Cycles, November 1987.

— "Emotional Cycles in Man" by Rex B. Hersey, Foundation for the Study of Cycles Reprint from Journal of Mental Science, January 1931.

— "Exploring the Forces of Sleep" by Erik Eckholm, New York *Times* Magazine, April 17, 1988.

— "Foundation Explores Mysterious Rhythms" by Mark Roth, Pittsburgh *Post-Gazette,* July 18, 1983.

— "Get On Your Success Cycle" by W. Clement Stone, Success: The Magazine for Achievers, July 1983.

— "Have Services Taken the Sting Out of the Business Cycle?" Business Week, April 4, 1988.

— "Hems and Haws" by Sandy Stevens, Cycles, March 1967.

— "Hydrological Cycles" by Wallace Stegner, Wilderness, Fall 1987.

— "Inside The Greenhouse" by J. I. Merritt, Princeton Alumni Weekly, April 19, 1989.

— "Is the Movie Industry Contracyclical?" by Diane C. Nardone, Cycles, April 1982.

— "Is the World Economy Riding a Long Wave to Prosperity?" Business Week, May 5, 1986.

— "It's Part of the Legacy of Being Human," Q. & A. with Dr. Henry Schneiderman, New York *Times,* May 7, 1989.

— "Just a Matter of Time" by Malcolm W. Browner, New York *Times* Magazine, September 27, 1987.

— "Mathematics of Sleep" by Steve Nadis, Technology Review, February/March 1987.

— "Measuring Your Personal Emotional Cycles" by Jeffrey H. Horovitz, M.D., Cycles, December 1986.

— "Motivations For The Study of Cycles" by Ralph V. Hagopian, Cycles, August 1967.

— "Music History in Five Five-Hundred-Year Cycles" by Warren Dwight Allen, Journal of Human Ecology, Vol. I, No. 13, 1951.

— "New Research on Light Could Be Boon to Sleep" New York *Times,* June 16, 1989.

— "Periodic 18.6-Year and Cyclic 11-Year Induced Drought and Flood in Northeastern China and Some Global Implications" by Robert Guinn Currie and Rhodes W. Fairbridge, Quaternary Science Reviews, 1985.

— "Political Cycles" by Gary Marting, Cycles, 35, 1959.

— "Political-Economic Cycles in the U.S. Stock Market" by Anthony F. Herbst and Craig W. Slinkman, Financial Analysts Journal, March/April 1984.

— "Possible Cycles in Temperature at Charleston, S.C." by James E. Vaux, Cycles, Vol. XXVI, No. 5.

— "Prediction of Long-Term Geologic and Climatic Changes That Might Affect the Isolation of Radioactive Waste" by Rhodes W. Fairbridge, Underground Disposal of Radioactive Wastes, Vol. II.

— "Prolonged Minima and the 179-Year Cycle of the Solar Inertial Motion" by Rhodes W. Fairbridge and James H. Shirley, Solar Physics, 1987.

— "Researchers Will Use Lasers to Study Earth's Water Cycle," Earth Science, Fall 1987.

— "Science of Cycles" by Patrick Huyghe, Science Digest, August 1983.

— "Seasonal Architecture" by Cleta Olmstead Boughton, Journal of Human Ecology, Vol. II, No. 1, 1953.

— "Seasonal Painting" by Cleta Olmstead Boughton, Journal of Human Ecology, Vol. I, No. 22, 1953.

— "Seven-Year Spirals" by Kelly R. Bennett, Cycles, March 1988.

— "Some Neglected Aspects of Accident Prevention" by Rexford Hersey, Cycles, January 1952.

— "Something Out There" by John Brooks, New Yorker, February 3, 1962.

— "Some Will Take Grim Delight in the New Recession" by George F. Will, International *Herald Tribune*, March 1989.

— "Sleeping to the Beat of the Body's Rhythms" U.S. News & World Report, June 15, 1987.

— "The Creative Function of Cycles" by Theodor Landscheidt, Cycles, May/June 1989.

— "The Cycle of the World's Great Religions" by Arthus Louis Joquel II, Cycles, April 1959.

— "The Cycle Outlook for Real Estate" by Richard Mogey, Cycles, May/June 1989.

-— "The Effect of Climate on Human Behavior in History" by Raymond Holder Wheeler, Transactions Kansas Academy of Science, Vol 46, 1943.

— "The Fifth Force" by Freric B. Juenemann, Research & Development, April 1989.

— The Magnetic Attraction of Periodicities" Science News, March 29, 1986.

— "The 9-Year Cycle in Social Disease," Cycles, July 1958.

— "There's a 54-Year Cycle to Rates" by Tony Reid, Toronto *Sun*, September 4, 1983.

— "The Seasonal Cycle in Quaker Speaking," Cycles, November 1959.

— "The Solar Cycle in Precambrian Time" by George E. Williams, Scientific American, August 1966.

— "The Solar Inconstant," Scientific American, September 1988.

— "The Time of Our Lives" by Michel Siffre, Unesco Courier, June 1987.

— "300,000-Year Record of World Temperature," Cycles, January 1952.

— "Tune To Your Body Clocks" by Wendy Murphy, McCall's, July 1988.

— "What Is It All About?" by Gertrude Shirk, Cycles, March 1962.

— "Wheeler's 'Big Book'" by Diane Epperson, Cycles, January/February 1989.

— "When The Sun Goes Backward: Solar Motion, Volcanic Activity and Climate 1990–2000" by James H. Shirley, Cycles, March/April 1989.

— "Why Does It Rain on January 23?" Cycles, August 1960.

— "Why Primo Levi Need Not Have Died" by William Styron, New York *Times*, December 19, 1988.

— "Worlds In Collusion" by Michael R. Rampino, Cycles, January/February 1988.

— "Writings of Raymond H. Wheeler," Parts 1–10, Foundation for the Study of Cycles, Inc., 1978.